BREAKER

HARLOE RAE

Cover Artist: BookCoverKingdom
(www.bookcoverkingdom.com)

Photographer: Rafa G Catala
Cover Model: Adrian Pedraja
Formatting: Champagne Book Design

NOVELS BY

HARLOE RAE

Reclusive Standalones

Redefining Us

Forget You Not

#BitterSweetHeat Standalones

GENT

MISS

LASS

Total Standalones

Watch Me Follow

Ask Me Why

BREAKER

This book is dedicated to Heather, Kate, and K.K.
For all the love, laughs, and unforgettable moments.
Thanks for being my beeches.

PLAYLIST

"Let Me Love the Lonely" by James Arthur
"More Hearts Than Mine" by Ingrid Andreas
"Love Runs Out" by OneRepublic
"Fearless" by Kat Perkins
"The Kill" by Thirty Seconds to Mars
"Till the Sun Comes Up" by Gavin James
"Can I Be Him" by James Arthur
"If We Never Met" by John.K
"Secret Love Song" by Little Mix
"If You're Over Me" by Years & Years
"Let It Be" by Imaginary Future
"Better" by Parachute
"You & Me" by James TW
"Stand By You" by the Pretenders

Listen on Spotify here >> shor.by/BreakerPlaylist

My heart is in the stars,
Beyond reach and reason.
He will never be mine,
And I will never love another.
—Sutton Olsen

"Tell me a happy something, Sutton."

I was only seven the first time Grady Bowen whispered those words to me. Cloaked by the black sky under a blanket of stars, it was easy to get lost. He didn't have any good memories of his own and needed to borrow mine. I would willingly give him anything.

Being infatuated with that boy was a beautiful curse. What could have been special didn't get the chance to bloom. He'd never see me as more than his best friend's kid sister. That was a hard lesson to learn, but not the most difficult.

Grady had always been struggling against the odds. Eventually he quit fighting and let his family's reputation own him. Try as I might, those influences were beyond my reach.

He didn't mean to break my heart. Or maybe he did. I shouldn't have made it so easy for him. Either way, our wrongs against each other carved new lines between us.

I went four years without seeing Grady—each one more painful than the last. That distance did nothing to dull my feelings toward him. But things are different now. Most noticeably is Grady. I barely recognize this man he's become. And that's the way he intends to keep it. Not that it really matters.

Grady Bowen stopped being my happy something long ago.

PROLOGUE

Sutton

Happy something #8: I love when clouds are extra puffy and big in the clear blue sky. It's fun to find animals in random shapes.

WET BLADES OF GRASS TICKLE MY ANKLES WHILE I SNEAK across the darkened yard. The squish of my flip-flops is the only sound aside from occasional crickets serenading me. My sandals slide along the dew and I almost stumble to the ground. Slowing my haste would be wise, but I can't allow reason to settle in. I'm already a short second away from losing my nerve.

The full moon watches my every slinky move. I keep my chin tucked to avoid the admonishment. But any attempt to escape the scorn is in vain. Every slight touch from the manicured lawn is a whispered warning.

This is a mistake.

Turn around.

He doesn't want you.

But I don't listen. Not this time. I've been ignoring my feelings for years. Tonight feels like my final chance. The only one I'll get, and the most vital. My heartbeat pounds faster with each hurried step. I wipe the sweat from my palms and pick up the pace. A single hanging light flickers above the front door. The low shine illuminates my target destination. I push forward, rushing to close the remaining distance.

The guesthouse is pitch black when I step inside. I don't bother turning on a lamp. I've memorized the path to his room over the years. His door is already ajar and I nudge it open wider. Moonlight filters in through the window, bathing the small space with a natural glow. I've never been more thankful for his lack of curtains.

Grady is sleeping on his back, granting me a clear view of his naked torso. Cut lines of muscle define his abs and chest. One strong arm is tossed over his face, shutting out the worry from sight. It gives me permission to continue my lazy perusal of him. A white sheet is draped low on his hips. I draw in a shaky breath and glance over his covered lower half. My imagination runs wild while feasting on the possibilities of what's hiding underneath. His soft snores carry over to me as I linger by the wall. The quiet noise beckons me to him.

My stomach twists to the point of pain. I wince at the sting, but shuffle closer. Another slew of caution slams into me. This feels like an invasion, but that still doesn't stop me. The floorboard creaks and Grady snaps awake. He sits up, scanning the room with wide eyes. His gaze narrows when he lands on me hovering just out of reach. The need to breathe burns my lungs, yet I remain frozen.

"What the fuck, Sutton?" His growl sends chills up my spine.

I knot my fingers together. "I didn't mean to wake you."

But that's a lie. He needs to be coherent for this to go

the way I hope. Being willing and agreeable are also important. I swallow down the bubbling nerves in a rough gulp.

"Why are you in my room?"

I almost wither under the intensity of Grady's stare. His green eyes gleam in the near darkness. I imagine their emerald color luring me under an unbreakable spell. The golden specks swirling within will smolder from the effort. I clear the dryness from my throat. "I, uh, wanted to see you."

"In the middle of the fucking night? There better be a damn good reason." The threat in his voice rings out, but I ignore it.

I study his stern expression, taking precious moments to peel away the hardened layers. Grady's eyelids are heavy with the remaining threads of sleep. Thick stubble coats his sharp jaw. Dark blond hair hangs over his forehead in messy clumps. His rumpled state makes him more desirable. That's a problem I don't need help with. I long to feel the rasp of his calloused hands over every smooth inch of me. The slight burn would surely set me ablaze.

Doubt creeps in the longer I stall on him. This boy has been through hell. Why am I considering adding more unnecessary drama to his plate? A hollow pang in my heart answers the rhetorical question. I can count on two hands the days we've gone without seeing each other. Tomorrow will change all that. I'm not ready for goodbye.

After a decade, the memory of how we met is getting fuzzy. Grady stumbled onto our property late one night. He ran to our house under the midnight sky and hid from the horrors that occurred at his home. If the walls of his trailer could talk, I'm sure they'd scream. Grady is broken and battered, abandoned by those meant to love him the most. But I've never let him down. Maybe he'll learn to rely on me one day.

Either way, he's an honorary member of our family. We

welcomed him with open arms and never let go. Grady and my older brother have been best friends since they were nine. He's unknowingly been the love of my life that entire time. If only he'd admit to feeling a fraction of the same. Or I had the guts to tell him.

Grady shifts on his bed. The squeak of springs drags my attention out of our past. I need to be focusing on the future. When I lift my gaze, he's still glaring at me. The desire to flee wobbles my knees. My courage is diminishing with each passing moment. This entire ambush will be a waste if I don't spit my intentions out. Crossing the line is up to me. I clench my eyes shut and let the words spill free.

"I want you to take my virginity."

Grady is silent for a few beats. I peel my lids open, watching the stacks of muscle in his shoulders flex with harsh breaths. The knot in my chest pulls tighter. My offering dangles in the few feet separating us. He just needs to reach out and grab me. But his lips pull into a sneer.

"Are you fucking joking?"

I cringe at his foul language. Grady's tongue has always been sharp. Even more so lately, especially with me. "No," I whisper. "I'm very serious."

"Go home, Sutt. We're not discussing this."

"Why?"

A tic of strain pops in his jaw. "Because I say so."

"Doesn't it matter what I want?"

"Has it ever?"

The answer is no. A loud, resounding boom meant to deter. But I don't hear it. I've been waiting all of my teenage years for this moment. I'm not letting it slip away.

"Just once. No one has to know."

His eyes flash with a streak of lightning. "How fucking nice. I can be your shameful secret. No fucking thanks. Find someone else to slum it with."

I almost smack my forehead. How could I be so dense? "That's not what I meant, Gray." This is not going according to plan. I lick my lips and search for a different route. "I want *you*, and always have. I've saved myself for *you*. My first time is meant to be with *you*."

Grady flops onto his bed with a groan. "People accuse me of doing a lot of bad shit, but I've never been a thief. I'm not stealing your fucking cherry, Sutton."

I'm shaking my head before he's done talking. Heat crawls up my chest and neck, but I'm already buried too far. "But I want to do this with you. It has to be you."

He scrubs a palm over his face. "Don't do this desperate act. Give yourself to a man who's deserving."

"I'm looking at him." This wall between us needs to crumble. I step out of my soggy flip-flops and instantly feel more at home. If I reach forward, my hand will skim his blankets. It's been years since I've felt the comfort—albeit platonic—of his arms. I curl my toes into the carpet at being this close again.

Grady glares at the ceiling. "Seriously. I shouldn't have to repeat myself, but I will. Go home, Sutt."

"Please, Gray." The two words trickle off my trembling lips.

His scoff echoes around the dark room. "Begging is far beneath you, Sutt. Keep that silver spoon in your mouth."

That has me clacking my teeth together. "Don't be an asshole."

"Then don't force my hand. Go back to your side of the fence. You don't belong in these bunks."

Something dark flips inside of me. "This is my property. I have every right to be here."

He grunts into a clenched fist. "Don't need another reminder of who reigns."

The strength that brought me here is beginning to crack

under his pressure. But a lingering spark ignites when I catch him staring at me. Grady rarely looks my way for longer than a casual glance. But the privacy of his bedroom is proving to make a difference. He doesn't conceal the way his eyes skitter across my exposed skin. There's unmasked hunger waiting for me there. That gives me a much needed confidence boost.

It's not an accident that I'm wearing a daringly low-cut shirt. The hem of my skirt is a few inches too short. Am I acting desperate like he claims? No doubt. Do I care about being the one pursuing this? Not in the slightest. Am I worried about being rejected? More than I care to admit. But that fear doesn't hinder me.

"Did you know that I'm leaving tomorrow?" I catch a brief glimmer of shock register across Grady's features. A twitch snags his eyebrow. His throat bobs with a heavy swallow. He rolls his gaze off mine, avoiding the truth. If I hadn't been standing so close, watching his every move, the reaction would be missed.

"And your point?" It appears he's choosing to address the wall.

"I'll be gone. We won't see each other anymore." I hold my breath while waiting for more honesty to show.

Grady's lips tighten. "So, you came for a farewell fuck?"

I wrinkle my nose. "Must you be so crass?"

"Don't act like this is a new development." His tone is flat and stiff.

I rub my temples. I'm beginning to see the massive error in my ways. But my heart is stubborn. "I always wanted things to be different between us."

"Sorry to disappoint." His tone reveals he's anything but.

I'm already waist deep. Why not wade a bit further? "It's not too late, Gray. I'm here now. This is what I've been waiting for."

"Wait longer. You're still a fucking kid, Sutt."

"I'm eighteen. Only two years younger than you."

He waves off my words. "Age is just a number. You're sheltered as fuck. Get out and experience the world before shackling yourself to the gutter. Get outta here before Jace finds you missing."

Rather than retreat, I erase the remaining distance to his bed. "I don't care about my brother."

Grady's snort resembles a bull. "I sure as shit do."

Of course he does. They might as well be related by blood, not just sentiment. Defeat appears in two large boulders weighing my shoulders down. He won't budge, no matter how hard I push. A seed of nostalgia plants itself in my mind. I find myself changing tactics as a last-ditch effort. "Tell me a happy something, Gray."

His chuckle is empty. "Nah, we're too old for that shit. But nice try. Don't have any spare joy to share."

I blink at the unshed tears slowly building momentum. I want to scream at him. Demand that he forgets the pain and anger for one second to see what's standing right in front of him. But I force the fire down. "Want me to tell you one?"

"Won't change my mind."

I glance away to hide my wobbling lip and wet lashes. "Will you at least hold me for a bit? Like you used to during storms?"

"Sutt—"

"Please, Grady. I never ask for anything from you." I scoot forward until my legs bump the mattress.

With a resigned sigh, he opens his arms. "All right, fine. Five minutes, then you're going home. C'mere."

I nod and quickly cuddle into his side. He smells of a hardworking man, that familiar mix of motor oil and fresh hay. I snuggle deeper while inhaling the scent of my dreams. "Remember the first happy something I gave you?"

Grady nods, his chin ghosting across my forehead. He doesn't protest while I tug us along some pleasant highlights. I fill the chilly silence with sunny chatter. Grady doesn't add to the conversation, keeping it one-sided. It's probably for the best. Nothing he shares lately is good.

My five minutes loop several times before I run out of steam. We're stuck at a fork in the road. Sad as it might be, I find myself turning in the direction that leads away from him. "I'll miss you, Gray."

A rumble rises off his chest. "Yeah? Try forgetting me while you're at it. You'll be better off."

I don't bother responding. With that final blow, a gate slams shut between us. The clang ripples through me, solidifying what I've been trying to deny. This is the end of us. But this has always been the story of a girl desperately in love with a boy. Irrevocably and unrequited.

I'm ready to leave these well-worn pages behind.

CHAPTER ONE

Sutton

Happy something #54: Setting a goal,
only to reach and surpass it.

I DROP MY CAP INTO THE BOX AND FOLD UP THE MATCHING GOWN. The maroon polyester slides across my fingers with a quiet whoosh. Another chapter of my life is coming to a close, welcoming new opportunities and adventures. That's what I keep telling myself about graduating college. If I'm being completely honest, the last four years raced by in a blur.

The gleam of spotless glass catches my eye. I pick up the framed diploma and smooth a finger over my name written in scrolling script. This piece of embossed paper represents so much. All of the credits and courses that give me a sturdy foundation. Valuable lessons that can never be replicated. Late nights of studying and missed hours of sleep. Perhaps most importantly, honed and sharpened skills that will advance me in a competitive field. My career is built on this degree. I'll be taken more seriously because of the time and effort spent earning it. The memory of a certain green-eyed boy glares at me. He didn't believe advanced education was necessary to be successful. That opinion isn't wrong, it just isn't mine.

The final feathers of my youth are strewn about campus. Not that twenty-two is old. But most of my reckless and rash decision making is behind me. That's what I'm claiming, at least. A streak of untamed impulsiveness remains. I'll never be able to shed my ability to make poor choices. Not entirely. Even now, as I prepare to become a professional and take on a more serious role in society, that stubborn strand lays dormant just beneath the surface. I feel that tightly wound coil waiting for an opportune moment to break free. Returning to my roots probably has a lot to do with that.

Without further dwelling, I set the frame in a box with the rest of my valuable mementos. I roll my shoulders in an attempt to alleviate the pressure building there. For every friction of excitement that zips along my skin, a daunting shiver follows. There's so much change coming and I can't seem to collect my scattered feelings. Returning home to begin my adult life isn't all roses and sunny warmth. There's one very large storm cloud waiting to crash down on me. Or maybe he'll continue avoiding my path. I've been made well aware that's one of his newfound specialties. And contradicting myself is one of mine.

It's discouraging, and more than a little upsetting.

"Whatcha doing, Sutt?"

The question efficiently stops me from traveling further down that dark road. I give my friend a small smile. "Packing what's left of my stuff."

"Ah, exhilarating. I just stacked up the last of mine." Harlyn peeks into the nearest box and looks back at me. Whatever she finds makes her squint, studying me with greater scrutiny than necessary. I try not to squirm as she digs deeper under my layers. She tilts her head at me. "You're not getting sentimental, right? We both know that's my job."

I wrinkle my nose, trying to hide the slight sting from the earlier reverie. The pungent aroma of cleaning supplies filters into my lungs. "I'm fine. It's just a big move."

Her lower lip sticks out. "And we won't be roomies anymore."

A familiar tug pulls taut in my belly. "Don't remind me. I'll be stuck with my parents for at least a month."

She swings an arm around my shoulders. "No luck finding a place to rent?"

"Nothing with immediate availability. The earliest opening was July, but most are August or later."

"Downtown or in the outskirts?"

I laugh at that. "Not sure there's a huge difference when it comes to Silo Springs. I found a few within a mile or two of Main Street. But you're well aware of how spread out everyone is. There aren't a lot of residential spaces in the heart of town."

"Saves room for all those adorable shops. And maybe your future office." She wiggles her brows.

That earns her a dry scoff. "An apartment will suffice for both purposes. I'll happily work out of my living room."

Harlyn shimmies away so she can face me. "Are you so excited to get Sunny Monday Solutions rolling?"

I bite my lip and smile. "I really am. It still seems a bit crazy to me. I never anticipated this outpouring type of response when I decided on my career."

A zing darts up my spine when I think about the clients already lined up. Being a media marketing manager might not be glamorous to some, but it's a dream for me. I'll get to help others achieve and increase sales while continuing to grow my own portfolio. This is my version of creative talent. Searching for authentic content to post that will highlight their products is only the beginning. Making sure their online presence is consistent and reliable is key for my success. Building their brand into something we'll all be proud of is the ultimate goal. I allow a ghost of a smile to tilt my lips while reciting the mental list.

"I honestly can't wait to dive in," I add.

"Those romance authors are lucky to have you. Maybe you'll get signed copies of their books as a bonus." Her eyes sparkle under the dining room lamp.

"A few boxes are already on the way. I need them for pictures. K.K. Allen is a whiz on Instagram and is showing me the ropes. She tossed in a personalized Center of Gravity paperback. That's my favorite. I'm already getting spoiled." I wink at her.

"You better share."

"Pretty sure your life is already packed with hearts and flowers. Foster is your real Prince Charming. That man stepped straight out of a fairy tale."

Her sigh is whimsical. "He really did. I can't believe we've only been dating a few months. It feels like so much longer."

I catch the pure joy radiating off her, wanting to soak it in. "Soulmates."

She leans against the table and folds her arms. "Can't fault fate. We're crazy meant to be."

"You're welcome, Miss I-Didn't-Want-To-Take-A-Spring-Break-Trip. I'm always happy to prove you wrong." I giggle when she sticks her tongue out at me. After shooting her an air-kiss, I swipe through the air. "Okay, enough mush. Are you all set to live in the big city?"

Harlyn makes a see-saw motion with her hand. "I guess? It's a bit intimidating for this country girl. But I'll adapt to the surroundings. I'm really excited about the school. Making a difference for those kids is what matters most."

"And you will. You'll be the best teacher that district has."

She's quiet for a moment, her laser-focus zoomed in on me. "Are you trying to butter me up?"

I toss out an exaggerated gasp. "What? No. Why would I be?"

"Because today is kinda sad." She shrugs. "And you're avoiding heavier topics."

"Not sure what you mean." But I totally do. I'm sure my expression is guarded. There is stuff I keep hidden, even from my best friend.

Harlyn huffs and blows some bangs off her forehead. "Is Jace happy you're coming home?"

Surprise widens my eyes. I wasn't expecting that. "Oh, I'm sure he's positively thrilled to get me back within spying distance. My brother is a pain in the ass. Even two hundred miles couldn't save me from his interference."

To call him protective is a massive understatement. Nothing would make that man happier than me remaining single for the rest of my life.

My friend quirks a brow. "Are we talking about your lack of dating?"

"And everything else where the opposite sex is involved." I keep my features flat.

She laughs. "Jace might be cause for a few failed flings, but there's another man who deserves more blame."

I press a finger to her lips. "Don't you dare."

"Mur yeuo fnew tits rurth."

"What was that?" I remove the flimsy gag.

"That Bowen boy still has you wrapped—"

This time I clap my entire palm over her mouth. Prickles erupt along the nape of my neck. Thinking about him always gets my body buzzing. "No. Absolutely not."

Harlyn rolls her eyes but stays silent. I pull my hand away. She smiles so wide that it reaches her eyes.

"We'll see how long you last being back in Silo Springs.

Does that one guy I'm apparently not allowed to name still live with your parents?"

I force out a harsh exhale. "Real clever, Hae. But no, thankfully. He moved into his own house."

"So, the threat of running into him is low?"

I bite my lip. Warmth spreads through my belly at the idea alone. "Can't promise that. He still works for my dad sometimes."

She walks to the fridge and grabs a bottle of water. "You know an awful lot about this phantom."

"Jace is his best friend. Even if I wanted out of the loop, I'd get reeled back in." I join her in the kitchen and pour a glass of iced tea.

Harlyn studies me while taking a sip. "Is that going to be okay with you?"

"It won't make a difference if I see him or not. I understand where we rest and our final score. Plus, he's become really good at keeping his distance from me whenever I visit. I'm sure it won't be a problem."

Not that it really matters. I have plans of my own. And they sure as shit don't involve Grady Bowen. I wince while the harsh lie rattles around in my mind.

Try as I might, my future will always have a designated space for that jerk.

I peek over at my roommate. The grin on Harlyn's face says it all. She's not believing the lines I'm spewing. Heck, I can't blame her. She bumps her hip into mine. "Well, I'll only be a quick text away if you need assistance."

"And several towns over," I mutter.

She waves me off. "A minor technicality. I'll always be around for moral support."

"That's one of the reasons I love you." I smile at her.

Harlyn holds up a finger. "Don't forget my cooking and cleaning skills."

"Foster is reaping so many benefits. He must be wild in the sack to keep you hooked."

A blush paints her cheeks. "As if you don't already know. And I'm not moving in with him."

"Yet," I tack on for her.

She chews on her thumb nail. "It's only been a few months."

"Of paradise."

"Never thought you'd be the one pushing for this." She shoots me a narrow side-eye.

"When it's right, why wait?"

Harlyn laughs. "You've been reading too many romance novels."

"Have to get my kicks somewhere."

Her lower lip pops out. "Aww. I want you to meet someone special."

My chest tightens with her words. There's only one guy I've ever imagined spending my life with. I grew up with stars in my eyes aimed at him. Loving Grady was instinct. The dislike part has been more of a slow burn. My lovesick heart is finally beginning to admit that he never saw me as more than a little kid chasing him around.

And here I am, about to take up permanent residence in hostile territory. Fingers effing crossed.

I mosey back to the table and fold the flaps of my final box. After adding it to the stack near the door, I dust off my hands. My dad and brother will be here tomorrow to do the heavy lifting. I turn around, surveying our shared space with a wobbly smile. The majority of our stuff is packed, but the couch and television remain.

"What should we do with our final night?" I ask Harlyn while still staring at the mostly bare living room. The wood floor shines from the unfiltered sunlight pouring through the windows. Not sure the place has sparkled so bright since we moved in two years ago.

Harlyn stands next to me, joining in the reflection of our apartment. "How about an epic Netflix binge? Then we can have dinner at The Tavern."

My stomach rumbles at the suggestion. "I'll miss their chicken stew and roasted potatoes. Oh, and the fresh baked bread."

She licks her lips and nods. "It's only a few hours to drive."

"I know." My acknowledgement comes out as a whisper. I glance away as my eyes get hot.

"It's going to be amazing, Sutt. You'll be so happy." She dips her face to peek up at me.

I can't hide my sniffle. "I'm just being overly emotional again. Don't mind me."

Harlyn grips my fidgeting fingers. "In a month, when you're planting roots into a new apartment, this will seem like old news."

"I suppose."

"You'll be surrounded by love and family. I'll make sure Jace keeps an extra close eye on you." Her grin is pure trouble. "Wouldn't want a shred of weakness to ruin all these goals."

That turns my mood in the opposite direction. "Urgh, please don't. He does more than enough without being encouraged. I'm hoping some woman has caught his attention so he'll leave me alone."

"It's more likely to catch a flying pig. He's not settling down anytime soon."

She's right, of course. My brother has the tendency to jump ship before the girl can suggest a second date. His commitment issues rival—

I shake my head. Dammit. All this Grady talk has him cropping up in every direction. I need to shove him to the recesses of my mind where he belongs. That's how I've kept my heart intact these last four years. The method will be my source for survival while battling our lack of physical proximity.

So much easier to say than do.

CHAPTER TWO

Grady

Happy something #67: Not having to look over my shoulder each second of every damn day.

I DROP MY ASS ONTO A STOOL AND THE SHREDDED LEATHER cushion groans in protest. The worn wooden legs can hardly hold my weight. Heaven forbid this dump springs for new chairs, or pay to update anything for that matter. A quick glance around Howlers is a flashback to an era before I was born.

A jukebox—the kind with vinyl records—rests near the entrance. Faded posters for movies that came out on VHS hang at crooked angles along the walls. There's a cigarette machine between the bathrooms. Each time I walk inside is a taste of living in the past, which is weird as hell.

Smoking hasn't been allowed inside this spot for decades, yet the stench still clings like the bad habit itself. The lights are low, hiding the poor decisions being made. But no one casts judgment. That's what I appreciate about this outdated dive. Everyone who steps foot into this place is on the same level. I'll fucking cheers to that all damn day.

As if hearing my thoughts, Decker slides a cold beer in front of me. I lift my chin in greeting. The bartender salutes and strides off to help another customer. The place has a few perks, shitty decor be damned. I lift the bottle to my lips and take a long swig. The bitter hops hit my tongue, making me feel right at home. A bit of tension eases from my muscles. This is exactly what I needed.

A cloud of lung-seizing perfume assaults my nostrils. I cringe against the sickly-sweet burn. A moment later, sharp fingernails dig into the flesh of my shoulder.

"Hiya, Gray." The scent is already suffocating me, and Trista's nasally whine makes my ears bleed. I'm sure she means for the pitchy purr to be seductive. The breathy sound only succeeds at grating on my nerves. I pry her claws from the fierce grip she has on me.

"It's Grady." I spit the words through clenched teeth. The reminder shouldn't be necessary.

Her responding giggle is acid in my veins. "You're so funny. We've known each other long enough that I can use your nickname."

Something black and dirty twists inside of me. The fuck she can. Only one girl calls me that and she's long gone. "Nah, Trista. Grady will do. Need something?"

The question is a courtesy she doesn't deserve, but I ask it all the same.

She twirls a lock of her bleach-blonde hair. "Want some company?"

A quick shake of my head. "Nope."

"Maybe you should think a little harder."

I snort at the innocent pout this chick is trying to pull off. Every man within a five-mile radius is well aware of the game she's trying to play. Most fall victim to the tempting ploy. But I sure don't.

Trista's fingers walk up my arm. "Come on, Grady. Just a drink."

The stool squeaks when I jerk away from her reach. "I'm all set. Go hassle some other sap."

"But Grady—"

A clap to my back is a welcome interruption. "Hey, brother. What's up?" Jace narrows his gaze at the scantily clad woman hovering by my side. "Am I intruding?"

I let my lips pinch with the threat of a grin. "Nope. She was just saying goodbye."

Trista glares at my friend. Several awkward beats pass where the three of us stare at one another. Without another word, she huffs and stomps off.

Jace eases down onto an empty seat. Smart move considering the likelihood of that shit breaking. Decker stops by long enough to pass him a cold beer. What can I say, the service is tough to beat.

He enjoys a couple pulls and leans an elbow on the bar. "Trista?" Jace whistles. "That chick has been after your junk since high school. You'd think she'd get the message by now."

I snort. "Her perfume is killing brain cells. That's gotta be it."

He taps his bottle against mine. "No shit. Smelling like a flower explosion isn't sexy."

And that's the truth. The most alluring scent is coconut with subtle hints of strawberry. It's the aroma of forbidden desire. Just the memory makes my dick twitch, which in turn has me feeling like a filthy asshole. I tug at the waistband of my jeans and groan. If the guy sitting on my left knew I fantasize about his little sister, he'd likely string me up by the balls. When I glance over, Jace is studying me closer than I'm comfortable with. I almost tell him to knock it off.

He tilts his head at me. "So, what's up? Surprised to see you around while the sun is still out."

I pick at the grease under my nails. "Ran outta paint for the Drefter house. Called it an early day."

"Ah, gotcha. How's the project going?"

"Smooth, as always. These jobs are all simple restoration."

He nods. "And your place?"

"That's a challenge I can appreciate." I smirk.

"Glad to see something makes you smile." The expression slips off my lips and Jace grunts. "Shouldn't have mentioned it."

I scowl. "Nah, that makes me feel foolish. It's just a house."

Jace grips my shoulder. "But it's yours. Free and clear. You're allowed to be proud of that."

I shake off his touch. "For now. I'm sure something will change that soon enough."

My mother immediately comes to mind. She's a deeper money pit than the foreclosure I snatched up at bottom dollar. That thought turns my stomach. The brew I'd been enjoying turns sour with an unpleasant gurgle. I finish off my ruined beer and slam the empty bottle down. Decker walks over but I wave him off. It's a one and done sort of afternoon. I stand and reach for my wallet. After settling up the tab, I turn to leave.

"Going already?" Jace calls from behind me.

I flick my gaze back at him. "Got shit to do."

My friend polishes off his drink. "Wait a second. I'll walk out with you."

I push open the door with him on my heels. My bike waits for me out front along the curb.

"Still can't believe you bought a motorcycle." Jace's chuckle is full of disbelief.

"Dude, it's been six months. The shock value is long gone."

"Not to me. It's one of those exotic fantasies for a man."

"That's way too deep. It's just a means of getting across town. This beauty is far cheaper than my truck to fill up. Maintenance is a breeze. A lot more fun to drive, too. And we both know you're just jealous."

His grin borders on ridiculous. "Fuck yes, I am. But my folks would lose their shit."

I straddle my ride and lift the stand. "Still so concerned about what mommy and daddy dearest think?"

Jace folds his arms. "Don't pretend you aren't. My mom is getting more gray hair thanks to your choice of transportation."

The never ceasing knot in my gut tightens. I keep my gaze on the setting horizon. "She shouldn't worry about me."

"But she does," he reminds in a tone too soft for this conversation.

"I don't need pity." The accusation rips from my throat.

Jace holds up a palm. "She cares about you, we all do. That has nothing to do with feeling bad for your stubborn ass. There's a huge difference."

I grind my molars until dust collects. "Whatever. I gotta go."

He scoffs and shakes his head. "Yeah, yeah. Always bailing whenever the terrain gets a little tough."

There's no good way for me to respond. I have nothing to say that will fix this. It's a problem I'm more than aware of. But when life continues to shove me down, finding the strength to steer on a better route loses appeal. I slide my helmet on and crank the bike to life. The sharp rip of the engine drowns out any protest Jace might be voicing. I rev several times with extra power, my grip punishing. With a swift kick, I race off toward home.

Main Street passes in a blur. I twist the throttle hard enough to send my bike up on one wheel. I'm being reckless, but my skin is itching for speed. To escape the sensation of being trapped. In the next second, I'm flying down the road far above the limit. This is the only way I truly feel free.

The yellow divider guides my way. I focus on that as everything else fades to black. The vibrations beneath me are soothing and with each passing mile, tension melts away. It's almost impossible to hear anything above the whipping wind and roaring exhaust. But I catch the blue and red flashing lights in my mirrors.

Fuck.

I make the effort to brake quickly, not wanting to further piss off the cop behind me. I steer my bike to the gravel shoulder and kill the engine. After tugging off my helmet, I blow out a heavy breath. This should be interesting.

The echoing slap of boots on pavement warn me of the officer's approach. I clench my eyes shut and search for patience that doesn't exist.

"Howdy, Grady. Know why I pulled you over?"

I let my head fall. Not him. Anyone but this deputy dipshit. I glare over my shoulder at Lance Fucking Morris, also known as the biggest douchebag in Silo Springs. How he became a police officer is beyond me.

"Not a clue, man."

Lance shifts closer and stares down his pointy nose at me. I fucking hate being on lower ground. He doesn't deserve to make me feel small. "I'm not your buddy, Grady. Be careful with who you're offending. You're speaking to an officer of the law and you will do so with some respect."

I offer him an exaggerated eye roll. "Yeah, whatever."

"Step off the motorcycle, sir."

"Oh, you've got to be fucking kidding me."

"Now," he snaps.

I pocket the key to my bike and swing off. A cocky grin curves my lips as I stand almost a foot taller than him. "Problem?"

Lance resembles a weasel when he squints. "Turn around, hands behind your back."

A laugh scrapes out of me, lacking any trace of humor. "For real? You must be joking."

He removes a set of cuffs from his belt. "Are you resisting arrest?"

"What the fuck am I being charged with?"

"Don't make this harder than necessary, Grady."

"This is bullshit," I spit.

But fighting is useless. This bully has a badge and will win in the long haul. I turn away painfully slow and offer up my crossed wrists. This isn't my first rodeo. I highly doubt it'll be my last.

Cold metal pinches my skin, far tighter than required. I shoot him another glare. "Is that really fucking necessary?"

Lance sneers. "Can't be too careful in my line of work."

I tug against the harsh bonds. "You're targeting me."

"Not hard to do. Like father, like son. I saw you pulling out of Howlers. Next time, try to avoid swerving."

Stinging heat rips up my spine. "I had one beer."

"Such a lightweight. No wonder you're such a fuckup. This town doesn't need you staining it's good name."

"You're such a shit, Morris. Worse than the punk-ass you were in high school."

Lance drags me toward his cruiser. "That might be the case. Big difference is I have the law to back me up."

"Isn't that fucking swell. You're a disgrace to the department."

He yanks open the rear passenger door and motions for me to get in. "It'll be a pleasure to book you with disorderly conduct and verbal assault."

I force myself to follow orders, swooping onto the leather backseat. "Good luck getting that shit to stick."

"Any amount of time with you locked up is payment enough," he says with a grin.

"What about my bike?" It's not my greatest concern at this moment, but a potential hassle might have him thinking twice.

He rocks on his heels. "Not my concern. Have one of your cronies pick it up."

Lance shuts me inside with a reverberating slam. I can already picture the metal bars sliding closed and caging me in a microscopic cell. Bile rises, the foul flavor singeing my tongue. I scoot forward and swallow the urge to retch.

"Hey, man. You don't have to do this. Just let me out and we'll go our separate ways."

He bangs against the bulletproof partition separating us. "Shut the fuck up, Grady. You've had plenty of chances."

The fuck I have. My luck ran dry when I was still in diapers.

Lance is quiet as he drives us to the station. I can almost hear his brain rattling with effort. He smiles at me in the mirror. "Did you hear Sutton is coming home tomorrow?"

Her name alone is a shot to my chest. Fuck, I almost double over. But my reaction is hidden from this asshole's view. To him, my expression rivals a stone mask. The harsh look has granted me a reputation of being cold and unfeeling. Maybe that's true. No one gives enough of a shit to dig deeper and see.

Except her. But she might as well be ancient history.

I'd leave this crooked, judgmental town if it wasn't for my mother. She's barely hanging on. Without me checking in, she'd waste away that much faster. Silo Springs has no hold on me beyond that. I scoff over the lie threatening to strangle me. There's another reason, far more profound and significant. That truth prowls below the surface. My mother isn't the only person I stay rooted in place for.

Try as I damn might, Sutton has a hold on me. Nothing will ever come of that unyielding grip. Especially with the shitty way I treat her. But I can't lower my guard. The bullshit indifference is my only defense to keep Sutton at arm's length. Nothing more will ever develop between us, but I'm tethered to her all the same. She's the only happy something in my life. Even with the distance we'll always keep between us.

So, I'm left in a city full of people who consider me the enemy. A worthless punk from deadbeat parents. There's no real value to my name. I haven't helped matters with my less than pleasant demeanor. Case in point as I sit in the bad end of a squad car.

"Did you fall asleep? That one beer must have been strong." Lance's scratchy tone drags me into the present.

My scowl reaches new lows. "I'm completely sober at this point, fuck you very much. Just not interested in chit-chatting with you."

He grunts. "You're stuck back there. Make the most of it."

I sag against the seat and stretch my legs. "Noted."

"I'm going to ask her out."

"Who?" I close my eyes. Since Lance mentioned it, might as well try for a nap.

"Sutton. Weren't you listening?"

I jolt to attention, my spine snapping ramrod straight. "And you're taking a shot at her?" The words taste like sewage.

"Why the hell not? She deserves an honest man. I can treat her right and provide anything she needs."

I fist my cuffed hands against the jab of harsh reality. He's right, of course. This douche was raised on the proper side of the tracks. He's from a family that happens to be stupid wealthy. The steady job is an added bonus. Still, he doesn't need to gloat.

A rushed breath hisses past my lips. "Good luck with that, buddy. I'm sure she met someone in college." The idea alone is a dagger to my frozen heart. Sutton will never be mine, but she doesn't need random assholes pawing at her. I can't have her. No one else should either.

Lance's pearly whites flash in the rearview mirror reflection. "I can be patient."

Flames spark to life in my vision. I don't give a shit about most things. People can do just about anything to me and it doesn't matter. I've already been through worse. One bright spot remains, and he's trying to take that away.

Sutton Olsen is the only source of happy I've allowed myself. She's an exception to most of my rules. But that's a secret I'll forever keep. It's douchebags like Lance that will use my attachment to her against me.

Involving her in this pissing contest was a very grave mistake. If this smarmy asshole attempts to lay a finger on her, he'll find it broken. Keeping Lance Morris away from Sutton just became a top priority.

CHAPTER THREE

Sutton

*Happy something #124: The smell of fresh cut grass,
especially in the morning.*

STEP ONTO THE PORCH AND INHALE A LUNGFUL OF CRISP AIR. That heavenly aroma rivals the rich hazelnut steaming from my mug. Streaks of morning sun filter through the luscious trees overhead. My mother's beloved rooster crows from his roost on the barn roof. Getting reacquainted with this lifestyle will take minimal effort.

After taking a slow sip of coffee, I continue surveying our slice of paradise. This sprawling land is a hearty dose of pure good, and a blessing for the soul. The fringes of apprehension fade with each passing moment. I stretch my arms out to the side, feeling the stress of finals and graduation and moving home vanish.

There's no sign of industrial smog or haze clogging the sky. The nearest glow from a stoplight is miles away. No buzz of bustling traffic can be heard. There aren't any skyscrapers visible along the horizon. Out here, it's just green grass and natural beauty.

Almost on autopilot, I hop down the stairs and relax into an Adirondack chair seemingly waiting for me. The sigh that escapes my lips can only be described as blissed-out. Acres of rolling fields span in every direction. Memories join my reverie, flickering within the rustic backdrop.

I can see Jace throwing baseballs into the flat tire that's still strung up on the large oak. My mom hanging wet laundry on the clothesline because nothing bought in a store smells better than pure sunshine. I squint and imagine my dad hauling a trailer, brimming with bales, toward the barn. And Grady, of course. He appears more often than anyone else. No surprise there. His presence is root-deep, like the very soil this house sits on. But one spot stands out against the others.

Our swing still hangs from the sturdy maple branch. Goosebumps pebble along my skin when I recall the brush of his hands against me. No one pushed me higher than him, in all the ways that mattered.

"Hey, sweetie."

The serene melody chases those thoughts up into the clouds. I shift to face my mother while she descends the stairs. "Hi, momma."

"You're awake early."

That earns her a laugh. "It's nearly nine o'clock."

Her brow lifts. "My daughter used to sleep until noon during summer break."

"Well, consider that habit shattered. I can barely stay in bed past eight."

She sits in the chair beside me. "Never thought that'd happen. Jace was always my wake-up call. But here you are, up and out before me."

I smile at her. "Glad I can still surprise you."

My mom nods and takes a drink from her mug. "What's on your agenda for the day?"

"Oh, let me see. Finish unpacking. Set up my schedule for next week. Contact my clients. That sort of thing." I shade my eyes when a blast of sunlight breaches the trees.

She brushes some hair off my forehead. "Don't forget to save space for relaxing and smelling the flowers. Kick your feet up, enjoy being home."

My mom isn't aware that I'd been wading through syrupy nostalgia mere moments ago. My limbs are loose and there's zero threat of strain. No troubles are finding me on this tranquil piece of lawn. Not yet, at least.

"Don't worry, momma. I'll have plenty of fun."

"Good. That's really good." She squeezes my hand. "Any plans to reconnect with old friends?"

I glance over, catching the slight upturn to her lips. There's a particular someone she's digging about. "Lacie and Molly stayed local. I'll get together with them soon." A lazy shrug accompanies my words.

Her nails tap on the armrest. "Anyone else?"

A huff escapes me. My mother is well aware of my prior crush on Grady. "Why don't you tell me?"

"He's around often enough." She doesn't bother hiding her smile.

The telltale flutters take flight in my belly. Traitorous butterflies. "Oh?"

"Mhm-hmm. He's such a big help to your father and brother."

Without realizing, she provides an easy out from this topic. "Where's dad? He was already gone when I woke up."

"At the office."

"On a Saturday?"

Her nose scrunches. "He's working on a major project. An impressive tool with a really complicated name that could vastly improve some farming system."

My mother is clueless when it comes to my father's job. I'm not much better. All the equations and calculations go straight over my head. He's a mechanical engineer with a specialty in farm equipment. Way back when, he led the team that created several enhancements for numerous machines. Because of their developments, the time it takes for plowing fields and harvesting crops and baling hay is cut in half.

"That's why they pay him the big bucks." I steer my gaze forward. A few upgraded combines and tractors rest near the barn. This isn't a fully functioning farm by any means. Our expansive property is more for recreation and leisure. But my dad loves his toys, and puts them to good use. Twenty acres of the rear fields are used for growing hay. I'm fairly certain cutting and baling isn't a chore for him.

She nods and rises to her feet. "I'm not sure your father will ever retire. He has the best of both realities."

"Lofty corner office by day. Sitting comfy on a John Deere at night. What more could he want?"

My mom laughs. "Precisely. I'll never tear him away."

"Not that you really want to." I rest my chin on an open palm, appraising her carefree expression. They're both living the high life. Why was I hesitant to move home? The reasons are beginning to blur.

She cups my cheek, swiping at the soft skin with her thumb. "We're very happy to have you back, kiddo. Truly. This town lost a lot of sparkle when you left."

I blink at the moisture clouding my vision. "Thanks, momma. I'm glad my old room was still available."

Her tsk is loud. "Please. You're always welcome and we'll never change a thing."

"Even when I'm forty?"

"Now you're just being silly." She walks toward the porch stairs. "I have to get started on my pies for bridge club tonight. Can I get you anything?"

"Want some help?"

My mom waves me off. "Nonsense. Enjoy your downtime."

I glance around. "I could definitely get used to this."

"That's great, dear. Holler if you need something."

"Will do, momma." I slouch lower in my chair, soaking up the morning warmth before humidity forces me inside. This is absolutely living the right way. I savor my final sip of coffee with a soft sigh.

I'm contemplating a refill when something in my periphery distracts me. A shadowed figure breaks through the tree line. The hulking presence is a storm cloud crashing into my serenity. I know who he is without him getting closer. The sight of broad shoulders and a scruffy jaw sets my heart racing. A lump the size of Wyoming lodges in my throat. I don't move, not sure I can. Breathing is already enough of a challenge. I'm trapped in this intense force field he's solely responsible for creating.

A tremor wracks every part of me while the ground tilts sideways. I've been back in Silo Springs for less than twenty-four hours. That isn't nearly long enough to prepare for him. But that doesn't stop his steady approach. The warm sunlight vanishes, my ability to hear and smell and touch disappear. My senses are consumed by the man straight ahead. Grady's presence takes up everything without him realizing the impact.

His stride is stiff, that guard he uses firmly in place. The sun glints off his dark blond hair, the length longer than I remember. I rub my fingers together, imagining the silky texture of the strands. He's so damn sexy. There's no use denying his appeal. The need to call out burns on my tongue. I can't let him pass by without saying something. It's been four lonely years since we've spoken. A piercing cramp attacks my stomach at that. Our silence ends now. My pulse roars as I part my lips. A pitiful squeak is all I manage to muster.

I catch the moment Grady sees me. His steps jerk to an abrupt halt. The wrench he's holding trembles in his grip, but he remains frozen otherwise. The space around us, the handful of feet separating us, hums with energy and seems magnetized. I can practically feel the electricity zipping along my skin.

Any hints of youth have been wiped from his features. The boy I grew up with is tucked safely in my memories. The man before me is solid and vibrating with intensity. Grady's body has filled out and gained enormous strength, that much is evident. Even with what looks like the weight of the world on his mind, he stands tall and proud. He's the embodiment of male power. But his towering frame isn't the reason for this stupor I'm caught up in.

His eyes steal the air from my lungs. I shiver at the haunting glimmer. Vibrant green that once flared with interest is eerily flat. The emerald hue is dull, swallowing any sign of golden flecks. There's no mischievous gleam. Zero promise of trouble. The lack of interest couldn't be more apparent.

Grady remains silent, disturbingly so, while continuing to stare. I'd like to hope he's cataloging the changes to my features, the same way I did to him minutes before. But his gaze bores straight through me. It's as if he doesn't remember who I am. I wonder if he even notices my unwavering attention. The lash is so painful that I wince.

Those frigid depths flick over me for barely a second, as if I'm small and insignificant. His empty stare makes me feel nonexistent. I've been pushed around and left behind, but never with this blatant lack of care. My absence didn't impact him the same way. As always, the bottomless longing locked in my heart was one-sided. Maybe I fell asleep and this is a nightmare. I blink in rapid succession. When I refocus, Grady is still there.

He stays on the gravel path, a foot from where the

backyard begins. I've never been more aware of distance. He's almost within reach. Dark purple smudges rest beneath his eyes. The skin is puffy and screams of exhaustion. Weariness appears bone-deep, but he'd never complain. The boy I knew had trouble sleeping. I wonder if this man still does.

I've seen Grady over the years, of course. Those quick glimpses were never long enough to snap a decent mental image. I wasn't able to get a good sense of his well-being during my visits home. He'd appeared to be doing well. Jace provided bits and pieces that told a similar story. It was safe to accept Grady was fine. In this moment, I'm realizing how wrong those assumptions were.

The chair quakes when I scoot to the edge of my seat. The slight movement seems to jolt him out of his own trance. Those green eyes narrow on me. His expression is thunderous, ready for battle. I almost expect bolts of lightning to streak across the clear-blue sky. Angry clouds will surely sweep in and release a torrential downpour.

My mouth is bone-dry. Probably because my jaw has been hanging slack since he arrived. I attempt to draw in a decent breath and clear the grit from my throat.

"Hey, Gray." The greeting is hardly more than a whispered croak, but he hears it.

A guttural rumble breaks from his chest. The tortured sound slams into me, causing heat to sting my eyes.

He doesn't give me the chance to say more. In the next second, he's turning on his heel and striding toward the barn. I consider chasing him and demand he talks to me. But my legs are certain to give out if I try to stand. Heck, my knees are wobbling without any added pressure.

I rip my gaze off his retreating form. Grady Bowen means nothing to me. But my sappy heart bleeds the truth. This man is bound to ruin me all over again. Will I let him?

CHAPTER FOUR

Grady

*Happy something #82: Having a shirt
without holes or a tattered hem.*

TURN LEFT INTO THE NEGLECTED TRAILER PARK AND EASE MY truck down the dirt road. The stench of overflowing septic tanks immediately assaults my nostrils. Ignoring the odor is something I've unfortunately grown accustomed to. Doesn't make this trek more pleasant. I'd roll up the windows but this old beater doesn't have air conditioning. Roasting in this hotbox is not a fine way to spend an afternoon.

The wheels protest over the rugged terrain. This driveway probably hasn't been grated in over a decade. Groundskeeping isn't high on the priority list around these parts. I steer my pickup into one of the designated spots and cut the engine. The sigh that escapes me is a scream of defeat. It's not even five o'clock and my body is begging for a break. I didn't bother going home to change after work. The paint splattering my clothes doesn't bother these folks. Hell,

I'm just happy to have shirts and jeans without holes. I glare at the neglected lawns surrounding me. Yeah, pretty sure no one will even notice.

Without further delay, I grab the groceries from the backseat. I step out and the damn grass reaches my knees. The chance that anyone has a mower is slim to none. I make a mental note to bring one by and clean up the parking lots.

Silo Springs is a thriving city in general. This corner of town is long forgotten, and should remain that way. Nothing good happens inside these withering mobile homes. The fact I have to keep stopping by this way twists my stomach. My mother has some sick attachment. Or she enjoys making me suffer. Most likely the latter.

I yank open her screen door, nearly ripping the damn thing off its rusty hinges. One more piece of trash to add on the pile of this dump. My mother isn't just letting herself waste away. This trailer is rotting from top to bottom.

Fresh stains on the carpet welcome me, but I barely pay attention. The fact I can take a breath without dry heaving is a small blessing. Whatever is causing a rancid odor is masked thanks to the air fresheners I bought earlier this week. I recall a time when she took pride in our home. Those days are long gone. The trailer I grew up in was a palace compared to this corroding heap.

After dropping the bags off in the kitchen, I go in search of my mother. I don't have to look far. Her limp figure is sprawled out on the saggy couch. I make my way over, being sure to avoid stepping on decaying spots in the floor. My mom doesn't stir with the noise I make. If I had to guess, she's been knocked out for hours. I drag over the only available chair and sit down.

"Ma?" I give her shoulder a gentle nudge.

She doesn't move. I watch silently for a moment, catching the slow rise and fall of her chest. The ticking bomb in my stomach fizzles out seeing the slight movement. I glance at the door, contemplating an easy exit. But guilt is a fickle bitch. I can't leave without making sure she'll wake up. What's left of my conscience keeps me rooted to this seat.

I shake her a bit harder. "Ma, can you hear me?"

My mother groans, the sound rough and dry. She shifts and peels her eyes open. That cloudy gleam in her detached gaze tells me everything I need to know. She won't remember this conversation tomorrow. I'm sure she got ahold of something strong. With a crooked smile, she shows off rotting, yellowed teeth.

"Hi, boy." Her voice rattles with effort. She makes no attempt to sit up, not that I expect her to.

Bile threatens to bubble up my throat, but I swallow the acid down. "Glad you're okay."

"Why wouldn't I be?"

Her question is ludicrous. I blink at her while trying to gather a response that doesn't resemble a bellow. Several deep breaths grant me the power to continue this shallow exchange.

"I can never be too sure," I grind out.

A bony wrist flicks in my direction. "No need to worry yourself over me."

Easy for her to say. I was shoved into the parent role at age fourteen. Why stop now? I scrub a palm over the stubble coating my jaw. "Yeah, well, you're my responsibility."

"That's your own stupid fault." She probably meant for those words to sting, but her tone is thinner than these weak ass walls.

"Never said it wasn't," I mutter.

"So, what do you need?"

I hitch a thumb behind me. "Brought you some food. Knew you were running low."

My mother inhales too sharply and begins hacking. Her

wet cough makes me flinch. She's bound to snap a rib at this rate. Once she gets the fit under control, I release the breath trapped in my lungs. She shoots me a pathetic glare.

"Stop wasting your money on shit I don't need. If you wanna help me out, leave cash on the table."

I've given her more money than I care to admit. She immediately turns around looking for a score, shooting it up into her collapsing veins. This woman can't stay clean to save her life—quite literally.

Insanity is defined as doing the same thing over and again, always getting the same results, but expecting something different. I've never considered myself a very stable man, but I know when to quit. I'm not playing this game with her.

"How about you eat something? I can make tomato soup." That's usually an easy sell because no chewing is required. But my mother's bleary eyes narrow further and I already have my answer.

She gives a harsh jerk of her head. A clump of matted hair sticks to her forehead. Shiny blonde has long faded into a dull gray. "I'm not hungry."

I hold up a hand. "Fine. Your choice."

"Damn straight. Not sure why you're always barging in here, trying to force shit on me."

"I won't apologize for trying to keep you alive," I spit in return.

Her lazy gaze drifts to the drooping ceiling. "Well, good luck with all that. Feel free to show yourself out. You're better off leaving me to rot."

The burger I had for lunch curdles in my stomach. There are many days I'd agree with her. But leaving my mother to die isn't an option I can manage, even if that's what she's trying to do. Her blatant dismissal leaves me with toxic thoughts and a daily dose of reality. Being in this dismal space is a black hole. Seconds and minutes get doused in molasses, sticking together without moving. It all ticks by so slowly I'd assume time is frozen.

What a fucking nightmare. Is this what I can look forward to for the foreseeable future? My current outcome is bleak as fuck.

Residential restoration jobs have me busting ass all day. The place I bought keeps me working late into the night. I get the honor of cleaning up my mother's mess whenever she goes on a bender. Can't leave out being wrongly accused of stupid shit on a regular basis. If I'm lucky, there's a barstool at Howlers with my name on it. But that's few and far between. I go home to an empty house, always alone.

What a damn fine way of living. Not that I'm really complaining. Anything beats the years when my pops was still around. I shudder at the memory. That man was pure evil. One glance at the wasting form of my mother is proof enough.

I've heard Camilla Soulle used to have her head screwed on straight. Many called her pretty, a real looker with several potential suitors. Then my dad moved into town, changed her last name, and ruined the woman she could've been. The revolving line of men following close behind certainly didn't help.

If only there was a sliver of relief to be found. I snort at that. My greatest form of comfort just returned to town. I never admitted it to her, but Sutton has always been my happy something. The only one that matters. Growing up, I'd needed those stolen moments with her, juvenile as they were. She gave me an ounce of hope that everything wouldn't turn out to be shit.

With her name, a rush of visions flood my mind. Time has granted her more beauty. How is it possible that she's even more gorgeous? She's grace and class and everything I'll never have. When I saw her sitting right in front of me, it felt like the fantasy I'd conjured up. Her bee-stung lips parted with surprise. I wanted to kiss the shock away, and steal her breath along with it. Those blue eyes bored into mine, peeling away layers of pain and reaching depths only she has access to. My heart had threatened to burst. Tumble out of my chest and land in her lap. She owns the damn thing, might as well hand it over. The beating organ is useless without her.

But I couldn't talk to her. What the fuck would I say? Sutton went off to school and made something better of herself. I'm stuck in the same shitty spot, spinning my bald tires. I meant what I'd said four years ago. She was better off forgetting about me. The uninhibited desire in her baby blues screamed the opposite. Fuck. What I wouldn't give to make her mine. Wrap her in my arms and own her like she once begged for. But no. I won't ruin her life. And that's what being tied to me would mean. I'd only hold her back.

When Sutton left, any good went with her. Four fucking years in the dark changes a man. I'm almost ashamed of the guy always glaring back at me in the mirror. Seeing her after so long was a tortuous gift. My eyes suddenly sting with unwanted heat. I cough and choke down the unexpected onslaught of emotion. I'm typically referred to as a wall of stone—impenetrable and imposing. In this moment, I feel the opposite. I'm that lost boy rediscovering his one source of true luxury. I cover my face and groan. Getting upset about this is pointless.

I've made sure to avoid the Olsen ranch ever since catching sight of Sutton. That doesn't stop the temptation from crawling beneath my skin. Every moment is an opportunity to test my control. It's been a week of torture. Knowing she's within reach and unable to do shit about it is a lethal strike. I'm not sure how much longer this can last.

A car backfires and the loud bang knocks me from my thoughts. Here I am, wallowing in a shallow puddle of pity. Again. Poor fucking Grady. I have no reason to imagine an existence with Sutton in it. I'll just continue doing everything in my power to ignore her. Eventually the pain will return to a muted roar.

My mother rolls onto her side. A cloud of musty mildew wafts over from the couch. She startles at the sight of me. "Oh, you're still around? Figured you'd up and left hours ago."

I've only been here for thirty minutes at the most. I suck in a deep breath, agreeing that I've overstayed this welcome. "I should be going. Don't want to disrupt you more than I already have."

That earns me a loose grin. She lifts a shaky finger, pointing over my shoulder. "Be a good boy and fetch me a cigarette."

Before I can even consider following through with the request, her eyelids droop and she's out fucking cold. It's as though she wasn't actually aware of my presence. Maybe she never really was in the first place.

Mother of the damn year.

I glance around the debilitated trailer, a string of silent expletives spilling from my lips. This is a part of my life, but it doesn't define me. I can't stand the sight a moment longer. The weak floorboards tremble under my weight when I stand. I lean down and kiss my mother's head. Hopefully she'll eat something after this high wears off.

I barrel outside while the entire trailer rocks on its crumbling foundation. Like a lifeline, my phone beeps with a notification. The screen lights with a text from Jace.

Jace: Get your ass to Bronc. I need backup.

I groan at the name of the bar. That doesn't stop me from hauling ass to my truck. Whatever he needs, it must be damn important.

CHAPTER FIVE

Sutton

*Happy something #91: Sitting on the end of a dock
with my feet in the lake.*

THE AMOUNT OF PEOPLE CRAMMED INTO THIS BAR ON A Wednesday is rather impressive. Everyone is seeking a bit of relief after a long day at work, me included. Through the front windows, the sun is beginning to dip lower in the sky. I swirl the pink concoction in my glass and take a sip. Strawberries with a bite of vodka burst on my tongue. A happy sigh escapes me while I settle deeper into the high-top stool.

"This was a fantastic idea." I glance at the two girls sitting beside me. "I've missed these cocktails."

Molly quirks a brow. "They don't have cosmos near campus?"

"Not like this." I enjoy another taste and lick my lips. "There's something extra delicious mixed in."

Lacie studies the contents of her martini. "Who knew

Bronco Buck could sling better fruity drinks than ritzy college joints."

That gets a giggle out of me. "I would hardly call them ritzy."

She motions around the dimly lit bar. "I'm sure they don't hang bras on the ceiling."

I snort into my glass. "Those add to the appeal. Satin and lace are always a good choice."

We all share a laugh.

"Oh yeah, it really puts this place on the classy map. A signature of sorts. I guess it makes ladies night more interesting." Lacie wags her brows.

Molly hums in approval. "They need something to keep us coming back. Especially if a hot guy is the one to take your bra off. But let's be honest, we don't have enough options to be picky."

"In more ways than one." I glance around at all the familiar faces. Finding a guy I didn't attend high school with is a challenge.

Lacie clinks her glass against mine. "Amen, sister."

"We can visit my old roommate for a change of pace. Harlyn lives in the big city," I tell them with a smile.

Molly's eyes grow wide. "Imagine all the fresh meat. Let's do it."

Lacie holds up her hand. "I second that."

"Okay. I'll find out what works for her. In the meantime," I pick up my drink and drain the rest, "let's enjoy ourselves in Silo Springs."

"To the extent that your restrictions will allow." Molly grins when I scowl. She lifts her chin toward the far corner. "I see your bodyguard is on duty."

A muscle pops in my jaw. "He's such a bulldog."

Molly nods. "I'd say. He hasn't loosened up one bit when it comes to you."

I can feel my brother's stare from across the bar. He's been holed up against the wall for over an hour. It's beyond ridiculous that he feels the need to keep such diligent watch. He desperately needs another hobby. I've never been reckless or irresponsible when it comes to men. Jace makes it seem like the opposite. Heaven forbid a guy shows interest and tries talking to me.

"Good evening, ladies." The lazy drawl comes from behind us. I peek over my shoulder and find Lance standing far too close. There's no sign of the police uniform I've seen him strutting around town in. This preppy version reminds me of the kid I graduated with. He's grinning at all of us, but his eyes are locked on me. I do my best to repress a shudder.

"Hey, Lance." Molly's greeting is all wispy breath and unbridled desire. Interesting.

His gaze skitters off me when he nods at her. "Hi, Molls."

She twirls a lock of her ruby hair. "Off duty tonight?"

"I'm still patrolling, just a different kind." He takes a moment to openly ogle us, licking his lips in an overly lewd fashion. *Gross.*

Lacie picks at her nails. "I heard you picked up Grady Bowen the other day."

My hackles rise with a resounding screech.

"Sure did. He was asking for it. Arrested him on several counts. It was a pleasure slapping those cuffs on him." Lance looks way too proud of himself.

Fiery heat fills my veins. "You did what?"

Lance blanches at the venom in my tone. "He deserved it."

I cross my arms. "I find that highly doubtful."

The surprise melts off his face, replaced by a fierce glare meant to intimidate. "You're still defending him?"

Lance's question is a cracking whip slicing through the space between us. Many would probably shrivel at this open hostility, especially from a police officer. But I'm not one of them. I sit up straighter and narrow my eyes.

"Of course. Grady is my friend." I nearly choke over the last word.

"What a fucking waste," he mutters.

"Oh snap," Molly whispers.

Her stare is latched on something over my shoulder. Hair on the back of my neck rises from that look alone. A shiver ripples through me regardless of the balmy temperature. When I follow her gaze, my stomach bottoms out. Grady is hovering a few mere feet away.

The clouds darkening his eyes can be described as nothing but livid. My heart pounds a furious beat, enraged on his behalf. The reason escapes me because all my concentration is centered on him. No man has the right to look so fine in a basic T-shirt and jeans. His hair is wet, the dark blond strands sticking up in messy disarray. Thick stubble makes him look older and rugged. Flexing muscles ready to fend off any threat. Grady Bowen is a delicious package and I want to rip off every layer that keeps him hidden from view.

It's been over a week since I saw him at my parents' place. I was beginning to believe the entire ordeal was a figment of my imagination. But here he stands, ready to unleash the fury.

I try to swallow, but my throat is too dry. How does he still have this effect on me?

"Can I talk to you outside, Sutton?"

That voice. Dear Mother of all that's holy. It's a soothing balm and an abrasive scrape within the same few notes. I tamp down a moan as the words roll over me.

One of my ass cheeks is already off the stool. "Okay."

But Lance blocks my path.

"What the fuck are you doing here, Bowen?" His tone is terse and accusing. I don't care for it one bit.

Grady's responding glare is vicious. "Is stepping foot on public property suddenly a crime?"

Lance grunts. "No."

"Then mind your own damn business." The growl booms off Grady's chest.

"I was here first." Lance resembles a petulant child, and the look is not sexy. The pout on his lips makes me cringe. When I glance over, Molly and Lacie have a similar reaction. Glad my redheaded friend came to her senses.

Grady prowls forward. "Doesn't matter. Sutton is coming with me."

When he puts it that way, I want to stay glued to my seat. Oh, who am I kidding. Having a moment alone with him is worth a little hit to my womanly pride.

I shove past Lance and follow Grady's imposing form through the crowd. My brother is wearing a shit-eating smirk as we move by him. I fight the urge to flip him off. It's abundantly clear he had everything to do with this intrusion.

Grady slams open the door into the alley. I trail close behind and prop myself up against the brick wall. The temperature has cooled off, the slight chill is blissful against my heated skin. He strides to the opposite side, ensuring the maximum amount of space is separating us. I ignore the burn that distance causes. What did I really expect?

His features are a steel mask of indifference. He's not giving anything away without me asking. I'm not sure why he bothered bringing me out here. A cramp tightens painfully in my belly. Why is this so difficult? The strain grows heavy in the air, a living beast determined to keep us apart.

Our silence expands and overflows across the narrow gap. My throat tightens and I rub at the growing lump. I finally glance up at Grady from under my lashes. An exhale shutters off my lips when I catch him staring at me.

"Hey, Gray." I repeat the greeting from last time we were caught in a similar standoff.

A tremor wracks his limbs. I wonder if he plans to ditch out again. But his feet remain planted on the concrete.

"Hey, Sutton." The sound is low and deep and deceptively soft.

I want to tell him so many things. Highlights from the last four years pile up in my mind, jamming the gears and leaving me silent. One sentiment stands out the most. I've missed him. The words claw up my throat, bubbling out beyond my control.

"I've missed—"

Grady speaks up at that same moment, shutting my confession down. "Glad I could steal you away from all the fun."

A furrow dents my forehead. "What do you mean?"

"I'm sure Lance was entertaining you with sordid tales. He's a damn snake."

"Did he really haul you in?"

He snorts. "Wasn't the first time."

I let my jaw go slack. "On what charges?"

"Bullshit. He didn't have anything on me. Chief Wilson released me within an hour of arriving at the station."

A bitter taste settles on my tongue. "Doesn't that count as a mark against Lance or something? He should care more about being a good cop."

Grady snares me with those bottomless emerald depths. "You worried about him?"

"Not at all." My tone leaves no room for argument.

"Could've fooled me."

I rub my throbbing temples. "It doesn't really matter. Is there anything else you wanted to discuss?"

"You sober enough to remember this conversation?" He straightens off the wall.

I roll my eyes. "I've had one drink, thank you very much."

"Wasn't sure how many Deputy Dipshit bought for you."

That earns him a smile. "Wait, are you jealous?"

"Abso-fucking-lutely. He was flirting with you."

I drop my mouth open with a pop. My ears whoosh with crashing waves. I had to be hearing things. "W-what?"

"Stay away from Lance."

"Are you giving me a reason to?" I have zero interest in hanging out with that dink. Getting more truth from Grady is what's important.

He shrugs. "I don't like it. Jace doesn't either."

"Why?"

"Because I said so."

I dip my chin. "I already have one protective brother. I'm not looking for another one."

That was the wrong thing to say. Grady steps into my space, his jaw working back and forth. Golden flames and green lava swirl together in his eyes. "I'm far worse than your brother."

"W-why?" That's a popular word choice for me today.

"I have far more to lose." His words settle into a deep, secret part of me.

"Tell me," I whisper.

He leans in, giving me a potent dose of woodsy cologne and uncharted territory. The line between us barely exists in this moment. I almost reach for him. But Grady blinks and the spell crashes to the ground. He steps away, leaving me cold and alone.

"What do you want me to say? That I'm sorry? I'm being an idiot? Because I'm not. My life is full of regrets, Sutton. The list is never ending. But there's one thing I'll never feel bad about."

A shiver skates down my spine. I don't need to ask, but my lips form the question regardless. "What's that?"

"Turning you down, Sutt. You deserve far better than a lowlife like me. I hope you found him."

I avert my gaze, focusing on a wash of purple and pink splashes across the horizon. "I did."

In my dreams, with the memory of him.

Grady is quiet for a moment, and the silence stretches further. I glance his way, finding him staring at me with an intensity that makes every fiber of my being light up. His soulful gaze can cure the worst pain. If only his mouth could get the memo.

He nods, the bob of his head a slow beat. "That's good. I told you to find a man. I'm not trying to be noble, or an ass. Even though that's probably the opposite of what you think. What's important is your happiness."

The romantic buried deep inside of me springs to life. Her foolish lips curve into a seductive grin aimed at the man who only has a frown for me. Such a twit. But maybe she's onto something. I nibble on my bottom lip. "Well, in that case, tell me a happy something of your own."

Grady offers a sharp jerk of his head. "We're done with that. Haven't heard one in years."

"Whose fault is that?"

"Mine, of course. We don't need to play the blame game." The light snuffs out from his gaze. My chest aches as I watch him disappear behind that damn mask of indifference. "Everything is my fault."

"That's not true." I shuffle forward, but he retreats further.

"Doesn't really matter, Sutt." He juts his chin toward the door. "Go back to your friends. Ignore that douchebag if he starts any shit."

I lace my fingers together. "Where are you going?"

"Home."

I want to know where he rests his head at night. I'm

desperate to hear him admit his jealousy again. I need more truths from him. The possibilities spin on repeat. But he turns away without another word.

"Hey, Gray?"

He pauses, but doesn't turn around.

"Don't be a stranger, okay?"

His shoulders bunch under the weight of my request. He looks back at me, the barest hint of a smirk lifting his lips. "No promises."

Warmth tickles my lower belly as the hum of his words caress me. I'll have to accept that. For now.

The initial Grady haze is fading and I become aware of our surroundings. Very specifically, a motorcycle that's parked right in front of me. The chrome glints under the overhead lamp. He approaches the bike and straddles the seat. I'm sure my eyes are bulging wide.

"Surprised?" He palms a gleaming black helmet.

I nod. "Yeah, a lot."

Grady strokes over some orange flames painted on the fuel tank. "It's dangerous and chaotic. Fits me well."

He doesn't give me a chance to respond. The motorcycle roars to life and he peels out of the alley. I stand there silently, gaping at the cloud of dust left in his wake. What the hell happened while I was gone?

CHAPTER SIX

Happy something #32: A home-cooked meal. Even better if there are others sitting around the table to enjoy the food with.

I SHOVE THE CROWBAR UNDER ANOTHER PIECE OF ROTTING WOOD. The old board gives way with a single pop. I toss it onto the growing pile beside me. Wash, rinse, repeat. I've been at this for hours and barely made a dent. At this rate, the wraparound porch will never get replaced. Much like the rest of this house.

My stomach grumbles with a loud protest, but I'm not ready to quit. I'm losing daylight by the second and need to get some semblance of progress done. Jace's recent offer to lend a hand is sounding a lot more appealing.

From his spot on the lawn, Bear suddenly snaps to attention. A low growl is already rattling from his throat. His head jerks to the side, ears pointing forward with rapt interest. Before I can blink, my dog leaps to his paws and tears off toward the driveway.

"Shit." I toss down my tools. "Dammit, Bear."

His howling bark echoes off the trees and I jog to catch up. When I round the house, Bear is rearing up on the driver's side of a red coupe. The glare from the windshield hides my trespasser's identity. I stride forward and squint at the figure behind the wheel.

No fucking way.

But there's no mistaking her beauty. Sutton's mocha hair shines in the setting sun, those golden rays streaking the dark tresses. A flush stains the smooth skin of her chest and neck. A large majority of my blood shoots south at the sight. I want to trace the path with my tongue. The semi in my shorts agrees with a twitch. A startled yelp drags me from the erotic fantasy.

Sutton is cowering in her seat, gawking at my dog's vicious snarl through the glass. She seems to be frozen in place. I catch the rapid breaths puffing off her lips. Those big baby blues are blown open wide while she absorbs the very high probability of being attacked.

I reach for Bear's collar and tug him off her car. He pulls at my hold with the force of a buffalo. I wince at the pressure on my sore muscles. Bear doesn't relent, attempting to break free by any means necessary.

She cracks open the window and pokes her head out. "Uh, hey there."

Bear bites at the air with her greeting. I haul him in tighter. "Hi, Sutt. Wasn't expecting you."

"Yeah, maybe I should have called."

"Would've been a good idea."

She eyes the vibrating hound at my side. "You're not gonna release him, right?"

I almost crack a smile. "That depends. What're you doing here?"

"Thought we could catch up. We used to be, um, friends."

"Did we?" That doesn't sound right to me. That term has never fit for how I picture her in my life. But the platonic label is what's best for her sake.

"I like to think so."

"All right then."

Sutton reaches over and lifts a bag. "I brought you dinner."

A mixture of melted cheese and garlic wafts over. Without hesitation, I suck in a deep inhale. Another rumble attacks my gut. Bear gets a whiff and releases a pitiful whine. Damn, she's reeling us both in.

"What is it?" The question is stupid. As if I'm going to turn her away.

"I made my mother's lasagna." She hoists the paper sack higher.

"You cooked?"

She nods. "I did."

"For me?" This deal keeps getting sweeter.

"Well, yeah." Sutton nibbles her bottom lip. "This used to be your favorite at our house."

A deeply broken piece inside of me twists painfully. "Can't remember when I had that last."

"Figured as much."

I glare at her assumption. "And why's that?"

"Looks like you've been occupied elsewhere." She nods toward the house.

Her soft tone soothes me in a way I can't reason with. The fire in my veins is tempered, but the lust boils hotter than before. This girl reaches me on an elemental level. I widen my stance to hide the evidence. "Yeah, I keep myself busy."

Sutton glances away, a furrow in her brow. "Is it okay that I stopped by?"

I want to tell her no. This is a terrible idea. Having her in my space is an invasion. There are no scenarios where this ends well. The word curls on my tongue, but I swallow it with a shrug. "Guess so."

"Can I come out?"

"Why couldn't you?"

She points at Bear. "Your dog doesn't like me very much."

"He's just protecting me." I ruffle the fur on his head.

Her twinkling laugh is a siren song, and I'm helpless against the pull. "I'm not a threat."

"You sure about that?"

Sutton's throat trembles with a rough gulp. "Yes."

I wave her toward me. "Come on."

Her movements are rigid and robotic. She creaks open her door at a pace that rivals paint drying. She steps out of the car even slower.

There's no fighting my chuckle. "You don't have to worry. I've got a strong hold on him."

Some of the strain falls off her limbs. "Okay. I'm not really afraid, but he seemed pretty determined to get rid of me."

I glance down at my trusty sidekick. "Most of that is for show. Not sure he'd really hurt anyone. He's a total softie with me."

Sutton doesn't look convinced. "What's his name?"

"Bear."

She smiles. "That's fitting. Can I pet him?"

"Go ahead and try." I tighten my grip on his collar.

"You're really selling it."

I lift a shoulder. "I don't get many visitors so this hasn't been tried and tested often. He's a guard dog. It's his job to scare off harm."

She shuffles another foot closer. "To keep you safe. You always wanted a dog."

These strolls down memory lane are bashing at my armor. It's a constant battle to keep my guard in place when she's around. I force my expression to remain stoic. "One of my best decisions yet. He's great company."

"And very handsome," Sutton coos while inching forward.

He yips and drags me her way. "Don't just dive straight in. Let him smell you first."

Sutton extends her fingers in Bear's direction. One sniff of her hand and his defenses crumble. In the next beat, Bear's tail is wagging in a happy dance. The final threads of his reluctance unravel within moments. His entire body begins wiggling with the type of joy that only occurs when he's gained a trusted ally. He scoots on his ass trying to erase the remaining space between them. His efforts are successful when she kneels in front of him. If she's not careful, one-hundred pounds of German Shepherd are about to be sitting in her lap. Lucky fucking mutt.

"Oh, you're such a good boy." Sutton scratches Bear behind the ears. Pretty sure he's giving her a dopey smile in return. She's been initiated into his inner circle and has no clue. Sutton is too busy fending off his slobbering kisses. Her giggle tells me she doesn't mind too much. "What were you worried about, Gray?"

"Pretty sure you were screeching for help a minute ago." I fold my arms. "Clearly I'm the one who overreacted."

Bear rolls over, offering his belly for a rub. He's a goner. I know the feeling well.

Sutton doesn't hesitate, finding a sweet spot that makes his hind leg shake. "Does he always warm up this quick to strangers?"

"The few he's met? Not at all. Bear still growls at Jace when he tries messing with me."

"He's a great judge of character."

I stare at her smiling face. The happiness radiates off every feature. "He certainly is."

She peeks up from under her long lashes. "Thanks."

I rip my gaze off her. "So, you found me. What now?"

She stands and nudges me, the playful move familiar. "Just returning the favor. Figure it's only fair since you sought me out last time."

"That was different." And her brother is really to blame, not that she needs to know.

"Well, yeah. Tracking me down at the bar was a bit unnecessary. But I'll let it slide."

"And I'll overlook your trespassing."

"That's a tad dramatic."

I signal to the open space surrounding us. "Never a dull moment."

Sutton follows the motion and a curious glint flickers in her gaze. "Can I have a tour?"

I'm not prepared for her question, or any of this. My vision narrows on all the flaws and scars littered about. What good is there to see? Then my eyes land on earnest baby blues. Those glittering pools draw me in, calming my breath. This is Sutton. She's the reason, my motivation, behind all of this. Why wouldn't I show her?

Because she'll dig too deep.

I shove the warning away, but shackles of doubt remain. "Won't the food get cold?"

She swings the bag in her grip. "We can nuke it. I don't mind."

"All right, follow me."

I turn on my heel and stride toward the backyard. Sutton's sandals slap against the ground as she hurries to catch up. Bear lopes off ahead, more than happy to lead the way. We pass by the house without pause. Those bare bones won't hold any interest. I continue guiding us across the lawn, the last streaks of sunlight painting the grass.

Her gasp triggers a tightening in my gut. Fuck, that

connection is a maze I'll never solve. A single sound scrambles my ability to function normally. Making it through this evening unscathed will be quite a feat.

"Oh my gosh." Surprise elevates Sutton's tone several octaves.

When I glance over, she has a few fingers pressed to her lips. She stares at the scene spreading out in front of us, a landscape of vibrant green and blue. I stay quiet and focus on the lake's sparkling surface. A zing rips up my spine while recalling the first time I saw this view. I bought the place thirty minutes later.

We stand in silence. The type that's comforting and easy to get lost in. I watch Sutton take it all in, from the rickety dock to a massive oak reaching over the shore. Wonder colors her cheeks the most beautiful shade of pink. She gobbles up every detail as if this is a decadent meal. Pride threatens to split my chest wide open. Maybe she'll want to visit more often.

I shake that idiotic thought away. Beautiful as the sight might be, she doesn't belong here. To believe she'd actually want to is ridiculous enough. I can't let myself fall into that trap.

"So," I burst the bubble. "What's the verdict?"

Her gawking continues. "This place feels familiar. Is that weird? Like a dream I've had. There's so much I love about it."

Every fiber in my body misfires. I'm winded without moving a muscle. I wasn't ready for that answer. Hell, I probably never will be. If Sutton looks hard enough, she'll see the truth.

She doesn't notice the war splitting me apart. "This is a hidden gem. Nice find, Gray."

"Are you sticking around Silo Springs?" The question trips out of my mouth without warning. Why the fuck should I care? But I do. There's no stopping it.

Sutton flashes those potent baby blues at me. I almost stumble from the magnitude. "That's my plan. Why?"

I cough into my fist. "Just curious. You went off to school. Wasn't sure if you'd land elsewhere."

A crinkle forms between her brows. "This is my home. Not sure I could plant roots in another city. I'll be at my parents for at least a month while looking for my own place in town."

"What're you doing for work?"

She beams at me. "I started my own business in media marketing. The large majority is done online so I can be flexible and remote. It's a lot of scheduling and planning. Building brands and selling products. Most of my clients are authors. Fingers crossed that I'll find an apartment near Main Street so there's a coffeehouse or diner nearby. But I'm not too picky." Sutton pauses with a huff. "Ugh, sorry, I'm rambling. I don't want to bore you."

That's the very last thing she's capable of doing. I could listen to her rattle off a list of job duties all night. She's clearly passionate about this. It gets my blood pumping hotter watching her be so animated.

I lock my jaw to contain a sloppy confession of truths. Instead, I tuck my chin and look away. "Nah, it's all good. I'm not surprised you've got a swanky job. I'm still roughing it in the trenches." I hitch a thumb over my shoulder.

"You're literally building a future, and I'm glad it's in Silo Springs. Who'd want to live anywhere else?"

I snort. "Plenty of people."

"Like?"

"Me."

Her eyes bulge in their sockets. "What? You're going to leave?"

"Well, not tomorrow. But eventually I'll be ready to go."

Sutton flails her arms out in front of her. "You have a slice of paradise. Where else will you find this?"

I dig the toe of my boot into the dirt. "I hear Minnesota has a lot of lakes."

"And cold ass winters."

"Doesn't bother me."

I can feel her penetrating stare on me. It takes all my strength to continue avoiding her.

"I figured you'd be a lifer," she whispers.

It would kill me to stick around, have a front row seat of her settling down and raising a family. I'm not strong enough to face that type of torture. Bile burns the back of my throat. "Nah. There's nothing locking me down here."

She flinches. "Oh. Guess that makes sense."

"Let's not pretend I have a reason to stay, Sutt."

"But what if you did?"

I comb through my shaggy hair. "I don't want to find out."

"Maybe you'll find one anyway." Her soft words attempt to revive a semblance of belonging inside of me. It would be easy to agree with her. I could beg her to be mine. She's capable of healing the hurt, being my one and only happy something. We would be whole, at least for a bit. But eventually she'd start resenting me.

I can't look at her. There's no doubt that hope is reflecting in her sky-blue gaze. "Doubt it. This town doesn't have room for me. Nothing has changed."

"I'd argue the opposite. Clearly we're different people." Sutton points at my bike parked in the driveway.

I squint at her. "You're right. We're practically strangers."

Sutton turns to me. "I wouldn't go that far. The boy I grew up with is hiding in there. I'd like to know the man you've become."

"That kid is long gone. He took everything decent with him," I mutter.

She's quiet for a moment. I've ruined this, mostly on

purpose. There's no point pretending we can have anything together.

Sutton's focus returns to the shore. "I'd like to be the judge of that."

A grunt doused in disapproval is all she gets in response.

"Well," she blows out a heavy breath. "Your property is beautiful."

The snarl of pressure calms as we veer onto safer ground. I try not to let the sag in my posture show. This I can handle. "But not the house?"

Sutton twists to glance behind us. Her lips part, but nothing comes out. She flounders with wide eyes and knotted fingers. I can almost hear the potential niceties she's trying to dredge up.

With a snort, I let her off the hook. "Just fucking with you. I know it's a mess."

"It looks more like a work in progress. And to be fair, I've only seen the outside." She quirks a brow.

I scratch the back of my neck. "Guess we should eat. Do you wanna come in?"

She's already treading backwards. "Thought you'd never ask."

CHAPTER SEVEN

Sutton

Happy something #108: Feeling the wind whip through my hair as I race my horse around the barrels.

MY BOOTS HIT THE GROUND IN A CLOUD OF DUST. THE SUMMER heat mixed with minimal rain is turning the arena's fluffy sand into compacted concrete. I'll have to water and drag the grounds before my next ride. Not that I have any intention of pushing Daisy faster than a relaxed lope. The need to turn and burn died with Pago. Any riding I do now is strictly for the sake of enjoyment.

I reach for Daisy's reins and loop them over her head, leading us to the hitching post. Her velvet nose wiggles against my pocket in search of a treat. With a laugh, I remove her bridle and pass one over. My horse chomps the apple wafer while I slip on her halter. I loosen the cinch and slide the saddle off Daisy's back. After grabbing the pad, I set both on the nearby stand. The movements come automatically out of habit, regardless of the months that have passed since I've done this.

The early morning sun gains strength as I drift a brush along her shiny coat. Her neck is still damp, but she's cooled off. May has officially faded into June and taken any remaining chill with the passing spring. Today will be great for the lake. Not that there's ever a bad one.

Memories from the other night filter in with that image. If I try hard enough, the lazy slap of water against the shore echoes in my ears. I wasn't sure what to expect when pulling into Grady's driveway. It wasn't the massive German Shepherd trying to claw his way through my door panel. When I got over the initial shock from Bear and stepped out of the car, all the air was yanked from my lungs.

His house is… *the house.*

It's a place I once described very vividly as a happy something. It needs a ton of work, but the bones are all there. I could see a new wraparound porch with two chairs sitting out front. The colonial pillars will need a fresh coat of paint but they're solid. I absently wonder if he plans to add a swing to that large oak by the lake. If Grady doesn't think I noticed, he's more lost than I pegged him for.

Daisy bumps my hip and those thoughts vanish in a whoosh. I'm stretching out the tremble from my fingers when she knocks into me again. She earns a soothing stroke down her blaze. I untie her lead rope and head toward the gate. "Ready to roam, pretty girl?"

The rapid clomp of her hooves is my only response. I pass over another treat and set her free. Daisy doesn't hesitate. She kicks up her hind legs and runs off to find our other horse. That spunk never translates while riding her. I let a giggle loose while walking to the barn.

"What's so funny?"

I lift a hand to shade my eyes. Jace is leaning against the fence, waiting for me to approach. I smile at him. "Daisy is feeling her oats."

He nods. "She doesn't get out much. I'm sure the exercise gave her a boost."

"She did seem overly eager for attention. What happened to all the lesson kids?"

"Mom still works with a few. They tend to choose Buster and his spots." He shrugs.

Our other remaining horse is an appaloosa and a favorite with kids. "Sad news for Daisy."

He nudges my shoulder. "She's got you."

"It was nice getting back in the saddle."

Jace's blue eyes laser into mine. "Do you ever miss competing?"

It's my turn to shrug. "That depends."

"He was just a—"

I hold up a palm. "Don't even start with that shit. You're not attached to animals, but I sure am. Don't pass more judgment about how I feel. Horses are like dogs—part of the family."

His scoff drives a stake through my heart. "To you, maybe."

"And every other little kid who has felt that bond." I continue striding toward the barn, more than done with this conversation.

Jace jogs to catch up. "Speaking of, we should get another dog."

"You mean mom and dad?"

Without looking at him, I know his gaze is set on the empty kennel. "Every farm needs at least one."

"No argument from me. Maybe a big breed that'll protect the land."

He grunts. "Pretty sure Maggie never chased anyone away."

A grin curls my lips recalling our old Yellow Labrador. "You're right. She loved everyone."

"I heard the Allen clan is raising Boxers."

"Or we could ask Grady where he got Bear."

His steps come to an abrupt halt. "You met his dog?"

I turn to face him. "Sure did. I went over to his place earlier this week."

"Why?" My brother peers down at me. I almost squirm under the pressure. "Wait. You're not still harboring that stupid crush on him, right?"

"What?" I cough to cover my gasp. "That's silly. I'd like to be his friend." *If nothing else,* I add silently.

Jace doesn't relent, seeing way too much. "Pretty sure he's not interested."

I rub at the slap his words hit my cheek with. "Blunt much?"

He folds his arms. "Just speaking the truth. I barely see Grady. He's been shoving a lot more distance between us lately."

"He mentioned leaving Silo Springs," I murmur.

Jace scratches at his smooth jaw. "That doesn't surprise me."

My stomach plummets to the gravel ground. "How could it not?"

His lips flatten into a thin line. "Grady has never felt at home in this town."

"He always has a spot in our family."

"Not sure that's enough for him," he admits on a sigh.

"I wish it was." I suck in a sharp breath, willing my eyes to stop watering.

"You're better off spending that energy elsewhere."

That doesn't sit well with me. At all. "But what about the house he's fixing up? Why spend all that time and effort if he's just going to leave?"

Jace hitches a shoulder up. "Turning a profit."

I furrow my brow. "It feels like a place to stay."

"So what? Why does this matter so much to you?"

"Because I care about him." His glare has me backpedaling. "Not like that. He's been close to our family for years."

"Well, you've been gone. Things change. Just leave him be."

That was my initial plan. Grady Bowen should no longer have a hold on me. I was supposed to ignore him the way he'd been avoiding me. But there's no resisting his steely exterior and hardened expression. Letting him go is a battle I'll always lose. I'm more likely to win the lottery and get struck by lightning in the same afternoon.

I release a slow exhale. "What happened to Grady?"

Jace's narrowed gaze snaps to mine. "Not sure what you mean."

"He isn't the Grady I knew. Not even close. Sure, he's always been guarded. This is something else entirely. He's different in a glaring and drastic way. Why?"

My brother is no dummy. He can read the reason I'm asking clear across my forehead. I'm sure he has similar concerns about our friend. It's impossible not to. I've buried the need to check on Grady. Four long years biting my tongue. But staying silent hasn't done me any favors.

Jace's exhale is forced. "People haven't been kind to him, Sutt. The majority have been really shitty, if we're being honest. There has always been a countdown to the point where he'd crack."

Heat creeps up my neck while I try collecting courage. "But he managed for the first twenty years in Silo Springs. How terrible were the last four?"

He keeps his eyes averted. "I'd say pretty damn bad. Whatever gave him a shred of happiness suddenly vanished. He stopped giving a shit. Can't really blame him, Sutt. Life hasn't been kind to Grady."

The blow is swift and direct. Does my brother see more

than he's telling? Maybe I deserve it. I left Grady behind, knowing full well he wasn't in a good place. But he'd made it perfectly clear I'd never be more than Jace's little sister. Even so, the toxicity of abandonment slithers across my skin.

Moisture clings to my lashes when I blink. I should have tried harder, for Grady's sake. A cramp twists my stomach and I drag in a sharp breath. If Jace doesn't already know my true feelings toward his best friend, continuing this conversation is bound to expose me.

I almost gag around the boulder in my throat. "How long has Grady been making furniture?"

"Nice, Sutt." Jace snorts over my abrupt change in subject. "That's just a hobby."

"He doesn't sell any pieces?"

"Why?" He chuckles. "You in the market for some chairs?"

"Maybe. I really like his dining table."

Jace gawks at me. "Grady let you inside his house?"

"Uh, yeah?" My voice takes on an unsure note.

"Huh. He never lets anyone go in there."

I quirk a brow. "Why?"

"Fuck if I know. Grady is really private about it."

"Okay? But it's just a house." That lie is easy enough to weave, even as the truth settles in my chest.

He shrugs. "Not to him. There's some reason he doesn't let people through the front door."

I dig my boot into the dirt. "Grady called it a mess. Maybe he's embarrassed to show people around."

Jace shoots me a look. "Get real. You honestly think that's a possibility?"

I tuck my chin. "No. He's never cared what others think."

"Only a select few," he muses.

A flurry of romanticized flutters attacks my belly. "Oh?"

He rolls his eyes. "Stop fishing."

Pretty hard not to when he's giving me the bait. But I bite my tongue. "All right, I'm sure there's a simple explanation. He probably doesn't want anyone stomping into his personal space yet."

"Nah, it's more than that."

Because it's special for us. The sweet whisper warms my cheeks. That reality seems too farfetched, like the dream it used to be. I shove that giddy notion away. But testing the theory seems necessary.

"Have you been inside?"

"He let me use the shitter once when I was there lending a hand. I don't think mom and dad have been invited over."

I force my expression to remain neutral. What does that mean about me? My pulse is a stampede of wild horses, making it difficult to hear beyond the pounding of hooves. I try not to let that little kernel expand into something more. But it's impossible. Grady barely hesitated before leading me into his place. This is big. So effing huge. I need to tread lightly, but remaining upright is a feat in this moment.

Jace plows forward with his revelations, unaware of my internal meltdown. "I shouldn't be surprised. Grady is a massive prick to everyone except you. He's never been able to deny you a damn thing."

I let my mouth pop open on a strangled exhale. There's no doubt my face is the shade of a ripe tomato. So much for keeping my attraction a secret. If I try to speak, the lid is bound to blow off this charade. I remain silent while the chaos in my mind rages on.

My brother tilts his head. "You okay, Sutt? Looks like a ghost spooked your ass."

I manage to pull myself together enough to form a mumbled response. "Something like that."

CHAPTER EIGHT

Grady

Happy something #41: Uninhibited bouts of laughter. I never hear that enough.

I TOSS THE WRENCH INTO MY TOOLBOX AND SLAM THE TRACTOR hood shut with a resounding bang. The afternoon sun is relentless, immediately searing my skin once I step out of the shade. Motor oil is a thick layer on my hands and shirt, evidence of the several dirty jobs I've done. There's only one answer to give when Barry Olsen asks if I can spare a few hours to fix some shit around his farm. I could never refuse the man who practically raised me. That responsibility doubled after my own dad was locked up.

The old log bench along the barn calls my name. I park my ass on the sturdy wood, reaching for the filthy rag tucked in my pocket. It takes a good five minutes to dig the grit out from beneath my nails. Not sure why I even fucking bother. I lift my ballcap and drag a hand over my matted hair. There's a damn laundry list of shit waiting for me at home. The only thing I want to do is sleep. But talking to a certain blue-eyed girl holds an inflated level of appeal. A nap is more plausible, but still highly unlikely. I grunt at my shitty choices.

My dry throat aches for something cool to ease the burn. A cold beer has never sounded better. Lucky for me, Barry keeps a fridge stocked in one of the sheds. I get to my feet with a groan and wander that way. Freshly cut hay and sawdust cling to the humid air, making the temperature even more sticky. The property is quiet. It's almost startling how calm and still the farm is. I'm sure everyone is enjoying a lazy Saturday as it's meant to be.

I adjust the hat on my head, tucking the brim low to shield the harsh rays. This summer is already proving to be hot as fuck. This weather might call for the voyage dive off my dock. I've been stupid to hold out. It's not like anyone else will join me. Not that I'd want her to. My boots stumble to a stop on their own accord. No fucking way. That is absolutely not happening. I roll my shoulders and shake that shit off. The happy something she whispered to me almost a decade ago is ancient history.

I duck into the building with a sigh, heading straight for the back wall. A breeze passes through the open doors. That slight wind is enough to ease the sizzle from outside. I grab a beer and pop the top, dropping my ass into one of the open camping chairs. Weariness seeps into my bones. Every inch of me is weighed down with a heaviness beyond normal limits. A moment of rest won't kill me. I tip the bottle to my lips and guzzle the final drops of cool relief.

Just as I'm letting my eyes fall shut, the shuffle of footsteps jolts me wide awake. Barry strides toward me with a wide grin stretching his weathered face.

"Hey, son. Didn't think you'd still be here."

I scrub a hand across the coarse bristles on my jaw. "Just finished. That orange Ford should be running the best a thirty-year-old model can. I also fixed the leak in the Deere."

"You're saving my hide. I can't keep up with it all any-more." Barry settles into the chair beside me, relaxing deep into the seat.

"It's not a problem."

"I'm sure you've got business to complete elsewhere."

That's very much the case, but being here isn't a burden. "It doesn't put me out. I have all evening to finish stuff at home."

Barry crosses his arms. "It might be time to consider hiring a ranch hand of sorts."

"Yeah? Or rope Jace into more. He can get the next round."

He snorts at that. "I won't hold my breath."

Me either, but that doesn't need to be said. Jace does plenty to help out. Mechanics aren't one of his talents. "More for me, then. I don't mind."

"You've always been a good kid, Grady. I'm grateful to have you around."

I tug the ballcap lower and avert my gaze. "I appreciate that, sir."

Barry toys with his own hat, the brim fraying and splitting apart. "None of that formal crap."

"Old habits and all." I knew plenty about that. Hell, we both did.

He presses a finger to his lips and releases a slow exhale. "How's your mama?"

I almost cringe at the question. She's not a topic I'd ever choose to discuss. I can't force myself to give her much thought. If I did, a lot of other dark shit would swoop in. But Barry has his reasons. They grew up together in Silo Springs. He watched the start of her downfall far before I was born. I flare my nostrils and shove out a breath. "Alive."

That earns me a raised brow. He gets a shrug in return. A lot of men don't talk about emotions and feelings, me very much included. Barry is the opposite. I can't count the number of conversations he's had with me on the subject. But I won't open up on this, even for him.

"I get it, son. Sorry to pry." He points to my empty bottle. "Want another?"

"Nah, one is enough. I should be going soon." I rub at a stain on my jeans, trying to force off the grime covering me. Just more evidence of how filthy I am.

Seemingly out of thin air, Sutton struts into the barn. That sweet reprieve from the sun dissipates as the temperature spikes. Hot fucking damn. The sway of her hips is a fluid motion that instantly snares me. Her tan legs are on display thanks to a tiny pair of cutoffs. All that smooth skin creates a certifiable hunger in my lower half. The craving is fierce and direct, an intensity only she can provoke. I gulp down the saliva pooling in my mouth.

Any signs of exhaustion I'd been experiencing vanish with Sutton's bubbling laugh. Her head tips back, exposing the sleek column of her throat. A cascade of dark waves spill down her delicate frame. My muscles flex with the effort of staying seated. I could easily scoop her up and haul us to the hayloft. The man beside me would probably have plenty to say about a stunt like that.

I belatedly realize she has a phone pressed to her ear. Finding out who's on the other side of that call becomes a necessity. She's giggling without restraint, clearly loving the recipient's voice. A furious green monster rises from my gut. If it's Deputy Dipshit, he's going to get acquainted with my fist before the sun sets.

The sound of a dry chuckle barely registers. "Don't waste more years, son."

I jerk my eyes back to Barry. "Huh?"

He lifts his chin toward Sutton. "I'm not blind. Neither is she. Don't sit around waiting for a moment that will never come. If you want more from her, get up and do it."

This man is my role model. The only father figure I have. My heart thunders with an impending storm. I can't possibly make a move on his daughter. No part of that statement is realistic. Admiring from afar is bad enough. Anything more is strictly forbidden, permission granted or not.

I rip off my hat and wring the fabric tight. "I'm right where I should be."

And that's the truth. We're on opposite sides of everything that matters. Sutton is across the room, safe and happy. She's talking to someone who brings her joy. All I've ever offered is bullshit and pain. I'll never deserve her.

Barry shakes his head. "Don't be a fool, kid."

Of all the people rooting for this, it shouldn't be him. I grind my molars. "It's better this way."

There's no missing his hollow scoff. "Suit yourself. Can I ask a favor if you're set on staying in place?"

I squint at him, trying to read his intentions. As always, Barry keeps shit locked behind an impassive expression. "Okay."

"Do you have thirty more minutes to spare?"

I didn't, but turning this man down wasn't an option. "Sure. What's up?"

He scratches at the stubble on his chin. "I've been trying to hustle with this second cutting. The fact we'll be getting three this season is a miracle. That square baler stalled in the back field. I should have replaced it years ago. Can I bother you to take a look? I need to call some folks and let them know their hay delivery will be delayed."

I'm out of my seat before he finishes talking. "Any idea what could be causing it?"

"Probably a bad belt or something jammed the engine."

"I'll check it out."

He stands up and claps my shoulder. "You sure?"

"Positive. I'm sure it won't take long."

"Feel free to drive the four-wheeler out there. Keys are in the ignition."

I nod at him. "Got it, boss."

Barry snorts. "If only you could be convinced to work for me."

"I owe you too much for that."

He waves me off. "We're not discussing that nonsense."

"All right," I mutter.

"I'll catch up with you in a bit. Thanks again, Grady." He pivots on his heel and walks outside.

A list of what I'll need begins to compile in my mind. I grab a clean rag out of the cabinet. At this time of day, I'll probably need a few to sop up the sweat and dirt. Those get tucked into my back pocket while I grab my tools.

The four-wheeler waits for me outside of the barn. After strapping down my toolbox, I straddle the padded seat. I turn my hat backwards and pull it low. The engine purrs to life, vibrating with power beneath me. I crank the throttle and dart off across the field. The wind whips through the thin cotton of my shirt. For a few precious moments, everything fades into a blur of multi-color nothingness. I can just be.

The square baler appears ahead of me and I pull up beside it. Barry wasn't lying about needing to replace this hunk of junk. The old machine is more rust than metal at this point. I'm surprised this model hasn't been tossed out sooner, considering the massive employee discount he gets. But he's sentimental. I'm sure there's a story behind this dinosaur.

I grab a socket, pliers, extension bar, and ratchet. At the very least, I'll get this piece of shit running well enough to finish the rear field. I lean inside the open front end to get an idea of what's wrong. Debris and nameless gunk cling to every available spot. I reach further to pull out some clumps of hay.

With a loud pop, one of the springs breaks in half. A whoosh of stale air is the only warning I get. In a split second, the baler's mouth slams shut. Two gnarly spikes latch onto my arm before I can blink. Blinding agony rips through my entire body. Raging flames erupt over every inch of me.

"Fuck!" I bellow the curse so loud my lungs burn. It's the last thing I remember before black spots fill my vision.

CHAPTER NINE

Sutton

*Happy something #131: Being able to help others,
no matter how small, is a wonderful gift.*

A BLOOD-CURDLING SCREAM RIPS THROUGH THE SILENCE around me. I pull the phone away from my ear to listen better. Harlyn continues talking at rapid speed, unaware of the interruption that's stealing my focus. I twist my head and wait for more shouting. A moment later, another agonizing howl shreds into my chest.

"I need to call you back." I end the call before she has a chance to respond. After shoving the cell into my pocket, I race toward the pastures. Cries of pain roar above my pounding heartbeat. I push myself faster, each inhale becoming fire in my lungs. The desperation fuels me to find a higher gear I didn't know existed. With each passing moment, the sounds get louder and more traumatizing. I can practically smell the horror looming just out of reach.

As I climb a small slope in the rear field, our old baler

comes into view. I see a pair of booted feet wrestling to remain upright. My throat clogs with an impending sob. When Grady is finally in sight, I fear the worst. He's practically hanging from the frontend of the machine. Two of the sharp teeth appear to be pierced straight through his forearm. From this angle, I can't tell if the metal spikes are stabbing through bone or muscle. Grady is trapped with no conceivable way of escape. I almost crash to my knees from the visual impact.

"Shit, shit, shit. Oh my God. Hold on, Gray."

Tears leak down my cheeks as I cover the remaining distance between us. He's no longer crying out, which raises an enormous red flag. I slam to a halt beside him and attempt to catalogue his injuries. This type of incident usually results in the loss of a limb. I'm no stranger to farming accidents. It's an occupational hazard around these parts. Malfunctioning equipment is far too common and one of the reasons my dad works so hard to engineer new parts. We have to plan for this. But this is completely different than anything I could prepare for.

"Gray?" I curl my hands into fists. All I want to do is hug him. That's the last thing he needs. What should I do? The blank I'm drawing is far and wide. I try to shake off the stunned fog. "Can you, um, talk to me?"

A muscle in his jaw pops. Grady isn't moving otherwise. He's frozen as stone, which is exactly what we're taught to do in these situations. Struggling can make the damage worse. His green eyes are flaring wide open, dilated and unfocused. He appears to be staring at nothing. There's a clammy sheen to his complexion, the color pale and ghostly. My mind scrambles with the proper steps I should be completing. I can't see past the helpless image of Grady. The daunting possibilities are fangs sinking into my neck.

A stinging slap of clarity knocks some much needed sense into me. I fumble while digging out my phone. The numbers are a blur, but I don't need them. I press the red button with a trembling finger.

"9-1-1, what's your emergency?"

My tongue is five times too large. "M-my friend is s-stuck in a hay b-b-baler. He n-needs help. R-right away."

"I need you to remain calm. What's your name?"

"Sutton."

"Okay, Sutton. I have assistance on the way. Is your friend breathing?"

I gulp down a lungful of useless air. It does nothing to ease the flames in my chest. "Y-yes."

"Okay, that's a good sign. Is he able to communicate?"

Grady's throat bobs with a forced swallow, but he doesn't speak. I bite my tongue while trying to trap another sob. Fresh tears gather in my lashes that I can't seem to blink away. "I'm, uh, not sure. He isn't saying anything."

The dispatcher hums softly. "That's all right. Don't force anything. Just stay with him."

As if I could possibly leave. The thought alone is inconceivable. I reach for his free hand and almost jolt backwards. He's cold to the touch, even though it's nearing ninety degrees outside.

"Stay with me, Gray." The plea drips off my quivering bottom lip.

Grady's grip on me is weak at best. I shuffle closer to inspect his gaping wound. Rivulets of blood flow out and puddle onto the grass. A pool of bright red is collecting, too big and spreading wider. I want to collapse under the weight of it all, and this isn't happening to me. I can only imagine the agony Grady is experiencing.

"Sutton? Are you still on the line?" Her voice is a distant buzz.

"Yes, we're here." I keep my gaze locked on Grady while answering her.

"Feel free to put me on speaker while tending to your friend."

I follow her suggestion robotically without pause. The screen lights up when I set my cell down. I watch the seconds tick by on the call tracker. It's been five minutes. Grady appears more ashen and despondent. The air grows thick and gray, a suffocating cloud descending upon us. I scoot forward, ready to do whatever is necessary to save him.

Where the hell are they?

The dispatcher interrupts my rising panic. "The rescue team is about two minutes out. Will they have any trouble finding you?"

I glance around at all the open space. "We're in the far corner field of my property. There's a trail they can take straight back. It's easily accessible. Tell the driver to follow the gravel path. Or they can take the private drive off Batron and Straller. That leads directly to us and might be faster. Either way, just hurry. *Please*." I'm on autopilot at this point, spitting out whatever information seems important.

"All right, Sutton. They'll be arriving any moment. Just sit tight." Her tone is measured and level, meant to soothe jagged nerves. But I barely hear the words over the rush of my pulse.

I squeeze the chilled fingers that are laced with mine. "Hear that? It's going to be okay, Gray. They'll be here soon." Even to my own ears the attempt at reassurance sounds like a hollow echo. I clench my eyes shut, silently chanting for them to hurry.

The wailing siren alerts me first. In the next beat, flashing lights appear in my periphery. An ambulance races up the small hill and across the pasture to where we wait. Through bleary eyes, I track the wheels bouncing over the rough terrain. I will them to speed up, impossible as that might be.

After what feels like an eternity, the red and white vehicle screeches to a stop beside us. Three men in blue uniforms hustle over, their arms loaded with necessities. One is carrying a massive wedge of sorts and shoves it into the mangled machine's busted front. The other two are fussing over Grady, shining a flashlight in his eyes and checking for a pulse. A shot of who knows what gets injected into his vein. Whatever it is must be strong because his body droops with a long sigh.

I do my best to follow their rapid and efficient movements. The knot in my chest grows with each tense second. One of them suddenly has his hand on a crank, ready to force the jaws open. I choke on a garbled gasp.

"Wait! Are you sure that's safe?"

The tallest guy snorts. "With all due respect, let us do our jobs." His deep timbre does nothing to set my concern at ease.

I bounce my gaze between Grady and these strangers. I wish he was lucid enough to tell me what's best. As it is, I can't process everything while keeping my sanity intact. Not sure why I bother trying. My opinion doesn't mean shit and they make the choice for me.

With a sickening creak of metal, the rusty teeth lift and release Grady's arm. With the spikes gone, his wounds erupt with blood. The two gouges are deep and resemble a poisonous bite. A tremor ripples through him, but he doesn't make a sound. The baler's lethal clutches drip with evidence of the attack. My lunch threatens to make a reappearance. I shudder and avert my eyes.

Grady sags against the man behind him, all the fight melting from his legs. Another paramedic slides a stretcher into place. He flops down onto the board, seeming relieved for the sturdy surface beneath him. His lashes flutter shut while he groans.

They strap Grady down as he fades in and out of consciousness. A river of blood continues to trickle down his arm. I gulp down another round of bile. The waves of nausea crash into the walls of my stomach. I've never had a weak gut, but this is Grady. Seeing him hurt crumbles any defenses I could attempt to conjure up.

They load him into the ambulance with seasoned finesse. This team is competent and capable. It's obvious they deal with this type of situation often. Sad, but realistic. The paramedics are talking at a rate I can't comprehend. Every other sentence includes a sliver of positive.

Missed the bone.

Not critical.

Can save the arm.

Permanent damage unlikely.

"So, he's going to be all right?" I hang back to avoid getting in their way.

The stocky one hops out and offers me a smile. "Yeah, absolutely. He'll need to visit the hospital to get patched up. But that's basic procedure. He's very lucky. Your boyfriend will be good as new in a few days."

My belly swoops at the title I don't have any claim to. That doesn't mean I'll correct him. I tuck some hair behind my ear. "That's really great news."

"He'll be out of it for awhile. Some of that is from shock and the adrenaline wearing off. It's a very common reaction. We're pumping him with morphine for the pain."

"There's no reason to worry?" But how can I not?

He shrugs. "Not really. But the doctor will run tests to be sure."

I give him a blank stare. How the hell long will that take? Grady will be suspended in the balance of unknown for hours. "Um, okay?"

The paramedic turns away without another word. That's it? But he motions for me to follow. I remain frozen in place.

He quirks a brow at me over his shoulder. "Are you coming?"

I blink at him while static buzzes in my brain. "Where?"

"To the hospital." His bland tone makes me feel as though this should be obvious. "You can ride in the back with him."

I inch forward. "O-okay."

He nods and walks off to the driver's side. I climb into the ambulance on trembling legs. My knees knock together as I sit on the cold metal bench. Everything is so clinical and sterile, except for the man laid out in the center. There's a cuff around his bicep. A single tube is attached to his uninjured forearm. They slam the doors behind me and the sound is deafening. It's just the two of us, one awake and the other zonked out. I've imagined us in countless positions. This was never on the list.

I reach for Grady's hand, clutching him in a tight grip. He's not aware of his surroundings. I doubt he can feel me sitting right beside him. I'm a mess, jittery and fidgeting from the inside out. There are probably unwritten rules about proper bedside behavior. I should be comforting him. But he keeps me grounded even during sleep.

The slightest pressure against my palm has me looking down. My heart leaps into the sky when I realize he's holding me in return.

CHAPTER TEN

Sutton

Happy something #73: Spending time with my brother's best friend, also known as the love of my life.

I SHUT THE HEAVY WOODEN DOOR, CLOSING OFF ANY FURTHER disruptions from the opposite side. Grady's discharge instructions run on a loop through my mind. This needs to be a stress-free environment. He's under strict orders to rest and stay off his feet for at least twenty-four hours. Keeping him still will be a challenge. He isn't allowed to do anything that will cause harm to the injury site. Strenuous activities are his livelihood. He won't stay put for long. But I plan to use the not-so-subtle art of persuasion.

Grady's soft snores draw me deeper into the room. I perch on the edge of his mattress and watch him sleep. Thankfully, he didn't have to stay overnight in the hospital. Once he regained consciousness, Grady immediately started bitching about being there in the first place. At that point, another dose of morphine had kicked in and he wasn't feeling any pain. Much like now. The doctors gave him a tetanus shot, stitched up his arm, and sent us on our way with a few prescriptions to fill. Whatever horse pill he was directed to take first knocked his ass out. And here he lies.

I brush the wispy hair off his forehead. He looks so serene without the stone mask. I could almost trick myself into believing he's at peace. But the deep purple smudges underneath his eyes appear worse. Maybe he'll be able to sleep easy for a bit.

His forearm is heavily bandaged from wrist to elbow. The gory sight hidden below threatens to turn my stomach all over again. I choose to focus my wandering attention on more appetizing sights. The dark scruff lining his angular jaw is a glorious distraction. I bet that stubble offers a tantalizing burn against sensitive skin. The soft area between my neck and shoulder tingle from that visual tease. A plain white tee does little to disguise his sculpted pecs and torso. The bumps and ridges are meant to be traced with a slow drift of fingers.

A slight shift of his hips lowers the sheet. That glorious happy trail leads to the promise of ecstasy. I'm privy to the fact that he's only wearing a pair of boxer briefs under there. A wicked infusion of heat enters my bloodstream. I curl my fingers into the blanket, wishing for something more solid. A thick steel rod encased in velvet would fit just right. I blink the image away. My creeper meter has officially reached new levels.

Maybe he needs some privacy.

Grady's voice stops me before I can move off the bed. A single garbled word drips off his lips and I nearly choke. There's no way he said what I think—

"*Sutton.*"

Well, that settles any doubt. Holy shit. My gaze scours his face, searching for any sign of alertness. I find none. It's fairly obvious that he's not lucid. But he's saying my name.

Very clearly. The sultry tune is more of a moan, in a seductive way. Those two syllables strum off his tongue in a song that leaves me stunned. That delectable purr reels me in. I'm helpless against the pull. I want him to keep whispering it, over and again, like a chant.

The bed squeaks with my slight movement. Grady's lashes flutter open, those emerald eyes cloudy and sluggish. I curse a blue streak for waking him. His lazy stare finds me hovering at an inappropriately close distance. This alone could be considered crossing a line. A few pesky inches between our bodies isn't suitable for friends. But maybe we're about to be more than that.

Does Grady remember dreaming of me? The green fire that's now illuminating his gaze suggests so. His languid perusal carves a path up my body. I can feel that trail, a hot brand covering every inch. Lust. Need. I cross my legs in an attempt to alleviate the ache. It doesn't work. The desire begins to boil in my veins. Soon it will hijack my entire system. From the looks of it, Grady is having a similar issue. The paper-thin sheet does a horrible job concealing his reaction to my proximity.

I clear my throat. My front row viewing party had to end eventually. Might as well get this over with. "Hey, Gray."

Grady lifts that fiery gaze to mine. Beyond the shimmer of lust, there's a smoky veil diluting the usually vibrant green. His lids are heavy, barely at half-mast. He slaps a sloppy palm onto my thigh. His fingers dig into me with the slightest amount of pressure. The movement is disjointed, and extremely unexpected. That's the only proof I need to determine that he's fucked up. The evidence is damning.

"Hi, Sutt." His voice is rough gravel, as if he's been sleeping for days instead of hours.

"How are you feeling?"

His fuck-hot gaze remains on mine. "Damn good."

I almost scoff. "Those pain meds must be powerful. You were stuck in a baler. There are over thirty stitches in your arm."

Grady doesn't spare his injured limb a glance. "It'll heal."

I flatten my lips. "That's not the point."

"No? Tell me what is."

"You're hurt, badly. Seeing you that way was petrifying." My voice trembles, revealing the fear. I've managed to tamp down the hysteria, but that crazy bitch is simmering just below the surface. My hackles would rise every time a doctor or nurse would enter the room. Unreasonable? Absolutely. Did that stop me? Not a chance. That fierce level of protectiveness was new to me, yet held a glimmer of familiarity. I've always wanted to shelter Grady from impending storms. Offering him a safe space came naturally. Those glaring facts will keep my ass parked in his house until he kicks me out.

His brows slowly crease, as though the thoughts are sluggish. "But I'm all right, Sutt."

"Because you're lucky. It could have been deadly. You scared the shit out of me, Gray."

"It's just a scratch. You don't need to worry about me."

"But I do. I always will, Gray."

He stares at me for a stilted moment. "Why?"

Hiding the truth would be safer. Spelling out the engravings on my heart will certainly lead to more scars. But I've never been smart when it comes to this man. "You mean a lot to me."

"It's the same for me, Sutt." Grady begins drawing small circles around my knee, the motion seems absentminded. The gentle caress from his fingertips should feel foreign. We've never exchanged anything of this caliber. These soft strokes offer a deep-rooted comfort. This is exactly what I need after the frantic events of this afternoon. Can he sense that on some elemental level? That soothing balm sinks directly into my bones and spreads throughout every part of me. I'm practically panting over that simple touch. Is Grady getting any satisfaction out of this?

"I like having you in my bed. Waking up with you is something I could get used to." His drawl is pure sugar, warm caramel dipped in chocolate.

An explosion of searing heat singes my cheeks. I fight the urge to dip my chin. "Oh?"

The sound he emits resembles a predatory rumble. I barely restrain a shiver. "You're the first girl to be in my room."

I flick a glance over the bare walls and minimal furnishings. If I didn't know better, I'd assume he just moved in. Or isn't planning on sticking around long. The second gives me pause. That may very well be the case. I try not to let that spoil this moment, pasting a grin on my lips. "Should I be honored?"

"I believe the honor is all mine." A loose smirk curls half of his mouth. That slow lift to his lips might be my undoing. The hitch in my breath rivals a foghorn. Attempting to hide my reaction is pointless. If the full-blown smile is any indication, Grady catches on quickly. He bathes the dim room in blinding happiness.

Good Lord, he's trying to give me a spontaneous orgasm. Is that a thing? Sure feels like a possibility. But pump the brakes. Who is this sweet-talking, panty-melter?

I take a closer inspection of this swoony charmer. Not an ounce of deceit registers in his expression. There's no stony edge blocking his emerald stare. His ironclad guard is nonexistent. Zero inhibitions block the sliver of space between us. Everything is on display for me to see. I should be the one to stop this. He's obviously not in his normal state and under the influence of hefty narcotics.

Who the hell am I kidding? Basking in a rare smile from Grady is a gift I won't take for granted. Appreciating from a safe distance will be the true challenge. I test my willpower by trying to evade the sneaky fingers inching up my thigh. But our skin is magnetized and moving is impossible. The golden specks in his eyes glitter at my failed attempt. Yep, he's onto me. I'm a goner.

As if there was another option.

The itch to comb through his shaggy hair tickles my fingertips. Would he lean into my embrace if I cupped his jaw? The tiniest bit of resolve stops me from acting on those impulses. But it doesn't stop my brain from working overtime.

I wonder if anyone else has seen this side of him. The romantic in me wants to believe I'm the first, and hopefully only. I shove the fanciful notion aside. "Well, you sure seem to be in a great mood."

That luscious bottom lip gets trapped between his teeth. I'd love to take a bite. As if hearing my thoughts, Grady rolls toward me. "Abso-fucking-lutely. Why wouldn't I be? I have a gorgeous woman within reach, ready to take care of my aches and pains."

This time I really do choke on my tongue. "W-what?"

The hand he has on my leg drifts higher. "You sound shocked, Sutt."

How could I not be? "That's an understatement."

"Stay with me," Grady croons.

"For the night?"

"For always." His gaze is smoldering. Damn, he's sexy. And irresistible. I'm liable to straddle his lap and offer him everything. But the chains of our past hold me hostage. I can't fall victim so easily.

"Why now, Gray?" Whatever painkillers he's on are proving to be an effective truth serum. I might as well use it to my advantage.

His blink is slow. "I miss the peace, Sutt. My slice of goodness."

The low tide of his voice whispers to my weakest spots. Those areas that have longed for the treasure of his affection. He's here, in this space, threatening to spoil me with tenderness. It would be so easy to give in and believe this could be true. He's offering the dream.

I want to rediscover hope and delve into endless possibilities. But what happens tomorrow?

Grady must feel my apprehension. Or maybe he wants to ensure my surrender. "Tell me a happy something, Sutton."

I can't stop the whimper that rips from my throat. It's been years—almost a decade—since he's asked. Tears sting my eyes as I'm transported back to a different time. Grady's thumb catches a stray droplet. It somehow feels like he's capturing far more.

A soft grin curls my lips. "I thought we were past that?"

His head jerks with a sharp denial. "I was lying."

I drag in a shaky breath. "That's not very comforting."

"Tell me, Sutt." He gives my leg a slight pinch.

I tip my face to the ceiling, picturing the warm sun beaming down. "Sitting under a large oak on the hottest summer days."

Grady groans, and I imagine he's picturing it with me. "I'm gonna build you a swing in the backyard." That's my breaking point. I turn away before a sob breaks free. He reaches for my hand, threading our fingers together. "Please don't go, Sutt."

I glance at him from over my shoulder. "What happens next, Gray?"

"We'll figure it out. Trust me." There's still an unusual shine to his gaze. Will he truly remember this conversation? Maybe it'd be better for both of us if he doesn't. Now I'm the liar.

I stare at him silently, so much traveling between us without another word. This moment is blistering with intimacy. I fear it will pop and everything will return to our strained normal. I can't let that happen. But Grady beats me to it.

"C'mere, beautiful. Be my girl." He lifts his arm and offers me access to that heavenly nook.

I want to weep at the possibility. Do I dare? It'll ruin me if he wakes up tomorrow with regrets. But I always choose to live in the moment. Following my intuition has never steered me wrong. That pesky voice has been rooting for Grady since I was seven. Why would I start refusing now?

Easy—I don't.

When Grady beckons to me again, I don't hesitate. Lowering myself into that divine gap fit for me is a decision I've always wanted to make.

CHAPTER ELEVEN

Grady

Happy something #17: The comfort of knowing dreams aren't always nightmares.

I PRY MY EYELIDS OPEN WITH A MUFFLED GROAN. THE ROOM IS bathed in darkness, further altering my sense of clarity. Bright light sneaks through the shaded window. That's the only clue I get. Probably doesn't help that my brain is sluggish, the gears dipped in sticky tar.

Taking stock of my situation requires more effort than usual. There's a bone-dry desert in my throat. Sweat dots my forehead. My shirt is drenched and plastered to me. The air is musty, but hints of strawberry and coconut linger. Damn, she smells better than a fantasy. At least there's one advantage to this shit-storm.

I glance down and catch the massive tent propping up my blanket. Morning wood strikes again. But this is stronger than the typical erection I wake up with. The desire coursing through me is laced with feverish need. Reckless lust pools in my blood, traveling south at dizzying speed.

I reach down to palm my cock and white-hot agony lashes up my arm. Shit, that's one way to receive a reminder. I glare at the offending wound. Any sign of injury is concealed by several layers of gauze. But I'm well aware of the damage thanks to the sizzling embers still crackling off my skin. I'd usually forego heavy-hitting medications, but this pain is quickly escalating into unbearable territory.

My forearm is blazing. My dick begs for relief. Everything fucking hurts. Except for the delicate weight plastered to my right side.

Sutton.

Her slim body clings to mine, as if she's keeping me glued in one piece. A humorless laugh bounces off my chest. I don't fucking cuddle. Being touched has never been my favorite. There are countless other reasons. None of them matter. Sutton's hands on me are the purest form of pleasure. This woman can snuggle against me all she wants. I'll never utter a complaint. Closing my eyes and soaking in the warmth is tempting as fuck.

My body is demanding too many damn things at once.

A glass of water and something for the torture to my limb are a great place to start. I attempt to inch out from under Sutton's embrace. She whines and nuzzles into the groove of my throat. I'm not going anywhere without her knowing. Not that it was really a choice with the pathetic state I'm in.

I feel the moment Sutton rouses. She stiffens against me, as if immediately realizing our position is more of a predicament. My cock twitches, giddy that she's alert and ready to play. I almost snort.

Nice try, buddy.

There's no disguising my physical response to having her beside me. If she hasn't noticed yet, it'll only be a matter of moments. Sutton will assume all I want is sex. She'll scramble away before I can utter a proper greeting. Not that I'd blame her. I'm rotten. She's pristine. Decent intentions aside, this won't end well between us. We can never last long term. But I'm not going to puss out and try erasing my confessions.

Before I can gather some semblance of an explanation, Sutton lifts her head to face me. Her baby blues are already shining with hurt. Dammit.

I tuck some hair behind her ear. "Morning, beautiful."

She relaxes with my words. The flicker of sorrow disappears faster than she can blink, returning her gaze to a vibrant shade. "Hey, Gray."

Sutton's shirt is wrinkled. Creases crisscross up her cheek. Her glossy hair is knotted at the ends. She's never looked more stunning, or appetizing if I allow myself to be honest.

Contrary to what most would believe, I didn't invite her to stay so we could fuck from dawn until dusk. Of course I want to be buried balls deep between her silky thighs. Any man with a pulse would bust a nut at the opportunity. But Sutton means far more to me than that. I'll eventually admit that to her. Maybe. For now, I need to dig us out of the tense silence.

I scratch my temple. "How'd you sleep?"

She nibbles on her bottom lip. "Really well. How about you?"

"Hard as stone." I smirk at the double meaning.

Sutton follows my line of sight straight down, to the bulge beneath the covers and into the gutter. Her eyes snap up to mine. I chuckle as splotches of red stain her smooth skin. She shoves my shoulder.

"Not cool, Gray. You're pervy in the morning."

I wince as jarring needles stab into my arm.

She slaps a palm over her mouth. Her eyes flare wide open. "Oh, shit. I'm so sorry."

"I'm fine." I grunt, attempting to shrug it off. The pop in my jaw catches her attention.

"Don't pretend on my account. I saw the gore and horror."

"You're shredding my man-card, Sutt. I'm not made of fucking glass. Give me some credit."

"Tough guy needs his ego stroked?" She winks at me.

I release a choppy breath. Try as I might, dredging up images of puppies and manual labor is falling flat. My cock is bound to punch a hole in the sheet at this rate. "I wouldn't say no."

Sutton skips her nails along my abs. She peeks up at me through lowered lashes. With a purposely slow lick, she wets her plump lips. "I'm so hot for you, Gray. I bet you're epic in the sack. Rattle the headboard until I'm screaming your name."

The air freezes in my lungs. Shit, is she serious?

She topples over in a fit of giggles. "Your face," she wheezes. "Oh my gosh, that's priceless."

If my arm wasn't torn to shreds, I'd swat that juicy ass and tickle the shit out of her. But retaliating isn't possible. Revenge will have to wait. I just lay still and let her joy wrap around me. The sound of her laughter is music to my neglected ears. She's playing a Grammy-worthy concert just for me. Maybe she'll continue blowing my mind by stripping naked and riding me to the highest peaks of ecstasy.

Sutton's twinkling tune dies off. The humor in her features fade, questions beginning to form behind those bright eyes. There must be something in my expression that tells her exactly what I'm picturing. Her breathing turns shallow. The rise and fall of her chest is a rapid beat.

"Gray," she murmurs.

I'm hypnotized by her mouth caressing my name. "Yeah?"

"What are you thinking about?"

I wrench my gaze off her. "Nothing."

She blinks at me, the shimmering enthusiasm clears from her blue depths. "Sure about that?"

"Have to be," I mutter.

A crease dents the center of her forehead. "Do you remember what we talked about last night?"

I lick my dry lips and nod. Begging her to stay is the first thing I've done right in four lonely years.

Sutton stares at me, unflinching and brave. "Please don't tell me that was the pills talking."

"That was all me, Sutt." But speaking of the scripts, my arm is still on fire. It feels like my skin is being ripped off as I continue lounging here. "Where did you stash those painkillers? I need to take something. And drink some water. Then we'll talk."

She quirks a brow. "Want me to grab your morning dose?"

"I can do it." A hiss rattles out of me while I try sitting up.

Her hand lands on my chest, pushing me down. "Allow me. I'm here to ease your aches and suffering."

As if I wasn't already hard enough. I'd pop a semi from that vision alone, fantasy or not. I settle deeper into the mattress. This reminds me of the old us, before shit got complicated and I destroyed everything. Inky darkness slithers in my veins. I always assume the worst, for good reason. But I know Sutton better than anyone. Or I used to. She's always been able to see through my bullshit.

Sutton reappears with an extra large cup filled to the brim and a prescription bottle. I gingerly lift my upper body into a position that doesn't cause stabbing misery. She tries handing me two pills. I open my mouth and wait.

She huffs. "Really?"

I raise my brows in answer. She drops the white tablets onto my tongue and holds out the water for me. My palms remain flat on the mattress. I lean forward until Sutton gets the message. The cool glass presses to my lips and she tips it up. I keep my eyes locked on her while swallowing the cool liquid. My throat screams in relief and I guzzle more. Our gazes never waver, the air crackling with restraint. When the cup is empty, she pulls it away.

"Want a refill?"

I flop onto the bed, feeling completely rejuvenated. "In a bit."

She returns to her spot beside me, sitting up with crossed legs.

"This is new." I trace the colorful flower on her ankle.

She tracks my movements. "I had it done in Cancun on spring break. My friend has a matching one."

"Who's this friend?" I try to tamp down my jealousy.

"Harlyn. We lived together in college."

I recall hearing her name. The green-eyed monster skitters away. "Ah, the dark days I know nothing about."

Sutton leans back, giving me an exquisite view of her tits. "I'm happy to fill you in."

There's only one question that's been plaguing me. I keep my eyes on her tattoo. "Did you go out a lot?"

"To the bar?"

"On dates," I supply with a grumble.

She tips her head back and laughs. "That's hilarious. You've met my brother, right? Somehow he managed to scare off all guys before I could even try."

A smirk brimming with satisfaction tilts my lips. I'll have to thank him for that. "Good. That's the way it should be."

"Yeah? And why is that?"

"You don't belong with any of them."

Sutton squints at me. "Dare I ask who does?"

No one, certainly not me. I can't force myself to spit those words. I'm such a pansy-ass when it comes to her. But she's the only one. I want to tell her as much. The catastrophe that would follow has me biting my tongue. "Didn't we cover this yesterday?"

"It could use repeating."

I can't find any regret, even digging to my very core. She should know how much I want her. I've been keeping my distance for her sake. All I've succeeded in doing is adding more torture. "I want to be the one who deserves you."

She nudges me with her toe. "I sense a but in there."

"Come on, Sutt. I'm all sorts of wrong for you." I curl the sheet into my tight fist. "You should be with someone like Lance." The words are gasoline to the flame already burning me up. Just thinking about it makes me want to punch his smug face.

"You don't mean that," she whispers.

My gut sinks straight into the foundation of this shitty house. "You're right, I don't. But that doesn't make you any less forbidden."

Sutton snorts. "Says who?"

"Me."

"Well, I disagree."

"That's why we've never discussed this before now."

Her lips flatten into a thin line. "And you're not budging?"

I scrub a hand down my face. "Even if I'm delusional enough to believe this could work, your brother will kill me. I'd like to keep my dick attached and out of harm's way."

"He has nothing to do with us."

"Easy for you to say. That guy has saved my ass more times than I can count. This would be the ultimate betrayal. You need to be sure, Sutt. Once you agree to be mine, there's no letting go. Not for me."

"That won't be an issue. I'm all in." She reaches for my hand.

I lace our fingers together. "Yeah?"

"Yes, Gray. In my mind, you've always been mine." Sutton leans into me. Her hungry gaze settles on my mouth. She parts her lips on a breathy exhale.

Kissing her would seal the deal. A simple exchange with permanent repercussions. "I won't push more boundaries until we talk to your brother."

Sutton jolts upright. "Excuse me?"

I shake off the arousal clouding my vision. "Is that a problem?"

She combs through her snarled hair. "Why do we need to tell him?"

"Wait, you want to keep this a secret?" I grind my molars.

She whips her head back and forth. "Not at all. But Jace doesn't have a say in this. The choice is ours to make."

"This is important to me, Sutt."

She shifts further away from me, scooting to the edge of the bed. Not having her wedged along my side is similar to losing a vital piece of me. But I let her go. I'll never force her to be trapped with me. "I've waited around long enough for you, Grady Bowen. I deserve to be with a man who will choose me over everything else, no matter what."

I cringe when Sutton uses my full name. That's a sure sign I'm in the doghouse. She's absolutely right, which is sad news for me. "I need to be sure nothing will get between us."

"That will only happen if we let it."

"Well, I'm already fucking up." No point in denying the obvious.

She purses her lips. "We're at an impasse. I'm going to leave. Try to rest while getting your priorities straight. I'll send precious Jace over to check on you in a bit."

Before I can attempt a response, Sutton slinks out of the room. The damage has been dished out. I better grab a spoon and enjoy.

CHAPTER TWELVE

Grady

Happy something #93: Finding people to genuinely trust and rely on.

THE ANTIQUE ROCKING CHAIR CREAKS WITH MY FORWARD motion. I'm out on my back porch, feet kicked up on the rickety railing, swinging to a gentle rhythm. My ballcap is slung low to shield the sun. There's a cold beer in my hand. I have no place to go. It's quiet and calm. Only the occasional chirping from a nest of birds greets me. The sticky-sweet scent of pine wafts over from the thatch of evergreens. I could get used to this laying low gig. My day off isn't turning out to be such a bad thing.

Other than Sutton storming out earlier. I'm hoping to rectify that situation soon enough. This afternoon has given me plenty of hours to reflect and strategize. The cogs in my brain are getting a tad sluggish. A nap will do me some good. Sutton did mention rest as part of my plan. I'm just following orders.

No one is around to bother me. A lazy lull captures my mind, slowing normal processing down even more. I slouch deeper into my seat. Sleep is beginning to pull me under when Bear's piercing bark breaks the silence. I crack open an eye to watch him take off toward the driveway. Whoever dares to show up here will either run off scared or figure shit out. I keep my ass planted in place.

A moment later, Jace rounds the house with Bear nipping at his heels. A dry chuckle escapes me at the sight of a grown man trying to outrun a dog. My friend has been trying to get on his good side for years. Sutton is the only one to instantly win my hound over. No surprise there.

Jace gives me the finger and a glare. "Real funny, asshole. How about you call off the killer?"

I whistle and Bear darts toward me. "He's harmless."

"To you."

"He just wants to play."

"By using my leg as a chew toy."

"Quit your bitching," I mutter.

He continues grumbling while plopping down in the other chair. "Not sure why your dog still hates me."

"You're threatening. Take it as a compliment."

Jace rolls his eyes. "Not sure that's a selling point."

"Don't overthink it. Beer?" I kick open the cooler next to me.

He reaches in and grabs one. "Thanks."

I lift my bottle to his. The bandage pulls tight around my injury and I wince.

"How's your arm?"

"Attached." But the hole in my black heart is bigger than ever. Sutton would heal all the broken parts. If only I let her. I take another swig instead.

Jace laughs. "I see you're in a talkative mood."

I flip my hat backwards. "Were you expecting social hour?"

"Nah, learned my lesson. Just wanted to check on you."

I gesture down my torso. "Still breathing."

"Sure glad Sutton found you when she did. The doctor said you lost a shit ton of blood."

The mention of his sister has my body locking up tighter than a steel trap. I'm not prepared to have that discussion yet. Spilling my guts will require a lot more booze, or courage. I don't have an abundance of either. Talking about the accident isn't pleasant, but it's better than him crushing my balls in a vice.

I scratch my jaw. "Uh, yeah. Guess it was a close call."

Jace chugs the rest of his beer and opens another. Good to know he's sticking around. "I see walking away relatively unscathed has lifted your spirits."

My frown deepens. "Had to be carted off in a damn ambulance."

"Could have been a hell of a lot worse."

"Shouldn't have happened at all. I was being careless." And distracted by a certain brunette beauty.

He's quiet for a moment, studying me too close. "What's with the mean-mugging? Beside the obvious."

"It's been a shit week."

"Anything I can do to help?"

Grant me permission to be happy.

But the asking price is steep. This could create a rift we won't be able to repair.

I squint up at the cloudless sky, imagining a blanket of stars. That vision sends me back to a different time. When a little girl with pigtails held the hand of a strange boy who randomly showed up at her house. No hesitation or fear. She's had ahold of me since that moment.

A lump of something fierce lodges in my gut. "Will any man be good enough for Sutton?"

Jace's head whips my way so fast I'm surprised it's still attached. "Why the hell would you ask that?"

I resume rocking in my chair. "Genuine curiosity."

"Is she fucking around with someone?" He's on the edge of his seat, ready to fly off the damn handle.

"Fucking relax, yeah? It's a simple question."

He glares at me. "Nothing about my sister is easy."

I grunt out a loud breath. "You're continuing to blow this out of proportion."

"You started it."

"What's with the temper tantrum? Did your period arrive early?"

"Don't turn this shit on me when you're the one with a sandy vagina."

I almost laugh. "You're such a tool."

Jace scoffs and crosses his arms. "Takes one to know. As if you have a damn leg to stand on. You turn into a snarling beast if another man comes within a mile of Sutton."

I shrug. "Learned from the best."

"Pretty sure it's the other way around."

I scrub over my mouth. He has a decent point. There aren't many people I care about in this world, but Sutton tops that short list. I'd lose my fucking shit if anything happened to her. Maybe that's a valid reason in my defense of all this madness.

A choking sound has me looking his way. "Holy shit, brother. Are you smiling?"

Am I? The slight lift in my lips lingers for another moment. "Huh, guess so."

Another strangled noise escapes him. "How strong are those pills you're on?"

"They pack a hefty punch. But I haven't popped one in hours."

"Sure about that?"

"Yeah, why?"

Jace hitches a thumb at me. "You're more loopy than a rollercoaster."

If that's the case, he'll think I'm insane regardless of what happens next. Might as well rip off the damn duct tape. I clutch my cold bottle in a tight fist. No more wussing out. "I'm in love with your sister."

His slack-jaw and bulging eyes are almost comical. "What the fuck did you just say?"

"I love Sutton. Always have."

He goes utterly still. "You better be yanking my chain."

"I'd have to find it first."

Jace's skin seems to glow with a reddish tint. "Not in the mood for your shit after that bomb. Are you fucking serious?"

I lock my steady stare onto his. "Deadly."

He narrows his eyes. "Why the fuck are you telling me this?"

"I'm finally ready to do something about it." Our future relies heavily on his shoulders. I wonder if he can feel the crushing weight.

His chuckle is hollow. "Does that include stabbing your best friend in the back?"

My stomach lurches and I swallow a mouthful of bile. "I'd never do that to you."

"That's fucking rich considering we're having this conversation."

I hold up a palm. "Calm the hell down. Nothing has even happened yet."

His jaw tics. "Sounds to me like you have plans to change that."

It's my turn to spit through clenched teeth. "I wouldn't have said anything if that wasn't the case."

He grinds a finger into the center of my chest. "You better be referring to more than just fucking her."

I smack his hand off me. "Don't degrade her that way."

His entire body starts shaking. "Me? You're the one talking about getting busy with Sutton."

I groan into my fist. "Will you knock it off? I wanna date her. Do things the right way. Take her out. Make her mine."

The sneer curling his lip says he doesn't believe me. "How fucking sweet. You're writing a fairy tale."

The raging bull inside of me snorts to life, pawing the ground and aiming to attack. "Stop being a dick."

Jace leaps to his feet. His meaty fists are twitching at the ready. "Wanna fucking go? You're already taking shots at me. Might as well make it official."

If he was any other man, I'd already have his ass pinned to the lawn. "Sit the fuck down. We're not fighting over this. You either approve or not."

"As if it actually makes a difference."

"It sure as shit does, especially to me."

To my surprise, Jace drops down into his chair. "So, what, you actually expect my consent or some shit?"

"That'd be nice."

"I can't fucking believe this." He rakes rigid fingers through his cropped hair. "How does Sutton feel about you? Have you even asked her?"

I drain the rest of my beer. "She's currently pissed as shit."

"Can't say that I blame her. I'm not your biggest fan at the moment. Seems to be a common theme for you."

"Thanks for the moral support, asshole."

"Not sure what outcome you had in mind," Jace mutters. "You two as a couple has never been on my radar."

I falter at his words. How can that be possible? His dad made it seem like I've been obvious as hell. "For real?"

He shakes his head with a scowl. "You boning my little sister wasn't something I thought to consider."

Another round of flames ignites in my veins. "Will you shut up with that? This is real for me."

"Well, excuse me. This is weird as fuck for me."

And this entire argument was going nowhere fast. I grip the armrest, taking a sick sort of comfort from the searing pain engulfing my injured limb. Any slim chance I had with Sutton dissolves in a putrid puddle of acid. What a fucking joke.

Jace clears his throat. "So, uh, what'd you do to make her mad?"

I blink off my pity-party. "I told her you needed to be okay with us being together."

He quirks a brow at me. "Figured you were feeding me bullshit with all that."

"Yes, this was all a fucked up ploy." I hang my head, suddenly wrung out and beyond spent.

"Already quitting? That's not a good quality for any relationship." He claps my shoulder.

I shrug off his hold. "Giving me advice now?"

"Thought you wanted the green light?"

"Yeah, something like that."

"That's actually really honorable."

I glare at him. "Don't sound so shocked. I'm not always an asshole."

Jace nods. "Sutton softens you up, that's for damn sure."

Toxic thorns prickle the back of my neck. "You can ease off the compliments. I might get a damn complex."

He lifts a foot onto the weathered railing. "I'm trying to turn this shitshow around, okay?"

"Could've fooled me."

Jace's steely-blue focus lasers in on me. "I'm not gonna lie, brother. This is creepy as fuck for me. I don't like the idea of my sister shacking up. Thinking about it makes me want to hurl. But if anyone is going to be with her, it should be you. There's no doubt you'll worship every patch of land she walks on. Your sorry ass will treat her like the spoiled princess she already is. I'm positive you're gonna do right by her."

My pulse ricochets faster than a ping-pong ball. I gape at him. "You mean that?"

"That expression?" He gestures to my face. "It looks like someone shot your dog. I can't be responsible for that type of misery."

"Don't agree out of guilt."

"Trust me, I'm not. You're a good man, Grady. One of the best I know."

Shit, my eyes are stinging. I cough over the annoying tickle in my throat. No way in hell am I crying. Not fucking happening. "Thanks, brother."

He crosses his arms and leans back. "So, when's the wedding?"

My lungs seize up just picturing my girl in white. I choke out a wheeze and spin my hat around, tugging the brim low. "A long way off, I'm sure. She doesn't know how serious I am."

"Chickening out?"

"Figured we would take shit slow, if anything happens at all."

"Thought this was a home run?"

I pick at a hole in my jeans. "I've got some making up to do."

He stands and stretches with a yawn. "Better get after her or someone else will."

I punch him in the gut. "Fucker."

Jace points at me while descending the porch steps. "Glad I could turn that frown upside down."

"No take backs."

His brow furrows. "Huh?"

I chuckle. "Never mind. Thanks for the blessing, man."

He tosses me a wave over his shoulder. "Don't thank me yet. Sutton still has to agree."

"Hey," I call out before he disappears from view.

Jace stops and turns. "Yeah?"

"Can I catch a lift?"

"Where to?"

I squint against the setting sun. "Your parents' place."

He motions me over. "Hurry up and hop in."

CHAPTER THIRTEEN

Grady

*Happy something #60: Listening to Sutton
make magic out of simple words.*

MY HEART POUNDS A BIT HARDER WHEN THE FAMILIAR MAILBOX comes into view. The headlights flash over that little red barn, a miniature replica of the one standing tall around back. I smooth a finger along the tattered seam of my cap just for something to do.

Maybe this should have waited until morning. I could've called Sutton and asked her to meet me tomorrow. Showing up unannounced might be overstepping my bounds. But she used to love surprises. More road disappears behind us, the property edge that much closer. Too late for second-guessing now.

Gravel crunches under the tires as Jace pulls over. The truck rolls to a stop before we reach the driveway. He slings his arm over the wheel and shoots me a grin. "We're here."

"Sure are." I glance out the window. Even in the near

darkness, bright-white fences and sprawling acres of land speak to me. My greatest escape.

"Feeling okay?"

I offer a slow nod. "Thanks again, Ace."

He lifts his chin in my direction. "Don't make me regret it."

"I won't." The words come out as a low growl.

"Good." He checks his reflection in the mirror. "I have a date of my own so get a move on."

I use that as an excuse to stall in my seat. "Anyone I know?"

"Nah, she's not from Silo. I swiped right. Maybe I'll get lucky."

"Or catch a case of crabs."

Jace laughs. "That's why I'm always prepared with extra protection. Wrap it up and stay clean. You can't hate on the game unless it backfires."

A shudder courses through me. "Don't need that shit anymore."

"So in love," he coos.

I flip him off. "Better than hooking up with a random stranger."

He gives me a pointed stare. "No one has an endless supply of convenient friends with benefits. Especially in a small town."

I don't have a response for that. It's been years since I relied on the empty embrace of a meaningless hookup. That shit gets old really fast. Trying to force myself to feel something good was a cheap knockoff. I lost interest after a few shoddy attempts. It was stupid searching for a slice of happiness with someone else, even for a quick release. But I never claimed to be logical.

That all changes tonight.

My sole source of peace is within reach, waiting right inside.

He taps on the dashboard. "Need a shove?"

I glance over at him. "Damn, you really are in a hurry."

"I'm shocked you aren't."

I tap my temple. "There's a lot to consider. I'm getting it all straight."

Jace makes a gagging noise. "Gross. I just remembered you want to see my sister naked."

"Not this again," I groan.

He smacks my chest. "Just fucking around. Go confess all your mushy feelings to her."

I pinch the bridge of my nose. "That's not helping."

"Whatever. Go do something." He makes a shooing motion. "Best of luck, man. Here's to hoping you don't crash and burn."

With that parting piece of positivity, I step out of the truck with a renewed sense of urgency brewing. Jace revs the engine and peels off like someone is chasing him. I fan the dust away from my face, adding a loud snort. Pretty sure he's the one hounding tail. I stand there for a moment longer, until his taillights disappear around the bend. His words from earlier still clang against my skull. This day has made a sharp turn for the better, and nightfall is about to put on the finishing touches.

Speaking of getting busy, the need to find Sutton thrums through me. My boots pound across the pavement with a hasty stride. I plan to grovel and beg and do whatever it takes. If all goes well, she'll accept my apology. We can ride off into the sunset and live happily ever after. I stop dead in my tracks. These pills are really fucking with me. Either that or I'm officially losing my mind. The latter is more likely.

Nothing is ever that easy. Wishful fucking believing.

I try to collect my thoughts, but everything scatters with the cool evening breeze. There's so much that needs saying. Where will I begin? Words have never been a strength for me.

Sutton was more than willing to talk enough for both of us. Growing up, she would follow me around and rattle off whatever story popped into her beautiful mind. Chores were never boring with her nearby. I let my lips lift with the hint of a grin. Listening to that lyrical voice will never get old.

But this is the start of us, a new beginning with a fresh outlook. Damn, I sound all whimsical and shit. Maybe Sutton is making me soft. Does she want me to be? Not sure that's possible for me. A slight twitch below the belt offers a solid reminder. I'm positive she'd prefer certain parts of me remaining hard. That's a topic for a later date, or maybe an hour or two.

I veer onto the brick path leading to their front door. The moon is wide awake, glowing like a beacon in a sea of black. Crickets serenade me while I hop up the porch stairs. I raise a fist and rap my knuckles on the heavy wood.

Shuffling footsteps sound on the other side. The door creaks open and Sutton's face appears. Any trace of makeup she was wearing earlier has been washed away. Her features are pure and clean and on display for me to see. Just the way I love her.

She remains silent, using those baby blues to peel away the layers of my armor. I'm almost weak in the knees from one look. Her quiet stare bores into me. A thousand needles prickle along my scalp. Who's going to break first? She gives me nothing, other than her soulful gaze. This girl always has a smile and warm welcome for me. But not tonight. I don't deserve those yet.

"Hey, Sutt." Reaching for her feels essential. My touch might not be received well at this point. I shove my hands deep into my pockets.

"Hello." Her somber tone is a dull blade, ripping at my flesh without mercy.

I swallow that bitter pill. "You look gorgeous. But that's nothing new."

She raises her chin. "Thanks, Grady."

My stomach tightens at that dig. She's not open for compliments—duly noted. I bury the sting and force myself further into the flames. "Are you busy?"

Sutton taps her fingers against the wood frame. "I was doing some posts and schedules. Work stuff."

"Can you spare a few moments for me?"

"That depends." A shadow of a grin dents her cheek.

"On?" I lean an arm along the wall, dropping into her space.

"What you have to tell me."

"I'll spill everything." I lick my lips. A thrill zings up my spine when she tracks the slow movement.

She lifts a slim brow. "How many secrets have you been keeping?"

I lost count. But there's no use spewing that. "None if all goes well."

"So confident."

"I prefer optimistic."

Sutton's gasp is soft, but it blasts through me with the force of a cannonball. Her parted mouth calls to mine. I want to keep surprising her, for the rest of our lives.

My gut plunges when she takes a step back. But her trace of a smile has me holding on. She tucks some hair behind her pink-tipped ear. "Do you, uh, wanna come in?"

My boots are glued to the stoop. No matter how much I care for her parents, we need to be alone. "It's too late for a proper date. But I still wanna take you out. Would that be okay?" I let my urges take control and twirl a piece of her silky hair. "Will you let me, Sutt?"

She sags into the door. "Where to?"

"A special place. We can walk to the meadow."

Another hitch shutters her breath. "O-okay."

"Can we go now? Or do you need to finish—"

"I'm ready," she blurts.

I blow out a long exhale. Thank the Lord for small miracles.

Sutton ducks by me onto the porch and shuts the door. It's my turn to be stunned. Her tan skin is illuminated by the overhead lights, giving me a mouthwatering view. A white tank clings to her round breasts and flat stomach. Her skirt is flowy, hiding those toned thighs I want wrapped around my waist. She's lush curves and sharp angles and made for me. My dick appreciates the sight, halfway to giving her a standing ovation.

I continue leering, a starving lion drooling over a meek deer. Sutton doesn't seem to care. There's a familiar gleam of hunger in her gaze. I'm struck by this moment, straddling a line that will change everything. I want to beat on my chest and announce that she's mine. But that isn't true.

Neither of us move, the seconds bleeding into eternity. Sutton twists her fingers until they resemble a complex web. I lift an open palm toward her. She stares down at my offering, the intention clear. Her shoulders bunch higher while she considers what this means.

The wind howls in my ears, lashing at me with promises of us. She can heal the hurt, be my one and only happy something. But that's for her to decide. "Take the leap with me, Sutty."

Her gaze jumps to mine at the old nickname. I haven't used it since we were young and childish. But a piece of our innocent past can bridge the hole that still echoes between us. She reaches out and slides our hands together, closing the gap with a delicate caress. The silk in her gentle touch mends the broken inside of me. I've been dealt a lifetime full of shitty blows. Whoever's in charge upstairs enjoys challenging me. But Sutton is my gift. The one piece that's always been right. And she's finally all mine.

I tug her into me. Any inch of space is a cold reminder of what no longer describes us. I press my lips to her temple. "Good choice."

She nuzzles into my chest. "It was the only one I could choose."

"Should we go?" I can almost feel prying stares boring into me through the window.

Sutton nods. I guide her down the stairs and onto the dark path. We walk side by side, our fingers tightly intertwined.

She scans the driveway as we pass by. "How'd you get here?"

"Jace dropped me off."

"Well, you're still in one piece. Must have gone all right."

I squeeze her hand. "He came around."

A spotlight from the barn catches the tension in her features. "What if he changes his mind?"

I let the corner of my mouth twitch. "He promised no take backs."

"What are you, twelve? Will you break up with me if he says so?"

The thunder in my pulse is deafening. "You're already agreeing to be mine?"

She bumps her leg into me. "I thought that was obvious when we stepped off the ledge. Refusing you isn't an option, Gray."

I pull on her arm, stopping us before we cross into the meadow. "But you can. Hell, you probably should."

"For a man who pretends to give zero shits, you sure do well with trying to scare me off. Stop attempting to convince me that this is a bad idea, Gray. I'll never agree with you." She brushes some hair out of my eyes. "Don't you see? I've been waiting for you to accept us."

"Fuck." A kaleidoscope of vivid color nearly blinds me. I wobble a bit from the impact.

Sutton grips my shoulder. Her brows knit together. "Should you be up and moving around?"

"I'm fine." A loose laugh tumbles out of me. "Shit, I'm fucking grand."

She leans in to study my expression. "Are you sure?"

"Yes. Even if I wasn't, this is more important." I steer us onto the worn trail that leads to our spot.

"And if you collapse?"

That has my feet stumbling to a halt. I lower my forehead onto hers, sparks flickering off our heated skin. "Always looking out for me."

She presses closer. "I'm upping my game after yesterday."

I loop my injured arm around her middle, hauling her hips into mine. There's no hiding my need for her. "Knowing you care does some crazy shit to me. It's difficult to keep myself in check."

Her gasp has my blood pumping south at a rapid rate. "What if I want you to lose control?"

"Sutton," I growl against her cheek. "You don't know what that means."

She drags her nails down my ribs, ending at the waistband of my jeans. "I'm ready to find out."

"I damn sure hope so." The threads of my restraint are beginning to fray. "But not tonight."

Her gaze searches mine. "What? You want to wait?"

"That's not why I brought you out here."

She slips her hand into my back pocket. "What's the reason?"

To look at the stars.

To find the good.

To be free.

To live happy.

But she's everything I'm not. Offering her one last

chance to leave burns up my throat. "You can do better than me, Sutt."

She shakes her head. "I already told you to stop. There's no such thing."

I rub my thumb across her lower lip. "Okay, I'm done fighting."

"About damn time," she whispers.

"I'm gonna make you proud of me. Proud to claim me as yours."

"That'll be easy. I already am, Gray."

No more words are necessary. I cup her delicate cheek in my clumsy paw. Sutton sags into my hold without hesitation. I tip her face up to mine, angling us closer. Her slow exhale blends with mine. A small taste won't hurt. I softly brush my lips along hers, more of a tease than anything else. That's all I planned for this to be. But she opens for me, a flower blooming under the sun. I delve in with pure lust boiling through me. Her honey flavor seeps into me, mixing with mint and citrus. My eyes practically cross while white-hot desire flashes in front of me. Her whimper is my undoing. I need more.

My fingers skim up her inner thigh, a coarse rasp against satin. Hot desire slices into me when she trembles. I fist the fabric of Sutton's skirt, yanking her into me. She tumbles against my chest with a gasp. I take advantage of her parted lips, diving in for another taste. She moans into my mouth. Her tongue licks at mine and I see a burst of the brightest stars.

Good Lord, this woman will be the end of me.

The zipper of my jeans is about to bust at the seams. I force myself to pull away. Sutton follows my retreat with a wheeze.

"W-what's wrong?"

"Fuck, nothing." I grip her hip, staving off another around. Just barely. "We just need to stop."

She bounces up on her toes, our mouths melting in a heated frenzy. I clutch a handful of her silky hair and tilt us into a seamless kiss. Oxygen leaves my lungs and all I breathe is Sutton. Her pure berry scent. All the sunrises and cloudless skies. Fresh cut grass and tree swings. Fuck, I get lost in all she is.

I rip my mouth away with a groan. "No more. Not here."

There's still a flush coloring her smooth skin. I get harder knowing it was me who put it there. "Now what?"

I drift a thumb up her jaw. "Wanna go for a drive?"

"You're awful adventurous this evening. Where to?"

I smirk at her. "We'll travel that road soon enough. Until then, I want you sleeping in my arms, in my bed, where you belong. Tonight and from now on."

CHAPTER FOURTEEN

Sutton

Happy something #89: Conquering new milestones and adventures. The more risky, the better.

I WAKE WITH A JOLT. THE ROOM IS DARK AND SMELLS HEAVILY OF rich pine. I'm in bed alone, the other side still warm. There's a shower running nearby. The muddled pieces of my awareness quickly snap into place. I smile wide, pressing two fingers to my lips.

The sheets are in a twist all around me, evidence of a great night. A searing blaze stings my cheeks at the reminder. I fan at my flushing skin, catching sight of my mostly-bare bottom half. But the scrap of silk between my legs remains securely in place. Much to my dismay, Grady insisted that we stall at first base and only kiss. My demands for more were met with steely resolve. I found a few cracks in his armor, though. He couldn't deny me everything.

We ended up sharing far more than a few innocent pecks.

My face and neck are chafed in all the best places. A

lingering reminder that Grady was there. Fantasies are born from that type of steamy make out session. A definite benefit was being graced by his near-nakedness. Only a tight pair of black briefs had concealed him. I wanted to shred that forsaken cotton with my teeth.

I glance at the glow coming from beyond the closet. The shower is still blasting at full power. Grady is in there, on the other side, without a stitch of clothing covering him. A solid plan forms in front of me, elicit and bold. The idea alone is an electric thrill skittering through me. I swing my legs over the edge of the bed. When did I get so daring? The provocative man within reach answers that without a word. I hear the water cut off, feel that stream abruptly end as if it's a vibration in my bones. The possibilities of what happens next loops a snug string around my waist. I scoot further on the mattress and almost slip off. A sudden whoosh rings out from the far corner, halting my haste.

The bathroom door opens with a billowing cloud of woodsy-scented steam. A freshly scrubbed Grady struts out in all his shirtless glory. Stray droplets speckle his tan skin. A few trickle down the cut muscles of his abs, and travel lower into the towel around his waist. The impressive ridge tenting the threadbare fabric is practically waving at me.

Good Christ.

There's a pool of saliva prepared to dribble out if I don't act soon. I swallow twice for good measure. I bite my lip, envisioning all the ways to make him messy. The list is endless, but three tiny words bounce around my brain.

Drop. The. Towel.

No doubt that's where things should start. Grady prowls toward me with a fluid stride. Too bad for me, that white cloth stays firmly knotted. Confidence broadens his already wide shoulders. There's no sign of pain or weakness. He appears to be in top virile form, capable of making me squirm with a single glance. I clutch at the pile of sheets for some false sense of stability. The material does little to hold me down. I'm liable to lunge forward and plaster myself to his chiseled chest. His eyes skewer me into place, as if he's able to read my wicked intentions.

I cross my legs, only to release them a moment later. I'm a jittery mass of pent-up yearning for this man. He better not think about trying to keep things tame again. Once I manage to regain a smidgen of wits, I'm upping my game.

Grady's stride doesn't quit until our knees bump. "Good morning, beautiful."

I walk my toes up his shin. "Hey, Gray. I could have joined you."

He tucks some hair behind my ear. "I didn't want to wake you."

"I wouldn't have minded. Wasn't it lonely in there?"

"It was."

"And now?"

An animalistic rumble rolls off him. "I regret letting you sleep an extra five minutes."

I'm having a conversation with his groin. How does he expect me to continue answering questions when he's standing so close, and at attention. "Uh, w-what was that?"

His body shakes with laughter. He tips up my chin with a gentle touch. My naughty gaze makes a lazy stroll up his torso and pecs, over the strong column of his neck, and eventually settling on the smoldering embers in his eyes. I gulp at the unfiltered lust brimming in those green depths.

Grady trails a finger along my scalding face. "If looks could speak, yours would be screaming my name."

I nod into his touch. No point opposing the obvious.

He links our fingers together. "Should we test my theory?"

I unhinge my jaw with a wordless pop. Can this really be so simple?

He kneels in front of me, the rough skin of his palms settling on my restless feet. My eyes nearly cross from that small amount of contact. His hands brush across my ankles and skim up my calves. The speed is a slow torture toward a distant edge. He reaches my knees with no sign of stopping. Smokey flames stoke higher with each passing inch.

His gritty tone strikes another match. "When I was a lost little boy, I wanted to hold your hand. As a punk ass kid, I relied on your kindness to survive the cruelty. As a horny teen, I craved the curve of your body against mine. Now I'm a man, and I want every single thing you're willing to give."

The hints of romantic sentiment get whisked away in a foggy haze. I'm wanton, needy and begging and unashamed. "P-please take me. You can have it all. I'm yours," I murmur.

He kisses the ticklish skin of my inner thigh. "Love hearing that, Sutt. You make me so fucking hard."

"Do something about it," I wheeze.

"Patience." His husky reprimand has the opposite effect. I scoot forward and his grip tightens. "Lay back and relax."

An unintelligible garble escapes me. I lower onto my elbows, keeping him in a direct line of sight. He's barely breached intimate territory and I'm already breathless.

His finger traces under the lacy edge of my panties. "These are pretty. But they'd look better in tatters on the floor."

My lungs threaten to seize from the lack of oxygen. How do I respond while losing ground with reality? I must be dreaming.

Grady isn't deterred by my silence. A satisfied smirk perches on his lips. He snaps the elastic on my ass and I buck up at the sting. His hoarse chuckle gives me goosebumps.

"So sensitive," he murmurs into my covered core. His breath is a furnace, blasting me with raw heat. The most private part of me is too empty, clenching at the prospect of what's to come. Only a thin layer of satin separates me from him.

I shift as he drags the silky fabric off my hips. Chilled air greets my exposed center, eliciting a hiss from me. He bunches the flimsy material in a fist and brings it to his nose. His inhale is loud and deep.

A squeak breaks out of me. Shit, that's so filthy. And I love it. Would begging him to repeat the process be weird? Do I actually care? I open my mouth with the plea. Grady's hungry growl stops me.

Erotic promises brighten his features. "Spread your legs for me, beautiful."

My limbs obey his command before I can process the words. He stares at my bare slit as if a priceless treasure has been revealed. My blood sizzles with what I can only describe as unadulterated need. The sheer wonder reflecting in his gaze has me wheezing. His eyes continue feasting on me while his thumbs part my folds wider. I want more of him, desperately so, but this visual foreplay is striking plenty of buttons.

Grady doesn't leave me hanging much longer.

His head dips between my stretched thighs. I attempt to get a grip on his slick hair, my nails sliding through the wet strands. That first teasing lick triggers a domino of sensations, igniting sparklers in my center and fanning out. A booming beat crashes against my ribs. I collapse flat onto the mattress with a long moan.

"Holy shit," I murmur.

His hum of approval vibrates through my core. Shockwaves zip straight to my curled toes. That earns him a drawn out, high-pitched whine. I watch through bleary eyes as Grady slowly swipes up my seam, bottom to top. The sound is indecent, a man savoring a favorite treat. My responding gasp encourages him to bury his face deeper. His tender strokes morph into lashing twists that has my head spinning. He zeroes in on my clit, hitting his target with masterful precision. With each loop of his tongue, I leap closer to sweet release. The promise of a climax to end all orgasms is just beyond my fingertips.

Grady grips my hips and drags me into him. My ass hangs off the bed until he changes angles. The back of my knees find purchase on his shoulders and he tilts me up. In this position, he opens me further for the taking. His tongue is a wicked spiral set on my detonation. Grady can show a tornado a thing or two with these skills. An intense increase of suction skyrockets me into the stratosphere. My thoughts fray into a tangle of nonsense.

"O-ohhhh, oh, oh," I chant the mumbled word until it's unrecognizable. He's lavishing my hypersensitive bundle with rapid flicks of his tongue. My vision goes fuzzy around the edges. The only thing I can concentrate on is Grady's mouth devouring me. "D-don't s-stop. I'm almost t-there."

A sharp bite to my pulsing clit is the final shove. My legs begin quaking as a tremor whips through me. The cork keeping me bottled up explodes with a shattering bang. I soar to the thunderous clouds, splitting in a hundred pieces. My eyes roll all the way back, lashes fluttering out of control. I'm a twitching puddle of elation, floating somewhere between reality and fantasy. I've never had this type of intoxicating pleasure thrumming through my veins. Anything before this moment pales in comparison.

Hot. Fucking. Damn.

I'm still attempting to regain feeling in my limbs when Grady pulls away. The grin he's wearing is the cocky assurance of a job well done. I couldn't agree more. Hell, this man deserves a raise.

I'm dizzy and seeing stars, but his handsome face flickers into focus. Grady wipes the back of a hand over his mouth, those emerald pools glittering with more temptation. I will my drained muscles to recuperate.

He sucks on his bottom lip. "Fucking divine. I'll gladly eat you for every meal."

I manage to cup his scruffy cheek. "I like the sound of that."

His lips drift along my thigh. "Breakfast in bed is my new favorite."

"You're dirty."

"Thanks to you. I get to have you on my tongue all day."

"Oh, that sounds even better. My turn." I try to tug him into me, but he resists. "C'mere, Gray."

A swift shake of his head follows my demand.

I try again, pulling harder. He doesn't budge. "Why? Where do you have to go?"

"Work." His tone rings with finality.

If my body was cooperating, I'd spring up straight. "What? Didn't you take more time off? You were just in a serious accident."

He frowns at me. "I need the money, Sutt. Sitting around on my ass isn't paying the bills."

"But you need to heal."

"Didn't hear you complaining about my well-being five minutes ago."

I glance away as fire singes my cheeks. "That's different."

He laughs. "Yeah, it's a lot more fun fucking around with you. Wanna play hooky?"

That gives me pause. Posts need to be scheduled. I think about the invoices piling up. I'm sure there's a stack of emails waiting for me. One of my clients is calling me at noon. I'm not sure where my phone is.

He must read the hesitation in my expression. "That's what I thought." Grady stands and the towel drops to his feet. He looms a foot away completely nude and apparently off-limits. I force myself upright for a decent view. It's a solid consolation prize, quite literally.

Grady turns and struts to the dresser. His ass is firm, sculpted male perfection. I want to nibble on those muscular globes. He peeks over his shoulder, very much catching me in the fine act of ogling. A smirk kisses his lips.

"Naughty girl. Keep staring and I'll never let you leave."

I squirm at the invitation.

"You like that idea?" He palms his dick, giving the iron shaft a leisurely stroke.

I nod. "Need a hand?"

Grady shakes his head, that girthy length still disappearing into a tight fist. "I can handle it. You give me plenty of material."

A pout sticks out my bottom lip. "Team effort?"

"Don't be sad. You'll get a turn."

That gets my blood pumping hotter. "Oh really? When?"

"I'll see you later."

"Says who?"

"Me. We're going on a date."

A giddy pitter-patter takes flight in my belly. "Are you going to tell me where and when?"

Another shake of his head. "All you need to be ready for is a shitload of wooing."

All argument dies on my tongue. Damn, I really loved the sound of that.

CHAPTER FIFTEEN

Grady

Happy something #103: Planning ahead for better days, no matter how stupid it seems.

I SLIDE ANOTHER PLANK INTO PLACE AND POSITION THE NAIL GUN. The hydraulic pop-pop-pop that rapidly follows has become more of a distant hum. It's been the same monotonous cycle all afternoon. Measure. Set. Nail. Repeat. I could've finished this section of flooring hours ago if my head was screwed on straight.

There isn't a lot I can claim to be good at and reliable for, but my work ethic is solid. Doing a job well gives me a boost of pride. I don't slack off or put in half-assed effort. My reputation is tarnished enough. More slams against me will land my ass in the unemployment line. That won't pay the bills I have piling up on my counter. Yet I don't reach for another piece of glossy oak. A small breather won't derail me much further.

The rubber mallet bounces off the wood beside me. I

wipe at the trail of sweat that's dripping down my temple. It's hotter than Hades in this house, even with all the windows open. The owner is paying us to renovate so he can flip this place for a nice profit. Air conditioning is out of the question. Cutting time is the priority, not our comfort while doing it.

Speaking of, seconds have never ticked by so damn slow. If time speeds up while having fun, that leaves hours to drag while nothing is happening. Here I sit with my head spinning in a thousand directions. Usually I credit myself with having the ability to focus until a task is complete. Working diligently while keeping my nose to the grindstone isn't asking for much. But there's no controlling my thoughts. Not today.

My mind has been wandering down a path that I'd been ignoring for too long. The floodgates burst open and any attempts at concentrating are utter shit. I'm a lost cause because of her. And I always have been.

Big blue eyes the color of a tropical gulf. Dark hair that hangs in loose waves, falling down to a slender waist. A lush pout that's still swollen from my kiss. Toned thighs squeezing my skull as I lick faster. What's a man expected to do? There's no ignoring her, even in my imagination.

"Yo, Bowen." The greeting bursts into my fantasy. "What's shaking?"

I look over my shoulder toward the voice. Cane leans on the doorframe with his arms crossed, looking relaxed and loose. His posture contradicts the mounting ball of pressure building in my chest. Must be nice.

There aren't many people I can stand hanging nearby for hours on end. I prefer being alone on the best days. Same goes for these jobs. But there are a few guys I've found to be tolerable. Cane is one of them. He's a decent carpenter and mostly keeps to himself. I appreciate my space. This guy is good about giving it.

He steps into the foyer, reminding me of his question. I

motion to the mayhem scattered around me. "Trying to put a wrap on this room."

"I just finished installing that southside window."

Why do I care? I lift a brow and drawl, "And? You want a cookie?"

Cane chuckles at that. "I need to take off. Wanted to see what you're up to."

I grunt. "You're looking at it."

He's not required to check with me before dipping out. We're on a level playing field, responsible for managing ourselves and the tasks assigned to us. There's no official foreman, other than the owner himself. He drops in weekly to check our progress but otherwise leaves us alone. It's a definite perk that we're not required to report on a daily basis. I get to rule my own post without someone hovering.

"Quittin' time for you soon?" He taps at his phone.

I glance outside, finding the sun still high. A quick scan around the living room shows rolls of matting and stacks of oak waiting to be placed. The floor is far from done. I could stick around another hour and get more boards down. Boss says to cut corners as needed. Visions of Sutton begin replaying, providing more than an adequate shove. Fuck it, I'll haul ass tomorrow. "Yeah, I'm ready to call it a day."

Cane is quiet for a moment, his gaze doing a slow sweep of the space I'm still crouched in. "You all good, man?"

I glare at him. Why is everyone so concerned about me lately? Do I have a stamp on my forehead requesting assistance? Didn't think so. I rise to my feet and face him. "Why wouldn't I be?"

He scratches the back of his neck. "Not sure. Trouble at home?"

"Oh, you got it." I might work with this guy frequently, but he doesn't know me. "Bear has been a real bitch to deal with. Nice try."

The easy expression melts off his face. "You don't have to be a dick. I was just asking."

"That's not necessary. I'm fine."

"Aren't fucking acting like it," he mutters under his breath.

A ripple of smoke swirls off my skin. I narrow my eyes into thin slits. "What's it matter to you?"

"Well, screw me for trying to be your friend."

A humorless laugh escapes me at his sudden interest. "I have enough of those."

Cane seems to be done leaving me alone. It's safe to say I misjudged his standoff behavior. He raises a palm. "Okay, whatever. Forget about it. Enjoy your night."

I jut my chin up. "Same to you."

"Going to Howlers. Cheers." He offers a limp salute before turning on his heel and stomping to his car.

I track his retreating form with a fierce glare. The tension in my muscles spiked with each passing moment. The throbbing pulse stabbing into my temples isn't helping. This afternoon just took a turn for the worse, and my mood is plummeting with the descent. Fucking awesome. The only thing stopping a spiral is my plan for this evening. Tonight will be better. And that's my cue to blow this joint.

Ferocious tidal waves whoosh in my ears while I storm from wall to wall locking the place up. All the materials remain in scattered piles across the living room. There isn't much use cleaning up at this stage in the game. With a resounding slam, I'm out of there. I remove my toolbelt with a harsh tug and sling the heavy leather over my shoulder. The gravel crunches under my boots as I walk to my truck. I toss my gear into the bed, metal banging loud enough to make an echo.

I've never been more thankful for the short trip to my house. Two songs have blared from start to finish through the crackling speakers when I pull into the drive. I hop out, alternating barks and yelps immediately cutting through the stillness. Bear is waiting on his hind legs when I open the door. Before I can consider petting him, he leaps forward and dashes into the yard with his snout to the ground. I allow the barest hint of a smile to tip my lips. That dog is good for the sour soul.

With my temper already unwinding, I trek upstairs. The unfinished projects littered along the way don't bother me for once. There's a new goal in my forefront. I need to push the reset button and wash this day off me.

It takes me less than ten minutes to shower and toss on clean clothes. I feel lighter on my feet while stepping outside. Bear follows close behind, making sure to mark every tree we pass. The humidity hasn't cracked and a fresh round of sweat quickly dots my brow. That'll make for an even better ride.

The detached garage is marginally cooler and offers a slight breeze. I stride to the far corner with a tremble twitching my fingers. There, still in the box, is a helmet. Shiny, pink, and another symbol of wishful thinking. Turns out that fleck of hope wasn't in vain, and is coming in handy if this morning was any indication. Dismal days forced me into wanting more from life. That's one of the harsh outlooks that kept me moving forward. It's a shitload easier to give up, my mother is realistic proof of that. But that small voice never quit whispering sweet promises of better moments to come. Sutton led me through my darkest points without even realizing. Or maybe she does. That connection between us hums in my gut. No more stalling.

I rip open the packaging and strap her helmet to the side of my bike. My foolish planning is beginning to pay off. No one has been on the back. She'll be the first, and only.

Bear paws at my leg, tilting his head to the side and giving me the pitiful puppy-dog eyes. I kneel in front of him and scratch his scruff. "Don't be sad, boy. I'm gonna pick up Sutton and go for a fast spin. We'll be back soon."

His ears lift and flick a bit. He adds in a whine for good measure.

I comb through the thick fur down his sides. Bear flops down and offers his stomach. I indulge him for a few minutes, scratching the spot that gets his leg spinning. With a clap, I stand and prop open the door leading to his run. "There. You can enjoy the great outdoors while I'm gone."

But he's done listening. Bear is racing back and forth along the chain fencing, chasing a squirrel or an imaginary bunny. I can't be too sure which one. A rumble rolls off my chest, releasing the remaining strain. It's going to be a damn good night.

Without overthinking anything else, I straddle the leather seat and walk my hog onto the driveway. I dig out my phone and the screen lights up with a plain background. Maybe it's time to change that too. I tap over to contacts. Sutton's number is the only one in my favorites, always has been.

Me: Where are you?

The three dots appear immediately. I smirk at that. Glad I'm not the only one jonesing.

Sutt: Steeped.
Me: On the corner of First and Hill?
Sutt: That's the place.
Me: Be there soon.

I pocket my cell before she responds. It's time to get my girl.

CHAPTER SIXTEEN

Sutton

Happy something #57: Making wishes on weeds.

THE RUMBLE FROM A MOTORCYCLE BREAKS APART MY thoughts and skewers the idle chatter around the cafe. That low roar rockets from the tips of my toes straight up. A streak of heat follows in its wake, goosebumps prickling my arms. I shiver and lift my gaze to the large bay window. There's a single headlight beaming at me, growing brighter as he approaches.

I nearly jumped from my seat when his text came through. Hasty might as well be my middle name. Grady messaged me fifteen minutes ago, but I wasn't sure how long he meant by soon. The idea of him showing up shoved an unpredictable twist in my smooth routine. I'd been semi-productive until that point. Most of that was due to my phone remaining silent. I'd been secretly waiting to hear from him since we parted this morning. But I refuse to be that clinging girl.

I'm no longer the lovesick teenager who would've done anything to be with Grady Bowen. A part of her still lives and breathes inside of me, but the woman I've become rallies louder. She demands stability and some perception of commitment before spilling her guts. There has to be a happy medium. This has happened so suddenly that a teeny tiny piece of me still needs confirmation. Silly as that seems considering this is Grady I'm referring to. He wouldn't deceive me.

We've reconciled, but there's plenty left unsaid. Maybe tonight will solve some of that. I'm comfortable letting things play out as they're meant to be. Confidence infuses my bones while Grady zooms closer to Steeped. Our potential is strong and bright. Being in a romantic relationship with him feels like a long time coming. It's difficult to remain calm and go slow. I want everything he's willing to offer, and that need burns through every part of me.

Grady will have the same from me in return. I'll be his rock. A pure source of happy somethings. His most reliable and loyal confidante. I'll always stick by his side. He'll want to let me in, completely and irrevocably. Gaining that level of trust seems like a feat, but his walls are already crumbling.

We bowed and bent toward each other without much fight. It's always been that way. Try as I might, which I really didn't, there was no resisting. That's why I couldn't handle being around before. Witnessing him avoid me on purpose was a shot of poison, infecting me with bitterness and toxicity. We're moving well beyond the opposite of that, I think.

I shake off the uncertainty, that flicker of insecurity tipping the scale. This is for real. He's pretty much admitted we're forever. But I should wait until we're officially settled to reveal any of this. That stops me short. There I go again, running off with wild ideas. This man stirs up a level of crazy I didn't believe lived inside of me. I lay a hand over my forehead.

Stay calm. Slow down.

That's probably the best place to start. But too many lost opportunities have slipped through my fingers. I won't waste more. Being with him—in any capacity—is all I truly need. Happiness is us blending together. Moving home to Silo Springs reignited our bond. And here we are.

I watch as Grady eases the bike to a stop along the curb in front of the main entrance. Is he coming in? Should I go out? Grady yanks off his helmet and turns those green eyes toward me. I blink at him. Can he see me? Does it matter? I collect my things in a rush and meet him on the sidewalk.

He's wearing a thin white tee that showcases his muscular build. His dark blond hair is mussed and messy. A thick dusting of stubble coats his jaw. Those seductive emerald pools beg me to dive in.

Mine. I clack my teeth and hope he doesn't notice.

Grady offers me a half smile. "Hi, Sutt."

"Hey, Gray." I'm a tad breathless, and not from dashing across a few feet of space.

All of those needs and desires from moments ago resurface. I stare at him, into those honest green eyes, and the words threaten to spill out. Somehow I manage to gulp them down. Well, most of them. Containment is essential for my pride.

"I'm extremely attracted to you," I blurt. "Like a magnet." I bump my fists together for visual emphasis.

That's what I choose to say? Out of everything? I almost smack my forehead.

Grady's laughter shatters my humiliation. "Fuck, you're sexy."

A scorching blaze wafts against my cheeks. I tuck my chin, but don't break our connection. Should I kiss him? Hold his hand? Grady makes a decision, tugging me into him by the belt loop. Two strong arms band around my waist and erase any bit of space between us. The answer was a hug, the best one ever. I purr against his chest.

My skin is still tingling from Grady's masterful ministrations earlier. Being this close to him again heightens the sensation tenfold. It's almost surprising my legs aren't trembling in anticipation.

"Don't get shy on me now." His lips tickle the shell of my ear. "I missed you."

"Missed you so much." I ease back a smidge to catch his stare. "How was work?"

Grady lifts a shoulder and I shift with the slight movement. "Decent. Didn't get shit done."

"No?"

"Had a lot on my mind." He rotates his injured arm, then winks at me.

I bite my lip. "Are you okay?"

"Much better now."

My stomach does a little flip that has me grinning. "So, where are you taking me?"

"For a cruise." His mouth skims my temple.

I lean into his touch. "To?"

"Somewhere special to me."

"Please not Howlers." I cross my fingers behind his back.

His upper body shakes with humor. "Ah, come on. That place isn't so bad."

I scoff. "For you. All the old bikers leer at any girl under forty when they walk in."

He squeezes my ass. "Can you blame them?"

I wiggle closer. His answering groan is the best reward. "I'm not trying to be a snob. But come on, Gray. That dive isn't swoony-wooing material."

"You have a good point, which is why we're not going there. But that bar saved me from some dark shit. It's one of my few escapes."

Crud. I want to rewind and take back all the negative stuff. "Really?"

His eyes bore into mine. "I'm not going to lie, this town sucks a lot of ass without you. I thought you'd left for good. Figured I'd be gone soon enough."

I swallow past the frog in my throat. "And now?"

"Things change."

"They do."

Grady nuzzles into the dip between my shoulder and neck. "You're gonna help me live my best life, Sutt. There's so much I want to share with you, starting with this spot tonight."

"Then let's get going. Should I follow you?" I suggest.

"No, we'll take the bike."

I glance down at my shorts and sandals. Not exactly motorcycle gear. "Umm, is it safe?"

He frowns. "I should've thought about your outfit." The strain melts off his features. "I installed custom foot pegs high enough to avoid the exhaust. You'll be okay, don't worry. We'll be careful."

I trace a narrow pinstripe on the rear fender. "I've never been on a Harley."

He shuffles us a sidestep toward the gleaming chrome beast. "Always a first for everything. You'll get used to it. Next time you'll wear jeans and boots."

I'm sure my eyes are blown wide. Next time? Apparently Grady has his own agenda. Not that I'm complaining.

A loud squeal on my left has me twisting in that direction. Molly and Lance are there, walking closer with a slow stride. Her face is lit up with glee. His is blank and unreadable, as if he's about to interrogate someone. He better not try any shit with Grady. I haven't gotten over doling out arrests for no reason.

"Oh my gosh." Molly's voice is more of a squeak. "Are you two an item?"

My gaze swings to Grady for the correct response on handling this. He doesn't hesitate, threading our fingers together. "Yeah."

I let my smile explode, showing off both rows of teeth. A few unmatched pieces slide together in my mind. Would it be awkward if I kiss him right now? His eyes focus on my lips and I almost lean in.

Molly bounces on her toes. "Steamy alert. I just knew this would happen. Didn't I say that, babe?"

Lance rolls his eyes. "You did, several times."

"Wait." I motion between them. "Are you guys together?"

Molly blinks up at him in that head-over-heels way. "Sure are. This is date number three."

Huh, interesting. Guess she wasn't put off after his behavior at Bronco. A genuine smile lifts my lips. "That's really great. I kinda got the feeling there was some interest."

She shimmies in place. "I'm bad at hiding my emotions. Heart on my sleeve and all that."

Lance grunts and loops an arm around her. How romantic.

Molly cuddles into him. "We're going to see a movie. Wanna join?"

Grady is a stone pillar beside me. I don't have to see his expression to know his preference. "Maybe next time. He's taking me for a ride."

Her mouth pops open. "Wow, that's so hot."

"Whatever," Lance mutters. "We're gonna be late, babe."

She lets him lead her along. "Okay, well, that's my cue. But how adorable will it be for us to double? Let's plan it, kay?"

I offer a wave without commitment. Grady remains silent, but he might as well be shouting his lack of interest.

"Bye, lovebirds," Molly calls. Lance practically drags her away without another word.

I scoot over to Grady's motorcycle. "On that note, shall we go?"

"Definitely." He reaches down and grabs a helmet. It reminds me of a jumbo gumball. "Here you go."

I take the offering with tentative hands. The pink bubble screams feminine. I don't want to assume, but this doesn't appear to be a helmet he'd let his buddies use. That only leaves other women. I barely conceal a cringe. "Thanks for letting me borrow it."

A wrinkle forms between his brows. "It's yours."

The tangle in my stomach smooths out with a swoosh. I suck in a sharp breath. "You got this for me?"

He nods. "I did."

"Today?" I lower the gift onto my head and fasten the strap.

He scratches the nape of his neck, looking almost sheepish. "Uh, something like that." Grady straddles the seat and pats the small cushion behind him. "Hop on."

I do just that while channeling an ultra-chic biker babe. But in reality, I'm sure my version of saddling up is clumsy and ridiculous. Whatever. I have many next times to improve.

He reaches for my arms and wraps them snug around his middle. "Hold on. Ready?"

I lace my fingers against his torso and squeeze every muscle available. "Yes." I add a nod for good measure.

The bike starts up with a deafening growl. With a seamless motion I'm jealous of, Grady cranks the throttle and sends us flying. A rush of adrenaline immediately floods me. I laugh and snuggle in for the ride.

Out here there's nothing except pavement and rolling fields. The wind tunnels through my helmet. All I can hear is a dull roar from the engine. I press my palms flat against Grady's abs. He inhales a deep breath, shifting my touch lower. I use that as permission to explore his upper body—within reason.

Grady responds by resting a calloused palm on my bare knee. His simple touch is a shot of piping hot lust straight to my lower belly. The bike vibrates beneath me, sending my synapses into a tailspin. I can hardly see straight. It makes me feel reckless.

I squeeze the metal between my thighs and release the death grip around Grady's waist. I tip back and spread my arms out the side.

"I'm the queen of the road," I call. The words bounce off my visor and disappear into the sky.

Grady pulls off the road and steers into an empty lot. It's difficult to see much, other than a wide open space. He shuts off the bike and all is still. I swing my leg over to dismount. Grady follows suit. With a quick click, he removes the strap under my chin. He hangs my helmet on the handlebar next to his. It's as though we've done this a hundred times.

He tucks a hand in his pocket. "What's the verdict?"

I comb through the snarls in my hair. "I'm in love. It's so freeing. Like riding a horse ten times faster."

He laughs. "That's exactly how I feel."

"Your steel steed. Maybe you'll let me take you for a spin on Daisy."

"I prefer wheels."

"Did I do okay on the back?"

Grady rakes a hand over his head, sending the dark strands to stick up in sexy disarray. "You're a natural. At the turns, you leaned with me like a pro. Horseback riding has given you natural balance. Your body is made for this."

Shit, that sounds naughty. "Oh?"

Fire licks up my neck while I consider what other hidden talents he'll uncover for me. Our conversation hits a lull and the silence surrounds us again. There's nothing except the distant sound of crickets.

"It's so quiet," I whisper.

"Almost scary, huh?"

I nudge his boot. "Not with you here."

He steps into me. "I'll always protect you."

"Good." I tip my face up and Grady presses our lips together. The kiss is chaste, sweet, and over before I can attempt to take things further.

He turns and lifts the seat, hefting out a small cooler. "I grabbed dinner."

Did you hear that? It's my fantasies knocking. This man is the end of me. "You're so thoughtful," I muse.

Grady threads our fingers together. "You bring it out in me."

We begin walking toward I'm not sure where. Letting him take control and lead has been in my favor. Why stop now. I feel the soft brush of cotton before seeing anything. A glance down proves my suspicion. I hadn't been looking in the right direction for our destination. It's all around us.

To anyone else, this would be an abandoned yard full of overgrown weeds. It's a happy something for us.

I scan the countless rows of dandelions. "What is this place?"

"An escape." His throat bobs with a thick swallow. "A reminder."

I tug on his arm, bringing us to a stop. "It's beautiful."

Grady's mouth twitches. "I was banking on you thinking so. Otherwise it's just a field no one tends to."

"Thank you for bringing me."

We sit in the center of a dense patch. Puffy white non-flowers form a perimeter around us. It's been at least ten years since we did this. I release a long exhale at the memories.

Grady unzips the cooler and takes out a few containers. He pops the lids, arranging everything between us. Cheese and pesto tortellini. Caesar salad. Strawberries and watermelon.

Unsweetened iced tea. More favorite things. Pressure builds behind my eyes. I blink at the blur in my vision. A utensil I can't see gets placed on my palm.

"This looks delicious," I manage to croak.

His gaze leaps to mine. "You okay?"

I'm nodding too fast. Accept the past, live in the present, and look toward the future. I'd planned on coasting. But impulsive adrenaline still pumps through my veins.

"So," I broach the subject that's been mixing me up. "We're really together? All in?"

The fork he's using freezes in midair. "Why would you think otherwise? Do you doubt me?"

"No." My answer is instantaneous.

Grady's face dips toward mine. "Then why?"

I stare at him, this man who's already giving me everything. My eyes don't waver. "Just letting my brain catch up with what my heart has always known."

"Hmmm," he murmurs against my lips. "That's a great answer."

I seal the remaining space. "Thought so."

He pulls away after a moment and reaches for my hands. "We rushed forward without talking much, but I figured that wasn't necessary. A chance isn't worth taking if it's not crazy. There's no true love without a little heartbreak. We sorted that out. No more pain."

A lump the size of Wyoming gets lodged in my windpipe. I sniff and keep staring at the wonder before me.

Grady wipes away the lone tear trickling down my cheek. "Sutt, you're all I've never had but desperately wanted. Happiness and peace and comfort and anything decent. You're the only one I'd choose, ever. If you didn't want me, I'd live a damn lonely existence. Lucky for me, that's not the case."

My sigh wobbles. "I'm the lucky one. You're agreeing to be mine. Really and truly."

"Always have been. There was never a choice, right?"

"Not since day one."

His mouth hitches upward. He plucks a dandelion out of the thatch of weeds. With a quick breath, he blows the fluffy seeds. The particles scatter in a floating wave. Grady reaches for another and holds the white puff close to my lips. "Make a wish."

I let my eyes slide shut. There's no thought involved. With a slow exhale, I silently ask him to take what I've always been willing to give.

CHAPTER SEVENTEEN

Grady

I CUT THE ENGINE, SENDING SPUTTERING RUMBLES TO RICOCHET off the garage walls. Exhaust and gasoline cling to the air. Above the pungent bite, barest hints of coconut and strawberries float to me. My mouth waters for another taste of her. I'm already hard and aching behind the confines of my zipper.

The continuous lust pumping into me is testing all sorts of limits. I'm already toeing the line, desperation clawing at me for release. My control is a rapidly fraying thread. The girl behind me holds a scissor.

Neither of us moves for several beats of my rapid heart. Her chest pushes into me with each rise and fall. A delicate palm wanders from my pecs down to the buckle of my belt. The significance of what's waiting just beyond reach rests in my lap. I can almost feel her there. That's enough to get my ass in gear.

After clambering from the bike, I help Sutton off her seat. There's a shy sort of smile curling the edges of her lips. I want to watch that expression spread into uncontrollable ecstasy. For now, I unclip her helmet and tug it off. Chocolate waves flow out, cascading around her shoulders. A fresh dose of coconut hits my system. I don't bother trapping my low growl. She should be aware of my fizzling restraint.

Bear's whining yelps break into our bubble. He sounds close to being tortured. I can empathize.

Sutton tiptoes over to the pained noise and peers out the window. "Should I let him in?"

"Probably, or he'll bust down the door."

She smiles and turns the knob. Before she can blink, one-hundred pounds of German Shepherd are gunning for her. Bear does his best to topple her. Sutton stumbles, but catches her balance. He doesn't relent and slobbers her with sloppy licks. Lucky mutt. She giggles, lavishing him with coos and sweet words. Bear eats it up and goes back for seconds.

My turn.

I whistle and Bear trots to my side. He gets a scratch under the jaw for that. I wouldn't leave her unless forced. She lifts her gaze to mine and I nod toward the house. "Let's go inside."

"Sounds good."

I place a palm on the small of her back, branding my spot. She pushes against me and fiddles with the hem of my shirt. We take turns pressing boundaries, shoving closer, playing an ultimate game of who teases best. She wins. I'm more than ready to raise the white flag.

We pause near the kitchen. I clear the rust from my throat. "Want something to drink?"

Sutton shakes her head.

"A snack?" I lift a brow with my suggestion.

"Dessert," she murmurs. A pair of fingers walk up my

torso. I catch her hand and dust a gentle kiss to her wrist. Sutton steps into me and lifts her chin. "In bed," she adds.

Those words snap the final threads of my control. I kick off my boots without finesse. The rubber bounces against something behind me. Sutton watches me, slipping out of her sandals.

I knead her ass and squeeze, hoisting her up against me. She cinches her legs around my waist and clutches tight. The slight bite of her nails digging into my shoulders makes me harder than titanium. I want her too fucking bad. That fierce need pummels me as fresh strawberries bloom on my taste buds. I'm a damn junkie for this girl.

Refusing to wait another moment, I smash our mouths together. Sutton gasps and opens for me. The sweetest heat meets me, a mix of mint and fruit and passion. She moans when I slide my tongue along hers. The siren call is my undoing. I stagger to the nearest wall, shoving her against the solid surface.

The new angle makes me hyperaware of our bodies aligning in all the right places. Tingles are already threatening to erupt in my groin. I'll never last at this rate. As if knowing my limits are being tested, Sutton draws my bottom lip between her teeth. The hint of sting flips a switch and releases lava beneath my skin. I'm burning for every part of her. I rock my dick into her core, showing her exactly what she's doing to me.

"I need more, Gray," she whispers at my jaw.

I smirk against her cheek. "Coming right up."

Sutton crosses her ankles along my lower back as I begin climbing the stairs. My room is dark and quiet, but not for long. I toss her onto the bed without warning. Her lithe figure bounces with the grace of a cat. She muffles a squeak and shoots me a playful glare. I quirk a brow at her, waiting for more. My girl never disappoints.

Sutton rises to her knees and crooks a finger at me.

"What do you need, beautiful?"

She points to the mattress. "You. Naked. Laying down. In that order."

"Really? You gonna take control?"

"For the first round." Her eyelids get hooded and heavy.

"Whatever the lady wants." I reach back and grip the collar of my shirt. It gets ripped off with one deft move.

She traces my upper body with ravishing hunger in her eyes. "That's very good to hear."

"You always get me, Sutt." I get to work on my belt, yanking at the leather and whipping it open. The button of my jeans pops and I nearly tear out the zipper. Threadbare denim drops around my ankles, leaving me in a pair of black briefs. She nibbles her lip and makes a circling motion at the garment.

"All of you."

Her sultry tone caresses me with silk. A shudder wracks my limbs, and I make sure she catches the reaction. I inch the fabric down, exposing slivers of skin with each second. The elastic band pulls lower and my dick bobs straight up with a salute. She tries to hide her shock, but there's no missing the widening of that ocean gaze. Her tits rise and fall at a hypnotic rate. I can almost taste her longing in the static air between us.

I hold my arms out, putting myself on full display. "Satisfied?"

"I'm about to be." Sutton's stare is fastened on my cock. I give myself a slow stroke for added impact. She gulps down a wheeze and gets to work. She whips her top off in a flurry. Those sinful cutoffs quickly follow. She's left in a matching bra and thong, the red pops against her tan. Having her in front of me in this nearly naked state should be a crime. I'm one lucky man.

Sutton shifts backward and pats the bed. "C'mere, Gray."

Her command is followed in a streak of speed I'm proud of. I settle against the pillow with my arms crossed behind me. Sutton's slow perusal is full of appreciation that has my cock twitching. She crawls over me, straddling my lap. I remain still underneath her. Handing over the reins has never suited me, but Sutton is different. In every conceivable way.

She leans forward, her long hair creating a canopy around us. Her lips press over mine with a tender touch. I arch into her for more and she smiles against me.

"Be patient," she whispers.

Now she wants to go slow? All right, I can play. I lower myself down and let her lead.

She trails a path of kisses down my throat, leading to my collarbone, and aiming lower. "What do you like, Gray?"

"You, touching me. Anything you do."

Her tongue flicks my nipple and I nearly bust from that alone. Keeping a lid on my arousal is going to test all limits. She continues her descent along my body, licking a scorching path across my abs and wickedly lower. One palm roams down and cups my balls. The fingers of her other hand wrap around my shaft. She hasn't used her mouth yet and I'm already leaking.

Sutton peeks up from her post with molten fire swirling in those baby blues. "I want to taste you."

Does she need permission? I part my lips with a jerky nod. But words aren't needed. In the next beat, she's licking at my tip.

"Christ," I mumble. "You're my fantasy, Sutt."

She swirls around my cock, faster with each pass. Her tongue is wet velvet against my steel. I prop up on my bent elbows, watching her devour me. Aside from her smile, this is the hottest view I've had the pleasure of seeing. I can officially die happy. Her mouth is my nirvana.

I try to relax in a reclined position, but that's impossible. She's a lit matchstick and gasoline to the flaming lust burning me up. I wanted to take care of her. This is the other way around. My head is spinning over what she's doing to me. I'm dizzy and disoriented without moving. Sutton finds a smooth rhythm, gliding her lips down my length and slowing drawing up. Damn, she's good and I'm instantly hooked. I'll never get enough of this.

On the next upward spiral, she releases me with a pop. Unbridled yearning reflects at me. "Show me what gets you off, Gray. I want to learn."

I lift my hips. "You're already doing it."

Sutton kisses my tip, not taking me in. "Teach me."

I'm not going to argue with that. My dick demands release and is ruling above brain functioning. I clutch a fistful of hair and guide her deeper. This change in angle allows her to take more of me. The impending orgasm curls at the tail of my spine, trying to break loose. I grit my teeth and force the release to recede.

"Fuuuuuuuck." The guttural growl rips from my throat. "Just like that, beautiful."

She hums in response, her lips suctioning full force around me. The vibrations in her throat zap straight to my balls. Telltale heat spreads through my lower half. I try to pull her off me.

"Baby, I'm gonna come."

A muffled groan is all I get in return. Sutton doesn't stop. Instead, she hollows her cheeks and sucks me to the base. Fuck. Yes. My girl isn't messing around by showing off her lack of a gag reflex. I buck my hips, striking the deepest point possible. She swallows and that's all the trigger I need. Warmth shoots out of me in spurts while I try to remain conscious. The edges of my vision get hazy. I'm going to pass the fuck out from a blowjob.

I come to my senses moments later, sagging against the mattress with the purest form of pleasure coursing through me. The grin Sutton is wearing says it all. I would clap if my arms would cooperate. There was no end of the line when it came to my desire for her. I want to savor her. Explore every inch over hours, throughout the night. She licks her swollen lips and purrs.

Oh, it's on now. I scoop under her arms and flip us so she's tucked underneath me. Sutton blinks up at me. Her mouth forms an adorable circle.

I give her a cocky smirk. "Your turn."

CHAPTER EIGHTEEN

Sutton

Happy something #178: Two broken
halves becoming a whole.

AN UNMISTAKABLE SMOLDERING ROARS TO LIFE INSIDE OF ME. There's a thundering that won't be silenced, not after this. My need for this man borders on desperate. The feeling clings to me as a second skin. I've always been ready for him. And he's finally hovering above me with our bodies locked in place.

I drift my palms up Grady's bulky arms, over those sculpted shoulders, and pause against his strong neck. "That was a smooth move, Gray."

He ghosts his nose along mine. "Are you impressed?"

"Very." My lower half rises to his on instinct.

"You're so sexy, Sutt. The things I want to do are indecent." There's no disputing his words. His desire prods at me. "Tell me to stop."

I toss my hair. "Never."

He shudders out a breath. "I'll never deserve you, but fighting us is no longer an option."

"It never should have been in the first place," I argue with a raspy exhale.

"Then to the gutter we both go." Grady kisses me, so soft and gentle. How could he ever believe that his intentions are otherwise?

"So long as we're together," I murmur.

"Indeed."

His lips meet the sensitive spot behind my ear and trace the column of my throat. He's being so sweet and attentive. I couldn't ask for better, especially for this. His dirty mouth was a delicious treat, though. Maybe I'll get a taste of that later.

Grady lightly snaps the strap of my bra, silently encouraging me to lift. I bow into him without hesitation. He reaches under me and flicks the clasp open with deft fingers. Satin and lace hit the floor after a quick toss. Grady wastes no time exploring my bare breasts. I gasp when he plucks a peaked nipple.

"You're stunning," he groans into my cleavage.

Sweat speckles my hairline, the temperature seeming to skyrocket. I'm feverish and restless and coiling with hot-blooded lust. This teasing will be the end of me. Air wheezes in and out of my lungs too fast. My tongue is sticky and useless, making speech difficult.

Somehow I manage to force a question past the pooling saliva. "What're you gonna do with me, now that we're in this position?"

Grady grinds his hips into mine. He's so hard against me, exactly where I need him. "I think you can guess. But first," his big body begins sliding downward, "I want you on my tongue."

I dig my nails into his biceps, halting the promising descent. "No."

He blinks emerald smoke at me. "Why not? Didn't hear you complaining earlier. Quite the opposite, in fact."

"That was different," I complain.

"Hmmm," he growls into the crook of my shoulder. "Has your hunger been sated?"

A torch blazes across my face. I squirm in his hold. He doesn't allow me to move a millimeter. That doesn't stop me from wiggling. "I want you inside of me."

"What happened to being patient?" He nips at my chin.

"I've waited long enough, Gray." With a few calculated twists of my hips, I begin lowering my panties.

He gets the message and removes the whisper of silk from between my thighs. The flat of his palm presses to my stripped center. I can feel the wetness that welcomes him there. The very essence of me is on display and prepared for his taking. Grady's answering groan has me automatically wrapping my legs around him.

"I'm ready for you. Take the empty away." I clutch at his forearms for an anchor of support.

Something naughty flashes in his light gaze. I curl my toes and latch onto him with an unrelenting grip. Grady smirks and takes advantage.

"I'm gonna make you scream my name, Sutt. Louder than before." A single digit skims a line down my seam. "I'm gonna show you everything that's been missing. What I've been foolish enough to deny us." He pinches my clit with the slightest pressure. I bow into him for more. "I'm gonna make sure you're always mine."

I guess that filthy side of him needed encouragement. I'm more than happy to oblige. "Show me."

He circles my opening with the tip of his finger. I push into his touch and he withdraws. The whine that trips out of me is almost pitiful. "Please, Gray."

The slow torture continues. "I love hearing you beg for me. It's a huge turn on."

"Please, please, please," I chant.

"Positive? I'm gonna defile you, Sutt."

My head knocks into his pec as I nod. "Why does that sound so hot?"

"You have no fucking idea." His voice is a ragged guarantee I want to hear on repeat.

I feel him there, nudging at my untried entrance. The need to tell him tickles my lips. I peek my tongue out, set on spilling the truth. An avalanche of emotion threatens to bury me. I flinch, just barely. Grady notices. A deep groove cuts between his brows.

I squeeze my eyes shut, unable to witness the unease reflecting at me. "Will it hurt?"

He goes utterly still on top of me. When his emerald eyes clash with mine, a storm is brewing. "Please tell me that question is due to the size of my dick."

I gulp at the thorny ball blocking my throat. "You're very huge." I grip the boulder of muscle in his shoulder. "Everywhere."

"Sutt, please tell me you didn't save yourself for me."

I blink at the stab of pain in his tone. "Yes, I did."

Grady places a delicate kiss on my bottom lip, granting similar affection to the top, ending with a sensual press that covers my entire mouth. "You're too good for me. I'll never measure up."

This big mountain of a man. He's still so unsure. I'll make it my life goal to prove his worth and pump confidence into him. But first, we need to cross this final line.

"That's for me to decide." I cross my ankles behind his ass and urge him into me.

Grady studies me with a caution clouding his features. I gently rub my hands over the wide range of his back. Straining tension melts off his body. The murky chaos clears from his stare, replaced with raw vulnerability. He lowers his forehead to mine.

"I love you, Sutt. So damn much," he murmurs against my lips.

Moisture blurs my vision with stinging heat. "I love you, Gray. Always."

"I'm gonna destroy us both." With a palm against my tailbone, he pushes into me. "But I'm too far gone to care."

His mouth locks over mine, tongues gliding together in a mutual vow of forever. He punches through that final barrier separating us. A rush of air hisses between my clenched teeth. Grady doesn't pause, and I'm thankful. My body stretches with a slight burn to accommodate his intrusion. I arch and shift in an attempt to alleviate the hurt. His large body trembles on top of mine. When he's seated to the hilt inside of me, I'm irrevocably his.

"Mine. You're finally fucking mine," he rasps at my temple.

"Yes," I answer into the groove of his neck.

He pauses. "Are you okay?"

"Don't stop." I rock into him. "I'm good, great even." The intimate connection we're solidifying makes up for any slice of agony.

"I take back my earlier thought." He kisses along my cheekbone.

I furrow my brow. "What was that?"

"When your mouth was around me, I thought it couldn't get better. I would die happy after being between your lips. But I was wrong. Because this, Sutt?" He plunges in with a smooth glide. "I would've missed out on heaven."

"We're made for each other." I've always known, but this proves my theory.

"You're perfect," he adds.

"For you." I lift my knees to the bottom of his ribs, allowing him to sink deeper.

Grady's strokes are slow and careful, sliding in and out

of me in measured thrusts. The prick of discomfort recedes after a few passes. I inhale spicy pine mixed with a salty kick. A serum of tingling bliss hums in my veins. I can definitely get used to this.

The room floods with our harsh breaths. He rolls his hips into mine, ratcheting me higher toward the sky. A rush of soothing heat twitches my fingertips. My skin is hypersensitive, every touch a jolt of pleasure.

I've pictured this too many times. My imagination didn't do us justice. Him inside of me, hard and pulsing, could never be replicated. Every fiber of my being claws at him with a bone-deep desperation.

"Never believed I'd have anything this good." Grady sucks on my earlobe, his panting breaths infusing me.

I twine my fingers in the hair at his nape. "It'll always be this way."

He nibbles at my jaw. "So damn amazing."

The bed creaks beneath us as Grady speeds up. He fills me to the brink of ecstasy. With another grind against me, a burst of white steals my sight. A spasm erupts in my core and I clamp around him. Grady groans, his sleek rotations becoming jerky.

The chords in his neck bulge. "Can't hold off much longer, Sutt."

I'm already teetering. Finishing the job won't take much. I dip two fingers between us. My clit is overly sensitive and screaming for attention. When I hit that needy bundle, an electric charge bolts straight to my toes. A few quick swipes and I'm gone.

The explosion is swift and powerful. I'm a seizing mass of wracking limbs and flexed muscles. A blanket of the softest velvet embraces me. Somewhere in the back of my mind, I can hear garbling nonsense.

At the last possible second, Grady jerks out of me.

Warmth spills across my stomach and chest. I can't help feeling marked, branded by this man. I'm almost shocked to find how much that thought gets me buzzing.

He drops onto me with a sputtering groan. The mess is our problem now. I comb through his sweaty hair, sweeping the wet strands away. My palm lingers and wanders to his cheek. He leans into my touch with a sigh.

"Hey, Gray."

His laugh jostles us on the mattress. "I love you so much, Sutt."

I kiss his nose. "Love you."

Grady rolls off of me, dragging my spent body into his. I'm warm and comfortable, satisfied in a way romance novels preen about. The afterglow is no joke. Within moments, I find myself drifting in some half-conscious state.

"Want to help me with something?" He slips his fingers through mine.

I snap into awareness with a slight shake. "Anything."

"I've always wondered if my shower is big enough for two."

I press my lips to his throat. "Thought you'd never ask."

CHAPTER NINETEEN

Grady

Happy something #6: A sense of belonging. What is that, anyway? Maybe I'll get the chance to find out.

WRENCH OFF MY HELMET AND GRAB THE HAT STASHED UNDER the rear cushion. After tugging it on, I swing my leg over the bike and stay put. The possibilities of what awaits beyond those walls is daunting. Avoidance is my faithful sidekick. I keep my ass glued to the leather seat as different scenarios pound into me.

There's a rampant fever raging through me on a constant basis. It's been a week since I stole Sutton's cherry. The shock hasn't worn off. A tremor rattles my hands just thinking about her beneath me, or in the dozen positions we've tried since. I swore to myself she was destined for better. She seems to think we're fated. That girl hasn't quit believing in me, no matter how hard I've tried to convince her otherwise. It's about damn time I truly get on board. I've been spending the past month, or more like fifteen years, thanking whatever greater power is watching out for me. Being graced with the privilege of calling her mine isn't a happy something I'll ever take for granted.

But my boots remain glued to the concrete. Why am I being such a pansy?

This beige house with red shutters is one of the few comforts I have in this world. I've been invited inside on countless occasions. There's no reason to be nervous, other than the explicit fact that our dynamic has shifted in a major way. Barry made mention of Sutton and me as a couple. Does he still feel the same? Will they truly accept me? Once I cross that threshold, questions will need answering.

The development of our relationship hangs heavy in the balance. I can almost feel the scale tipping against my favor. Blaming the delay on getting swamped at work or being a chicken shit coward is the easy way out. But I'm man enough to admit my fear of rejection. Not only from the family who raised me, but the girl who owns my heart and every happy something. I refuse to trap Sutton with me if Alice and Barry deem me unworthy.

I've tried convincing myself to not give a shit. It's easy enough to do—to the point of habit—with every other aspect in my life. That's not possible where these people are concerned. They're the only ones I care about. Their opinion and approval means everything to me. I've been good enough to be Jace's friend and a loyal farm hand around their property. That's a far cry from dating their daughter.

Our love has to be strong enough. I'm twenty feet tall when it's just the two of us. My girl has a way of boosting me up when others try knocking me over. She's always been great at that. After seven days of keeping her to myself, it was time to be a respectable man and face the folks. She finally convinced me to come over for family dinner, like the old days. This is how I find myself lingering outside of her parents' house.

The front door opens, revealing Sutton with a beaming smile aimed at me. Her dark hair glitters under the fluorescent lamp. Damn, she's beautiful. "Thought I heard you pull up. What're you doing out here?"

I straighten off my bike. "Just thinking."

She shuffles forward and leans against the railing. "About?"

"Being here." I wipe off my clammy palms and release a long breath.

Sutton's sigh can be heard from across the yard. "Gray, give me a hug."

My feet are moving before she's done talking. I'll never refuse her. Five quick strides and she's tucked in my arms. I press my face into her hair, feasting on coconut and strawberries. "Missed you, Sutt."

"I missed you so much." She clutches the front of my shirt in a tight fist, bringing the fabric to her nose. "How do you always smell delicious?"

"You're biased, but I approve."

"Nope." She takes another long whiff. "Any red-blooded woman with a pulse would agree."

I kiss her forehead. "There's only one I want to impress."

"Mission accomplished." Hooded baby blues peek up at me. "Tell me what has you hovering on the stoop."

I haul her tighter against me. "Just worried things are too good."

Sutton rests her chin on my sternum, forcing me to stare. "Do you doubt me?"

I almost flinch. "Never."

"Do you doubt my parents?"

That takes more thought. In the end, I give her another harsh jerk of my head.

"So, what's the issue?"

"That bad shit is ingrained soul deep, Sutt."

She places a palm on top of my pounding heart. "Believe in us, and them. They accepted you long ago. You're already a member of our family."

The door behind Sutton swings wide. Jace pokes his head out, finding us twisted tighter than a pretzel. A gagging sound erupts from his throat. "Quit with the PDA. I'm gonna puke."

Sutton huffs. "Oh, please. Like you're one to talk."

Jace wags a sloppy finger between us. "Very different circumstances."

"Don't be a dick," I mutter.

He grunts. "Don't make me regret my decision."

Uncertainty returns with a roar. I grind my molars until the taste of chalk hits me. "Such a fucker."

"Mom and dad are wondering what's up. Stop cuddling and get your asses inside." He doesn't bother shutting the door after his retreat, assuming we'll follow.

Pressure collects at the base of my neck. Jace is providing an adequate reminder of why I've been hesitating. His crude welcome is how I predict the rest of our evening will go. But I'm done shying away from my happiness.

Sutton tugs me toward the house. "Ready?"

I stare down at our clasped hands. "More than ever."

The smell of peppered fried chicken offers a warm reception as we step into the foyer. My stomach growls at the aroma of a favorite meal, close second to Alice's lasagna. There's a rejuvenated pep in my gait while I lock eyes on the kitchen. Sutton's bubbling laughter pops me out of the food trance.

"Glad you agreed?"

I duck to whisper in her ear. "Thanks for planning this."

She slants her upper body into me. "I'd like to take credit, but my parents did the heavy lifting."

A twinge pulls taut in my stomach. I shouldn't be

surprised in the least. Barry and Alice have always done their best to include me. This is further proof I shouldn't need. They'll never neglect me, unlike the rest of this town. A cold bucket of shame dumps over me. I've been an ass for ignoring their previous invitations.

Alice notices us entering the room. Her light eyes get glassy as she checks me over. She opens her arms wide, motioning me in. "I'm well aware that you're not a hugger, but humor me? It's a special occasion."

Is it? Not like I'd argue with her. I shuffle forward and allow her to wrap me up. She only reaches the top of my chest, similar to Sutton. A solid ten seconds pass before Alice pulls away with a trembling smile. She wipes at her wet cheeks. "I'm very happy you're here, Grady. We've missed you at our table."

"Thank you for having me." I tuck my chin.

She pats my jaw. "You're always welcome in our home. I hope you never forget that."

I appreciate that she doesn't guilt me for separating myself. It's been four years since I ate a meal with the Olsen's. Not because they didn't offer. They did, almost incessantly. But nothing was the same. I couldn't be surrounded by them with a frozen heart. That would have thrown me over the edge.

Alice turns to the stove. "Take a seat. Dinner is almost ready."

"Do you need help at all?"

She waves me off. "None of that. Take a load off and relax."

"Positive?"

Alice tsks. "Yes, shoo. You can cook next round."

I lift my palms and ease backwards. "You've got a deal."

"Want a beer?" Sutton moves to the fridge.

I nod. "Sounds good."

She pops off the cap and passes me a frosty bottle. I swallow a couple swigs, the chilled liquid soothing my parched throat. It takes effort to hold in a groan. Something about a cold brew always hits the spot. Sutton sidles up and bumps me with her hip.

"Where should we sit?"

"You decide."

She chooses a chair against the wall, tapping the one beside her. "C'mere."

I edge around the table and settle onto the wood seat. Sutton reaches for me, threading her fingers into mine. This is all new. But to be fair, my place in this family has changed. It's kicking off with a fresh outlook. That's something I need. I lost my sense of belonging for too long. I didn't fit with them anymore. Not without Sutton's smile across from me. Now we sit side by side, our palms clasped tight. I lift her hand to my lips and dust each knuckle with a kiss. She's brought me back.

Animated chatter steals my focus. Barry and Jace round the corner with two stacks of grilled corn cobs. Another gurgle rises from my stomach, earning a laugh from the older man.

"Well, that's a compliment to the chef. Great to see you, Grady."

"Likewise, sir."

He shakes his head, but doesn't comment on the title I can't quite drop. It's a tough habit to break. This man deserves respect. I want to give that to him by all means possible.

Barry wraps an arm around my shoulders, adding a clap to my back for good measure. He glances from Sutton to me, a smile brightening his expression. He nods at our joined hands. "About damn time you kids figured things out."

I gape at him and begin sputtering some excuse.

He lifts a finger. "Don't hold back on my account. I already gave my permission, not that you need it."

My heart threatens to overflow at the kind gesture. I smirk at Sutton and she beams at me in return. "That means a lot to me, and us. Thank you."

He grips my shoulder again. "Whatever makes my children happy. That's a parent's dream."

The knob of pressure lodged in my chest loosens with a long exhale. I really needed to hear that. Jace doesn't share in his father's enthusiasm, but he doesn't shovel out more digs at us. I'm calling that a win. A quick succession of beeps interrupts us and I'm saved from further inquisitions. Great timing.

Alice sets down a bowl of potato salad and a massive platter of chicken. Damn, we're eating good tonight. We serve ourselves and don't waste time before digging in. A steady flow of conversation goes around between bites. I've returned into the fold without a hitch.

"How's work, Grady?" Alice grins at me with the question.

I finish chewing and wash the food down with a sip of beer. "Picking up with the peak of summer. I already have another restoration lined up after the Drefter project."

"Oh, I'm happy to hear that. It's about time people take notice of your skill sets. Sure is difficult to find honest and dependable contractors."

Barry hums in agreement. "You've definitely come a long way from pounding crooked nails into the horse stalls."

I choke on an inhale at his praise. Those are great memories. "Had to learn somehow. Thank you, sir."

He chuckles. "You know better. I let it slide the first time. One of these days you'll call me by name." His gaze slides to Sutton beside me. "Or something more personal and far less formal."

A ball of warmth spreads through my chest. Is this topic really coming into the light?

"You've found a true calling," Alice interrupts. "Not everyone has the patience to learn a trade."

Barry is bobbing his head along with her words. "Don't I know it. There's no one willing to stick around for odd jobs. I was spoiled with these two." He points a fork between Jace and me. "Precise craftsmanship and dedication to the business is a dying breed."

"You can still count on us, pops. Whatever you need. Right, Bowen?" My friend nods at me.

Glad he's not holding a grudge and the layer of ice is thawing. I find myself offering a wide smile. "Absolutely. I enjoy the mechanical work. There isn't much of that with my contracts. I consider it an honor to work around the farm. Just let us know."

Barry raises his brow. "I'll hold you to that."

"I sure hope so," Jace replies. "Gets me out from behind my desk for a while."

"That's what you get for going the corporate route," I joke.

He grunts. "Yeah, yeah. The ladies love my suits."

"Not this girl." Sutton wrinkles her nose.

Jace glares at her. "You don't count as my target audience."

"You're the only one who does for me," I whisper against her temple.

Her cheeks flush a beautiful shade of pink. She bites her bottom lip and sighs.

"And there goes my appetite," Jace mutters.

Alice swats his arm. "Be nice. You're just jealous."

He rolls his eyes. "Sure, let's call it that."

Barry wipes at his mouth with a napkin and looks my way. "Heard from your mother lately?"

The air in my lungs turns sour. The answer is no. She's been gone whenever I've tried to visit recently. I drop off a load of groceries and leave without pause. It's hard to remember when I stopped concerning myself with her whereabouts over a decade ago. She'll go on benders for weeks on end without a care except pumping the poison into her veins. I had to sever ties to save my own sanity. Doing the bare minimum is about all I can handle these days. That doesn't keep the guilt at bay.

My silence must tell him everything he wanted to know. "Well, I hope she checks in soon. But enough of that." He pushes his empty plate away.

"Dessert?" It's no shock the question comes from Sutton.

Alice rubs her hands together. "I have all the ingredients for s'mores. Who's up for a bonfire?"

A chorus of agreement erupts from all of us. I feel right at home.

CHAPTER TWENTY

Sutton

*Happy something #66: Reading ghost stories in the dark,
under a blanket with a flashlight.*

I ALLOW MY EYES TO SLIDE SHUT FOR A MOMENT WHILE A COOL breeze kicks up. A heavy sigh follows close behind. The oppressive heat is finally wilting with the waking moon. This summer has already reached record highs and we're only halfway in. That muggy humidity brings the temperature to unbearable limits. Having a slight chill tickle my skin is a pleasing reprieve. Without that break, sitting around a bonfire would border on torture.

A fresh burst of bright orange and yellow flames crackle to life in front of me. Utter contentment hangs in the air, just beyond my reach. I avoid the glowering shadow looming on the edge of my vision. Easier thinking than doing. That pain in the ass doubles his efforts at stabbing holes into my bliss.

My parents hit the hay thirty minutes ago, leaving me alone with Grady and Jace. All was well until my boyfriend tugged me onto his lap. My brother has been shooting daggers at us ever since. That doesn't stop me from perching proud on Grady's thigh. Jace needs to get over it.

My brother releases another obnoxious groan. I toss my hands up, more than done with his hissy fit. "What's your deal? I thought us being together was fine with you?"

"What gives you the idea that I'm not? Did I say something to offend you?" He shoots me a smirk.

"You don't have to talk. That surly expression is plenty."

He yanks the brim of his hat lower. "Excuse me for caring. I've been protective since you were born, Sutt. Cut me some damn slack."

"For real, man?" Grady's voice is pure grit behind me.

Jace folds his arms. "It's still weird as hell."

"Well, this is happening. Get used to it." I paste on a toothy smile.

My brother scrubs over his face. "I'm doing my best, thanks for asking."

"Try harder, Ace." Grady slouches lower and tucks me further into his hold. He's definitely making a statement with that move. My brother would be blind to not notice.

"Let's move on," Jace mutters.

I snuggle against Grady's chest. "Great plan." And by that I mean find somewhere more private for at least an hour. Maybe half of one would do My man is a wizard, between the sheets at least. The telepathic message I'm sending him isn't computing. We remain seated, facing the firing squad.

Grady clears his throat. "How was your most recent right-swipe?"

Some of the tension melts from Jace's posture. "Meh, she was decent."

"Will you see her again?"

"Doubt it."

"She didn't hit the spot?"

Jace chuckles. "That wasn't the issue."

"Ah, shit." Grady snorts.

He shrugs. "Good for a one and done. Nothing more."

My attention has been bouncing between them. My brother's last comment stops me short. I wrinkle my nose. "You're so rude."

"Don't hate the player, Sutt. I'm just a pawn in the game."

I roll my eyes. "Keep telling yourself that."

He nudges my foot. "Not all of us are fortunate enough to find that special someone, especially so young."

"I'm twenty-two." The urge to stick out my tongue is strong. I keep it reeled in for maturity's sake.

Jace cocks a brow at me. "And been doodling hearts with Grady's name since you were seven."

My face feels hotter than the July sun at noon. Dammit. "You're such an ass," I grumble.

Grady strokes a finger down my fiery cheek. "Nothing to be embarrassed about, baby. I've loved you just as long, plus another day."

"Not possible."

He taps his temple. "You're always up here."

Jace whistles, effectively ruining our moment. "Fuck, that's so sweet my teeth hurt. Didn't peg you as a romantic soul, Bowen."

"Find the right girl and anything is possible," he returns with a glare.

My brother flicks his gaze my way. "I'm too busy keeping tabs on your ass to ever settle down."

Grady tightens his grip around my waist. "Not your problem anymore, Ace. I got her."

Jace seems to size him up for a moment, which is effing hilarious. A bright grin splits his face a moment later. "That you do."

My brother's moods are giving me whiplash. I rest a palm on my forehead. Maybe his floozy app will ding and he'll leave. A girl can hope. Grady nips at my ear and growls, "All good, Sutt?"

I giggle. "My sugar rush is fading."

"You only had two s'mores. How about another?"

He's such a smart man. Who am I to resist? I reach for a roasting stick and shove two marshmallows on the prongs. My mouth is already watering when I lean forward toward the pit. I hold the pair of white puffs over a patch of glowing coals.

Grady rubs my shoulders. "You're concentrating awful hard on this."

"One wrong move and I scorch them. This is a hidden artform."

I feel his laughter. "A little char adds flavor."

"Not the kind I like."

"I'm intimately aware of what stimulates your taste buds. Lucky for me, you seem addicted to my specific brand and the erotic assortments I offer."

A shiver races through me when he presses at a tender knot in my neck. I bite back a moan. "I really am. It was instantaneous."

"That's what I thought. Don't spoil your entire appetite on food." Grady pinches my ass and I yelp.

I narrow my eyes at him, but the threat is empty. There's no time for retaliation. I pull my skewer from the pit, inspecting the cooked confection wedged on top. "See? They need to be toasted to golden perfection with a gooey middle. That optimal crispy-soft combo."

He passes me a chocolate square and two graham crackers. We get the trifecta assembled without missing a beat. I squish everything together until white fluff oozes out.

"Looks like splooge." I laugh at my own nonsense. No

one else makes a peep. I hold up my creation for Grady to see.

He sits forward and rotates my ass on his lap. His head tilts in my direction. "Did you just say splooge?"

I giggle again. "Sure did."

"Who says that nastiness anymore?"

"It's making a comeback."

"I doubt that very much."

"There are stickers and everything."

Grady's jaw goes slack and he sputters. The rest of his features morph into a horrified expression from the possibility of my words. "No way would anyone buy those."

"This just keeps getting better," Jace chimes in.

"Hush up over there," I scold. My focus returns to Grady. "It's funny swag stuff."

"Splooge? Nope. Not believing that."

I poke his chest. "Since when do you pay attention to the book world? One of my author clients used it in her new release. Pour Judgment is slaying the charts. I own a personalized copy. If you're nice, I'll read you an excerpt. Heather is hilariously innovative. Figured I'd try it out."

He grunts and shakes his head. "You're sexy as fuck, Sutt. My love for you is endless. I can forgive you for most things. But please, never utter that word again."

I jut out my bottom lip in an exaggerated pout. "You're no fun."

Grady's eyes resemble radiant emeralds glittering in the flames. "I'll have you regretting those words later."

"Promise?"

"Without question," he rumbles.

I rip my gaze off him before this escalates beyond my raveling control. As a distraction, I take a very unladylike bite of s'more. An indecent moan tumbles out around my mouthful of sinful sweetness.

Grady glares at the dark sky. "Killing me, Sutt."

"Turnabout is so fair." I lick my fingers after polishing off the decadent treat.

"Maybe we should be going," he suggests. I can feel him hard and ready beneath me. His obvious reaction to me releases a fever under my skin. This man is hauling an extremely impressive package. I wiggle my hips to torture both of us.

"Sutt," Jace interrupts.

A gasp escapes me at the sound of my brother's voice. I'd almost forgotten about him. That's the power of Grady. I sit up straight and shove all dirty thoughts aside. "Um, yeah?"

"How's living with mom and dad?"

Talk about a bucket of ice water. I send him a flat look. The truth is I haven't been sticking around past dark in the last two weeks. But my brother doesn't know that. His sudden interest is almost alarming. What's he hinting at? I ignore the pricking of goosebumps along my arms. "Fine. Why do you ask? Thinking about moving in?"

He tips his head back and laughs. "As if. I have my own place."

"So did I. This was always meant to be temporary." That reminds me of my conversation with Harlyn yesterday. I glance back at Grady. "Are you still curious about my college years?"

His grunt says it all. "Is that even a question?"

"I was thinking we could meet up with Harlyn and her boyfriend this weekend. If you're interested."

"Sure. I should know them if they're your friends."

I press a hand flat to his chest, the steady beat meeting my touch. "They're awesome. I wish we saw each other more often. Living with Harlyn was a blast. She has plenty of dirt on me."

Jace leans forward, resting an elbow on his knee.

"Speaking of your wonder years, how's the apartment hunt, Sutt?"

Grady chokes on his sip of beer behind me. I glance at him over my shoulder. "Are you okay?"

He wipes droplets off his face. He juts his chin at my brother. "That depends on how you answer his question."

I look at Jace before returning my gaze to Grady. "I'm still searching."

A hollow scoff is my response. "The hell you are. There's a very permanent spot for you in my bed."

I crinkle my forehead. "But that's your house. I need my own space."

"Are you serious?" The question comes from Jace.

Grady's body goes rigid underneath me. "Not your business, Ace."

"You'll never tell her."

"The hell I won't." Grady's hand roams up and down my thigh. "Just been waiting for the time to be right."

"Nothing better than the present," my brother shoots back.

What is it with these two? I yank at my hair. "Oh my gosh, you guys. Stop talking in circles."

Jace and Grady are glaring at one another, doling out a silent pissing match. Neither move or utter another word. We might be here all night at this rate.

My brother stands up abruptly and dusts off his hands. "Well, my work here is done."

I gape at him. "Now you're leaving?"

He shrugs. "Plenty of moonlight left. I'll be at Bronco if you need me."

After he's out of sight, I turn fully towards my secretive boyfriend. "What's he talking about, Gray?"

His exhale blows the stray strands off my face. "Come on, Sutt. Doesn't my place seem familiar to you?"

A memory of my first visit filters into my mind. I recall all of the similarities to a certain happy something. There's no denying the resemblance. My voice is barely a whisper when I murmur, "Yes."

"And why do you think that is?" His green eyes are locked on me as he prods.

My heartbeat booms to a staccato beat. "You liked my ideas?"

He shakes his head, a slow motion I track with a steady gaze. "I wanted to build that dream for you, and us."

I gulp at the pressure quickly building in my throat. "W-what?"

He cups my jaw. "You heard me, Sutt."

"Why are you the sweetest man ever?" I clasp my palms to his cheeks.

Grady presses his lips to mine. "You deserve the best. I'll never stop trying to be that for you."

I sniff and blink off the moisture from my lashes. "You're already perfect, Grady Bowen. If you get any better, I'll feel extremely inadequate."

He barks out a laugh. "That's not possible."

I lift an eyebrow. "No? What if I disagree?"

"Then I'll spend hours proving you wrong." With the stealthy moves of a panther, he scoops me up and rises to his feet. One strong arm is banded under my knees, the other cinching around my shoulders. This hold screams of protection. I'm safe and not going anywhere.

"Sounds like a promising compromise." I nuzzle into him.

He tightens his grip on me. "You're coming home with me to our house. That's where you belong."

A tremble wracks my limbs. Bossy Grady is pushing all the best buttons. He gives me a cocky smirk that tosses another torch on the blaze in my core.

Better indeed.

A thought occurs to me as he hustles across the yard. "What if we didn't end up getting together?"

He gives me a fast jerk of his head in response. "I don't want to consider that as a possibility."

"Only a few short weeks ago, you were hell bent on keeping me away."

Grady snorts. "I was being an asshole."

It was difficult to dispute the truth. But I still give it a shot. "Well, things certainly had changed. There's no blaming you. Negatively speaking, what was the alternative?"

His nostrils flare. "Maybe I would've sold the house and moved away."

"You'd actually leave? Give our home to someone else?"

A muscle in his cheek jumps. "That was my plan. Not sure I ever would've gone through with it."

I bury my face in his shirt, inhaling smoke and fresh pine and a man always meant to be mine. My fingers twist in the fabric and cling on for extra security. "Well, it's a damn good thing we'll never have to find out."

CHAPTER TWENTY-ONE

Grady

Happy something #27: Playing board games. This wasn't a tradition in my house, considering we never owned any.

THE FOLLOWING SATURDAY, WE DRIVE 70 MILES NORTH TO meet Sutton's friends. Having my girl clinging to me while we fly down the freeway is a great way to spend an hour. That might've been my favorite ride yet. An electric buzz hums in my veins from having her lush curves pressing so close. But there's no time for sneaking off to a secluded area.

I press a palm into the dip low on Sutton's spine. That notch at the base of her back is fit for my hand. As if proving my silent claim, she pushes against my subtle touch. The smile she graces me with over her shoulder is icing on the damn cake. My woman loves the possessive parts of me.

We walk across the brewery parking lot with the sun beaming behind us. This is the type of day meant to be spent outside. Bottom Up Brew House appears to be a great place to do just that.

"How'd you hear about this spot?" I tuck her into my side as we wedge through the entrance.

Sutton bumps her hip into mine. "Harlyn lives nearby. I guess it's her new stomping ground."

"This isn't one of the many bars you frequented?"

She rolls her eyes. "Very funny. No, all of those clubs are by campus. This is the first summer Bottom Up has been open."

"Maybe you'll show me a favorite haunt one day."

"Other than Bronco Buck?" She flutters her lashes at me.

"Smart ass. I want to fill in the gaps. There are four years worth of memories I'm missing." I raise my voice above the growing chatter enveloping us.

The mid-afternoon crowd is gathering, with more pulling in. There's a taco truck boxed in along one side. Fried cheese and spiced meat pepper the air. An array of picnic benches, iron tables, and lone standing stools decorate the concrete patio. Most of the seating is already taken. We manage to snag an open space with four chairs and a small slice of shade.

"Popular area," I say.

She nods. "It's close to downtown. Being on the outskirts has benefits."

I glance up and around, taking in the view. "I can see the appeal. This industrial style awning is a nice touch." I motion to the slatted wood structure above us.

Sutton follows my line of sight. "You're such a carpenter."

"Thank you."

"Do you want me to set up a website for you?"

I kiss her red-stained lips. "Sweet of you to offer, but I don't need all that. Simple and easy works for me."

She swipes a thumb over my mouth. "You're the furthest thing from either of those, Gray."

"For you, Sutt. Most barely give me a second glance or assume the worst. You're the only one who sees me as anything more."

Her sigh is long. "Sucks for all them. I'm living the best life with you."

"And that's all I care about," I add. She nibbles on her bottom lip. I tug on the plump flesh being held hostage. "What's on your mind, Sutt?"

She peeks over at me. "Did your mom come home yet?"

Sutton is well aware of my mother's disappearing act. She's a saint for letting me vent about all the problems that woman causes. I bob my head. "Her neighbor called me this morning. She stumbled in at the ass crack of dawn. I guess she looks even worse than usual. It would probably be best if I check on her tomorrow."

"Want me to come with you?"

"You'd do that?"

She reaches for my hand. "Of course, Gray. I'll always support you with everything."

I suck in a choppy breath and glance off into the distance. "Are you sure?"

Her fingers squeeze mine. "Positive."

My swallow is rough. "Okay. I'll warn you, the sight isn't pretty. She's harsh reality in the cruelest form."

She offers a timid smile. "I can handle that. Don't worry about me. I love you, Gray. Let me be there for you."

I ghost my mouth over hers. "I love you so damn much, Sutt. Having you with me will make all the difference. I want to share all my truths. No more hiding."

She closes the remaining distance between our lips for a quick kiss. "Glad we settled that."

"Me too, baby. You amaze me."

"Look, I found them." A feminine tone comes from in front of us.

I lift my gaze and catch a couple approaching us. The woman tugs her guy along, dodging groups of people standing in their path. Her bright pink hair stands out in the masses. She's sporting a huge grin aimed at Sutton. I take a wild guess and assume this is Harlyn.

My girl blinks at this newcomer, her jaw going slack. "Oh my gosh. You finally went through with it."

"Whatcha think? Too crazy?" Harlyn tosses some neon curls this way and that.

Sutton stands and wraps her friend in a hug. "You're stunning, as always. The color suits you. Now that vibrant personality of yours can really shine."

She winks. "I figured why the heck not, right? If I ever wanted to go pink, it needed to happen before school starts. Come September, I have to be professional."

"I'm sure the kids would think you're cool."

"Maybe, but I need tenure before taking big risks." Harlyn laughs at her own words.

Sutton crosses her arms. "Oh, whatever. The principal is already halfway in love with you."

"Hopefully not too much," the man beside Harlyn grumbles.

She cups his jaw. "She's a her, cowboy. And super married. Nothing to worry about."

"I'm happy to see the bubbling bliss hasn't worn off," Sutton coos at them.

"Not in the slightest," Harlyn agrees. Her gaze slides to me. "Speaking of, who do we have here?"

Sutton baulks and turns to me. "Whoops, sorry. It feels like you should already know each other. Gray, this is Foster."

He pops out from behind Harlyn, offering me a wave. "Howdy."

I nod at him. "Hey, nice to meet you."

"And this is my college roomie, Harlyn." Sutton hitches a thumb at her.

Harlyn remains quiet, giving me a long once-over. I cock a brow and wait for her appraisal. She taps her chin, squinting closer. This ought to be good. "So, you're the illusive Bowen."

"Grady," I correct.

"Right." She elongates that single word until her breath runs dry. I brace for more sass, but she surprises me with a wide smile. "I'm happy to finally put a face to the name."

"Likewise," I respond.

Harlyn's eyes sparkle. "Sutton talks about me?"

The girl in question gives her a shove. "Don't be a dork. Of course he's heard about you."

"And all the trouble we caused?" Harlyn adds.

Everything inside of me stretches taut, until I'm liable to snap. "Is that so?"

"You're so bad, Har. Knock it off," Sutton scolds her. Her baby blues lift to me. "We were harmless. She's joking. Mostly."

I trace a line down her jaw. "Not sure I believe you, Sutt. I'm sure the guys were always chasing your ass. Hell, they still do."

"Oh, they definitely were," Harlyn chimes in. "She had to beat them off with a stick on the daily."

Sutton huffs. "Talk about an exaggeration. That's not true at all."

"That sounds like my worst nightmare." I curse a stream of expletives into my fist.

Harlyn laughs. "Don't ruin this for me. I finally get to mess with Sutt about a man."

I glare at the cloudless sky. "I'm beginning to regret this trip down memory lane."

Sutton pinches her friend's elbow. "Please stop. You're gonna scare Grady off."

"Yeah right." Harlyn snorts. "I doubt that's possible. Just check out the way he's staring at you. His protective stance further proves my point."

I startle at her observation. Heat prickles up my neck. "Uh, what?"

She flicks her wrist. "Don't be embarrassed. Sutt never looked twice at any guy. She refused to admit it, but this girl has always been totally obsessed with you. I'm relieved to finally meet the one who owns my bestie's heart." She leans forward and whispers, "I approve."

Sutton hides her face behind a hand. "I didn't tell you to reveal all of my secrets."

"Isn't that the point of this gathering?" Harlyn lifts a brow.

Sutton's sheepish gaze flickers to mine. She offers a light shrug. "You wanted to know about my college years. This girl was an essential part. She didn't know much about you, but clearly read between the lines."

I kiss her forehead. "Love that you couldn't forget about me. Even when I was an ungrateful asshole. I couldn't let you go either, Sutt."

She steps into me and tugs at the hem of my shirt. "Not even for a moment."

"Gah, you two are so presh. I'm a happy witness." Harlyn's voice is soft, but bursts our bubble all the same.

Sutton winks at her. "That's how I've always felt about you and Foss."

"Dreams are coming to life left and right." Harlyn clasps her palms together.

"As if we planned this or something," Sutton giggles.

"Oh, remember that night our freshman year?" Harlyn begins recalling some event I wasn't around for.

Foster clears his throat. "Thirsty?"

"Fuck yes, man."

"Let's grab a round of beers. The girls can catch up without us."

"You're speaking my language."

I follow him to the keg station set up in a far corner. We have to dip and dodge our way through the endless throng. Soon we won't be able to weave from one side to the other. Straight madness. The bar is finally in sight after getting my personal space tested far more than I care to admit.

I stand next to Foster while a line quickly forms behind us. It belatedly occurs to me that I don't know Sutton's alcohol preferences. I missed out on learning what she likes. A pile of bricks land in my gut. Damn. I scrub a hand over my mouth and glance over the choices.

Foster must notice the panic in my expression. "You okay, man?"

"Yeah, just thinking. What do you recommend?"

"They brew a killer IPA. Harlyn likes their blueberry sour. I think that's what Sutton would drink."

"Sold." I repeat the order when it's my turn. The bartender fills two mason jars and passes them over. With a deep sigh, I turn and face the fray. Foster takes the lead again, people immediately bumping into him. We eventually make our way back to the girls. It's some sort of miracle I didn't spill half our beers along the way.

Sutton makes grabby hands at the deep purple concoction. "You know me well. This looks right up my alley."

"Foster pointed me in the right direction. I figure fruity shit is always a good choice."

She blows me a kiss. "You'd be correct."

I settle on the chair next to her, across from Harlyn and Foster. We all lift our glasses and clink them together. "Cheers," we all say in unison.

"Should we play a game? They have a bunch inside.

Monopoly could be fun." Harlyn is already half out of her seat at the prospect.

Foster's face takes on a gray shade. "No way, not again."

"Oh, come on," she prods. "It'll be fun."

He shakes his head. "Nope. It's too competitive. I can't handle you at that level."

Sutton starts laughing. "Right? She's always cool as a cucumber until hotels start being built. I agree with Foster."

Harlyn slumps in her chair. "That's lame."

"Do they have Life?" I find myself asking.

Three pairs of eyes focus on me. Sutton leans on my armrest. "Maybe. Is that what gets your vote?"

I shrug and drop my gaze. "It always looked fun. Getting to choose your path and see what happens. I've never played."

Sutton stretches for my hand under the table and applies some gentle pressure. I drag my gaze up to hers. She smiles, her stare a calm blue ocean inviting me in. I'll gladly go. "Then that's what we'll do."

Turns out, board games are a lot of fun. Who the hell knew? Certainly not me. An hour later and I'm the official winner. But with the girl sitting beside me, I was already coming out way ahead.

CHAPTER TWENTY—TWO

Grady

Happy something #63: Finding an escape that lets me forget. Even for a few moments.

THE PUTRID STENCH OF ROTTING LIFE WAFTS INTO MY OPEN windows. I do my best to cover a cringe. There's no stopping the bone-snapping force that locks up my joints. I clutch harder at the steering wheel until my knuckles are white. This was a mistake. The evidence is strewn about the trailer park between piles of trash and hollowed out vehicles. This place is haunted with the worst memories, many of them my own.

My balding tires struggle across the overgrown terrain. The main drag is even worse than a short month ago. I swerve into the first available spot and shift my pickup into park. Above a pair of squawking crows, I can almost hear the old engine sigh. Not that I'm really listening. Nothing registers over the vicious evil plaguing my mind. Inky black sludge paints my vision until I'm left in total darkness.

Sutton doesn't belong here. This type of ugly should never touch her. I'm gutted and weak. What worth do I offer? I glare at the rusting dumpster through the windshield, refusing to face the horror marking her features. There's no doubt her regrets are stacking higher than the abandoned bags of garbage.

"We should leave," I growl.

In my periphery, I see her head swivel toward me. "What? Why?"

"I don't want you to see the worst of it."

She rests a soft palm over my flexing forearm. "Gray, look at me."

A poisonous thatch of thorns grows in my throat. It takes the remaining control I have to swallow past the pain. I allow my eyes to wander her way. What I find waiting in her expression steals the air from my lungs. There is no pity or embarrassment. I don't see shame glimmering in her blue gaze. Her stare is steady and doesn't waver, filling me to the brink with peace and love and everything good. I match her intense focus and take a deep inhale. Only the purest hit of strawberries and coconut greet me. This woman pulls me away from the wreckage, saving me from the worst version of myself. My exhale is a quiet stutter.

"Thanks, Sutt."

"We're a team, Gray. I'll never spook from anything so long as you're by my side. That should go both ways."

I manage a jerky nod. "It does."

"Good. Let's go see your mother." She hauls one of the grocery bags onto her lap. The swift move proves the strength in her tone. My girl isn't going anywhere but inside as planned.

I grab the other sacks and hop out of the cab. Sutton meets me at the tailgate. Her plaid summer dress matches the tropical ocean in her eyes. Shiny dark waves ripple in the slight breeze. It's no surprise that she's stunning, a blinding bright spot amongst the corroded rubble.

"Love you, Sutt." I swoop down and place a kiss against her temple.

She leans into me. "I love you, Gray."

Those three words inject me with enough confidence to face forward. The four wheels that hold up my mother's home have been flat since she moved in. I don't concentrate on the other crushing qualities as we walk along the grassy path. A few long strides and we're at the front door. The new hinges I installed gleam in the sunlight. I smile at that while knocking on the metal frame.

Sutton grips my arm when I step onto the single stair leading in. "Shouldn't we wait for her?"

"Nah." I shake my head. "I just like to offer a bit of warning, just in case."

A furrow dents her forehead, but she doesn't comment further. We enter the dimly lit room in silence. I ignore the foul odor of rotten eggs that assaults my nostrils. My stride falters when I catch sight of my mother sitting on the couch, a wide smile aimed at us. Talk about a rare bout of lucidness. I could trick myself into believing this person is a stranger. The flash of grotesquely decaying teeth provide damning evidence on the contrary.

I dredge up my voice. "Ma?"

"Hey, boy." She straightens against the cushions.

"You okay?"

She angles toward us, her expression warming another degree. "Of course. What're you doing here?"

I blink at her. Once more to be sure the sight in front of me is real. She's still there, awake and grinning. I'm seeing this clearly. Her question worms its way into my mind.

"Brought you some food." The bags I'm holding suddenly weigh a hundred pounds. I heft them higher and carry the loot into her kitchen.

Sutton follows my shaky gait. "All good?"

I shrug. "Uh, yeah. This isn't the sight that usually welcomes me."

"But she's alright?"

"Guess so." I peer over Sutton's shoulder. My mom is staring at us with a shrewd gaze. The typical glaze is absent, leaving a spotless view of her green eyes. I'm well versed on how to handle the woman who occupies this trailer. This seemingly pleasant version is a foreign concept.

She lifts her wrinkled chin at me. "Whatcha whispering about in there? Come sit down, boy. Bring your friend."

I grab Sutton's hand and thread our fingers together. We shuffle to the couch with obvious hesitation shackled to our ankles. I draw us to a halt a few feet from where she sits. My mother tsks, blowing some wispy strands off her face.

"I'm not gonna bite, kid. Don't be such a chicken shit."

That sounds familiar. I release a suspended breath. Her words, harsh as they might be, soothe the bite of unease nipping at my heels.

I spend a moment studying her, attempting to peel away the superficial layers. "How're you feeling?"

"Like roadkill, not that it's any of your concern." Her gaze skips to Sutton. "Who's this?"

"My girlfriend." I tuck her behind me on instinct.

Her eyes remain locked on Sutton. "You Barry's girl?"

She nods. "Yes, ma'am."

"Don't bother with that formal shit." My mother shakes a boney finger at her.

Sutton's gulp is audible. "S-sorry."

"No reason to apologize. We just aren't too fancy in these parts. Isn't that right, Grady?"

Her underlying meaning is a dirty film coating my skin. I scrub at the residue it leaves behind. Getting a clean break from this snake pit is a lost cause. But there's no sense responding to her cutting remarks. My mother should know I won't stoop. She tosses me a haughty sneer regardless.

"Such a puss," she accuses. "Not sure what this beauty sees in you."

Sutton gasps and clutches the fabric of my shirt in a tight fist. I grind my molars until a deafening crack pops the silence. "That's our cue to go. Enjoy the food. Make sure to eat something."

"Now, now, don't be getting all pissy. I'll behave." The smile she plasters on is brittle. Being nice and respectful has never come natural for her.

I almost call bullshit. This woman has never asked me to stick around longer than necessary. She's probably ramping up to beg for some cash. Bummer for her, I'm fresh out. I fold my arms and widen my stance. "Why? So we can have a friendly chat?"

My mother ignores me, her attention returning to Sutton. She pats the couch and a cloud of dust rises. "Come sit with me." She shoots a pointed glare at me. "Be a good boy and fetch us some tea."

I choke on the stale air. Tea? Since when does this woman drink anything except liquor? Yeah. Fucking. Right. This situation smells worse than a polluted swamp. Leaving Sutton alone with her, even for a few minutes, doesn't sit well in my gut. A gurgling protectiveness rises up and I remain rooted in place.

A shrill whistle cracks through the dank air. "You deaf, Grady?"

My mother gets an eye roll for that. She knows damn well I'm not. The digs will get her nowhere. I cock a brow and wait her out.

She makes a shooing gesture. "Why are you just standing there? We're thirsty."

"Pretty sure I can handle whatever you're about to say.

There aren't any secrets between us." I point at my chest before gesturing at Sutton.

My mother scoffs. "Get real. We're just gonna have a little girl talk. No boys allowed."

I look to Sutton and she shrugs. Her lips form a few words that I'm pretty sure are meant for reassurance. I hitch a thumb over my shoulder. "I'll be right over there. Holler if you need me."

"We won't." My mother is already facing my girl, icing me out.

And with that, I'm officially dismissed. I barely hear their quiet murmurs across the room. Instead of obsessing, I busy myself with finding two clean mugs and the kettle. It's shocking that my mother owns a teapot. A canister on the stove snags my eye. The contents smell minty, but there's an underlying aroma I don't trust. I won't be letting Sutton drink a sip of this questionable shit. If my mother wants a dose, that's her choice.

A soft giggle from the couch has me spying. Their heads are tipped close together. My mother pats Sutton's cheek. All I can do is stare. I've never received that type of open affection from her in my twenty-four years. Not that I'm surprised. Sutton gets the good from everyone, even a washed up junkie.

The bubbling boil alerts me before the sharp hiss begins. I fill the cups with steaming water and drop a leafy bag into the one for my mom. With quick strides, I make my way back to them. I set the two mugs in front of them on the table.

"Thank you, Gray." Sutton sends me a sweet smile.

I lift my lips in one of my own. "You're welcome."

My mom makes no move to touch the beverage. "Uh-huh, yeah. Thanks, boy."

"Good talk?" My question is to both of them, whoever wishes to answer.

"She's a good egg, Grady. Don't fuck it up." My mother beams at Sutton.

I snort at her words of wisdom. Stellar advice from mother of the year. "I plan to keep her around for always."

Sutton dips her chin, a deep flush coloring her face. "Likewise."

My mom sits silently, her gaze growing distant. Before I can comment, she blinks and the haze is gone. "It was nice meeting you, Sutton. Enjoy the day. You too, kid."

"Well, I guess we're free to go," I joke.

My mother reaches for her pack of smokes. Sutton scrambles off the sagging cushions as if something bit her. That's very possible in this hole. I loop an arm around her waist and lead us to the door. Mother dearest offers a weak wave with a flick of her lighter.

I almost cough from the rush of semi-fresh air as we walk outside. A comfortable silence envelops us. The last hour swirls through my mind on a rapid spiral. I'm not sure what to make of anything that occurred inside those four walls.

When we're settled back in the truck, a deep exhale escapes me. I sag against the lumpy seat. "That was really strange."

Sutton buckles up and turns to me. "Yeah? She seemed to be in good spirits."

"Exactly. That never happens."

"Huh. Guess that's odd."

I glance at her from the corner of my eye. A sad sort of smile curls the edges of her mouth as we pull out of the lot. "You okay, beautiful?"

"Yes. It was a bit sad, but also sweet."

I nearly swerve off the road. "Did you just refer to my mother as sweet?"

Sutton giggles. "I did. And she is."

"What in the world did she say to you?"

"Nothing outrageous. I think that little conversation was her version of sniffing me out. Making sure I have honorable intentions where you're concerned."

I can't stop the burst of laughter that booms out of me. "That's hilarious, Sutt. I doubt my mother gives a single shit about me or my life."

She strokes a finger down my cheek. "She told me to take care of you."

"That's comforting considering she never did."

Sutton hums. "She wasn't shy about pointing out her list of faults."

"Only took her several decades." My tone is bitter, a sour taste on my tongue.

"I think she wants the best for you, in her own twisted way."

"Why couldn't she tell me herself?"

She looks out the window at the passing fields. "That's on her. Maybe she's ashamed. Years of neglect and abuse. Sometimes it's easier to share all that with a stranger."

I release another heavy breath. "Whatever. I just hope it wasn't too much on you."

Sutton grabs my free hand. "I'm happy we went. This was a good thing."

"Maybe you need a refresher of what that word means." I lift our connected palms, kissing her wrist.

"What're you suggesting?"

I wink at her. "A new happy something. Anything you want."

Her hips wiggle in a sexy shimmy. "The possibilities are endless. Let's start with swimming."

That gets a low chuckle out of me. "Out of everything, that's what you want?"

She walks her fingers up my arm. "Diving off your dock."

My chest warms at the memory of a talk we had so very long ago. We never got to jump in the lake together. Turns out her suggestion is the greatest one.

Sutton leans across the space separating us. "Oh, and by the way? I lost my bikini. Hopefully skinny dipping isn't a deal breaker."

CHAPTER TWENTY—THREE

Grady

Happy something #37: Having the power to be numb.

THE Monday morning sun is threatening to blister my skin and it's barely nine o'clock. I almost miss the stuffy confines of working indoors. A quick glance along the outer wall promises a large shaded area thanks to the huge oak nearby. I should hit that patch of relief after a few more sections. What I wouldn't give to be neck-deep in the lake with Sutton again. Having her slippery body gliding over mine was the most satisfying happy something my dirty mind could ever conjure up. I palm my junk, cursing the persistent desire sizzling through me. It's hot enough without adding more flames.

After adjusting myself, I grab another piece of flimsy plastic. I'm finishing up the siding this week. Lighting and appliances after that. I have to stain and install the trim. Finishing touches in the bathroom. That should wrap up the restoration. The end of this project is finally in sight.

I'm about to nail another portion in place when my phone begins vibrating. An unknown number flashes on the screen. I stare at my cell for a slow beat. The decision to answer wobbles my hand. With a resigned sigh, I swipe across the green line.

"Hello?"

"Is this Grady Bowen?"

"Yeah." I'm already preparing to hang up.

"My name is Patricia. I'm a nurse at Springs Regional."

Everything screeches to a halt and my vision tunnels to the ground. "What happened? Is Sutton hurt?"

The woman clears her throat. "You're listed as the emergency contact for Camilla Bowen."

"She's my mother." This isn't the first time urgent care has called me about her. It probably won't be the last.

"Camilla was rushed to the hospital a couple hours ago." Her tone is flat, as if she's reciting a shopping list. That jaded indifference probably comes with the job.

I rub at the grit in my eyes. "Did she overdose?" I can only imagine the stash she dug into once we left yesterday. That woman isn't cut out for sobriety. That momentary glimmer was a glitch.

"The toxicology results aren't completed."

I want to tell her that's not necessary. Anyone in this town can fill in the blanks. And if not, her health history is more than extensive. "When can I pick her up?"

They usually watch her overnight, depending on the severity.

The nurse makes a strangled noise. "This is serious, Mr. Bowen. The doctor on call has just finished initial diagnostics. It's been recommended that you get here immediately."

"What's wrong with her?"

"That information will be shared with you in person. I'm at liberty to tell you that her condition is considered critical.

"Can I talk to her?"

"That's not possible. She's unconscious, sir. I repeat, her situation is urgent."

The salvia in my mouth turns to mud. "Uh, okay. I can be on my way shortly."

"Very good, Mr. Bowen. We're on the third floor. Check in at the front desk when you arrive."

"Okay," I repeat.

She ends the call without further instruction. I glance at the blank screen while possibilities stack up. They've never told me to rush over. That's definitely new. A prickle of unease worms up my neck. I scratch at the odd sensation. It's probably nothing. But that doesn't stop the cement from sinking in my gut.

My steps are robotic as I walk into the house. The nurse's words continue playing on repeat. This is more serious than an overdose. She's knocked out. The information can only be shared in person. Hurry my ass up.

Cane is crouching in front of the rear staircase. His blond head bobs with steady movement, as if he's listening to music. All I hear is the nurse repeating my mother's critical state.

"Hey, I need to leave."

He glances at me over his shoulder. Whatever he sees on my face makes him recoil. "What the hell happened to you?"

"My mom," I mutter.

Cane nods, knowing enough about my past not to question me further. "Take care, man. I'll get everything sorted here."

"Thanks." I sound drained, even to my own ears. The battle with my mother is exhausting and gruesome. I barely dredge up the willpower to drag my ass outside.

The drive to the hospital whizzes by in a blur of static. It's only thanks to some miracle that I don't end up in a ditch. I'm not sure how my truck gets parked. The bright blue sky has been replaced with gloomy clouds. How fucking fitting.

I hold onto these insignificant details, relying on them to push me onward. My boots echo on the scuffed linoleum as I enter the emergency room. A security guard waves me in the direction to a bank of elevators. When I get out on the third floor, another lobby greets me. A woman smiles from her spot behind a cluttered desk.

"May I help you find something?"

I blow out a stream of foul air. "I'm looking for Camilla Bowen. She was checked in earlier."

The woman's eyes grow saucer-wide. "Uh, yes. She's in 313. Very last door on the left." She lifts an unsteady finger toward a narrow hall.

I follow the gesture, a sick intuition twisting inside of me. "Thank you."

My stride is comparable to a snail as I edge down the long walkway. I watch the numbers increase with nausea churning faster in my stomach. It takes several minutes to reach the correct room. Those three bold digits mock me. What waits for me beyond this barrier? Only one way to see.

I push the door open with a cautious hand. The space is cloaked in darkness, shades drawn and lights off. Antiseptic and bleach suffocate me. I suppose this sterile stench beats the smell of death. My feet shove forward on their own. The rest of me is trying to process what I'm seeing. I pause halfway to the bed.

My mother looks so peaceful, frozen in sleep. Only the soft rise and fall of her chest alerts me that she's still alive. That slow rhythm is cathartic. Relief floods out of me in a cascade and my knees threaten to buckle. I stumble to the nearby chair, dragging it to her side. An array of machines beep and buzz. Tubes are taped along her right arm. There are colorful wires sprouting out from the top of her gown. So much is happening, yet nothing at all.

I grab her left hand and suck in a sharp breath. Her skin is ice cold. I press her freezing palm between both of mine. We've been in this situation before. The similarities aren't lost on me. But the differences are blaring louder than a foghorn. She's hardly moving. The ashen hue of her complexion is more pronounced. Her cheekbones jut out to a crude degree. Purple bruising is forming along her jaw. An eerie chill slithers across my scalp. I leave my eyes trained on her still form, waiting for more signs of life.

Someone knocks on the door behind me. I turn and find a man wearing blue scrubs poking his head inside. He's older than me by at least ten years. The way he steps into the room speaks of his authority.

"Mr. Bowen?"

I squint at him. Being called Mr. Bowen is beginning to skeeve me out. That doesn't mean I'll correct him. I'll take an upper hand if he's passing them out. "That's me."

He moves closer with an outstretched hand. "I'm Doctor Potter, one of the physicians supervising this floor. You can call me Miles. I'm responsible for your mother's care while she's with us."

"You're the one who ran all her tests?"

Miles shifts to the end of her bed. "I did."

I wait for him to elaborate. He doesn't. "And?"

"May I be blunt?"

"Please," I mutter.

He glances at her before sliding his gaze to me. "Your mother's health is very poor."

"No shit, doc. I'm well aware of her addictions. Tell me something new."

"I'm talking about more than her bad habits."

A cramp attacks my muscles. "Such as?"

Miles leans against the mattress, facing me dead on. "She's suffered from a massive stroke. From what I can tell, there's irreversible damage to her heart and lungs. Her scans and X-rays are a mess. There's almost no brain activity. To break it down in the simplest terms, your mother's body gave up fighting."

I hear his explanation, but not really. My ears are packed with cotton. There's a low thrum pounding into my temples. Rancid bile crawls up my throat. I squeeze my eyes shut and force the vomit down. "But she's gonna wake up, right? I can take her home tomorrow?"

His sigh is a sinking ship. "I'm afraid not, Mr. Bowen. We're doing our best to keep her stable, but she's unresponsive to treatments. She hasn't regained consciousness since being admitted. Her system is in shutdown mode. The machines are keeping her alive."

"So, she's dying?" The crack in my voice tears straight through me. I don't bother hiding my wince.

"Yes, Mr. Bowen. I'm very sorry."

I don't look up to find the matching sympathy in his eyes. The death sentence is a sledgehammer to my ribs. The reflex to wrap an arm around my torso rattles the shattering bones. "What happens next?"

Miles straightens off the bed, swiping at his tablet. "That's entirely up to you. She's not in pain. We'll continue measuring her vitals as needed. Usually we recommend spending time with her, say goodbye and make your peace. We have a chapel on site if you'd like to pray or talk with a minister. There are a few local grief groups that meet regularly."

His suggestions bounce off the bulletproof wall I've slammed down. "That won't be necessary."

The silence stretches a mile long. I'm about ready to leap from my seat when the doctor takes a step toward me. "When you're ready, we can take her off life support."

Is anyone ever ready for that? What a fucked up control

system. I pinch the bridge of my stinging nose. "Just like that?"

"Again, I'm sorry there isn't more we can do. Your mother was very sick, Mr. Bowen."

Was.

He's already talking about her in the past tense. Fuck. Pressure roars behind my clenched eyelids. None of this should be a surprise. She never took care of herself. If I'm being honest, she was hellbent on doing everything possible to end her life prematurely. All the drugs and booze were bound to catch up with her.

"Do you think she knew?"

Miles chews on my question for a moment. "Did she ever mention her health? Not feeling well?"

I snort. "We didn't have that type of relationship."

He nods, a glimmer of understanding dawning across his features. "A prideful woman."

"More like loose cannon." I scrub over my face, reality beginning to crash down from the ceiling.

Miles hums. "Well, her charts make no mention of regular appointments or general check-ups. Considering the condition of her organs and the severity of disease, I'd say she was either ignoring the issues or self-medicating enough to not notice."

And isn't that the gist of her existence. Damn. I dip my head, slouching low in the chair. Words stick to the roof of my mouth. What was left to say?

The good doctor must read my mood. "Please stay as long as you'd like. There's no reason to rush. Are there other relatives you need to contact?"

I offer a limp shrug in response. Anything more might break me.

"If so, feel free to do so now. There's a nurse station just down the hall. They can call me if necessary."

"Got it," I mutter.

He pats my back. "I'm very sorry you ran out of time with her. Take comfort in knowing she's no longer suffering."

But is that really true?

The door closes behind him with a soft click. We're alone, cocooned in endless silence. The steady beeping from her monitor spikes my own pulse. The urge to run and never return surges into my veins. I can't fucking handle this. My heart screams for comfort that only one person can give. The phone slips off my clammy palm. I grip the plastic until it's ready to crack. Mincing words has never been my specialty. With trembling fingers, I type out a message.

Me: I need you, Sutt. Now. My mom is dying. She's at Springs Regional. You have to be here.

CHAPTER TWENTY-FOUR

Sutton

Happy something #51: Finding freedom in letting go.

AN INDESCRIBABLE PAIN RIPS INTO ME WHEN GRADY'S TEXT COMES through. It's as if we're connected by that electronic ping. Everything he must be feeling pours into my soul. His grief and suffering become mine. Tar pumps into my limbs and standing up is a chore. A tortured whimper quivers off my lips. I struggle to regain a normal breathing pattern. Tears are already racing down my cheeks.

I don't bother responding to him. We'll be together shortly. I spin in two fast circles, trying to get my brain screwed in straight. Other customers inside the diner are turning to stare. Let them look. I couldn't care less about the hush falling over the small restaurant. Their faces blend into a single mask of intrusion.

After packing up my shit, I haul ass to the car. The engine rumbles to life with a sharp crank of my wrist. I type in the address and stomp on the accelerator. The drive should take me fifteen minutes. I make it to the hospital in eight.

My thoughts are a scramble as I breeze through the sliding glass entrance. I scan the lobby with urgency. The thundering in my ears echoes like a frantic pack of buffaloes chasing me. The tiled floor ripples and tilts beneath me. Shit, maybe I need to slow down. But the clock is ticking, each second a swift strike across my frazzling nerves. If I'm this spooked, Grady must be a complete mess. I yank at my hair and dart forward. A woman at the greeter desk takes pity on me.

"Miss? Are you all right?"

I'm certain my eyes resemble full moons. "No."

She motions me toward her. "Who are you searching for?"

My legs wobble as I stagger over. "Camilla Bowen."

A couple taps on the keyboard follow. A frown twists her features. "Oh, I see."

"What?" My voice is shrill.

She refuses to meet my gaze. "She's on the third floor in room 313."

"O-okay. Can you tell me about her prognosis?"

The woman is shaking her head before I'm done asking. "Nope. That's not my job. There will be a doctor doing rounds this afternoon."

I furrow my brow. "All right. How about some directions?"

She prattles off a laundry list of turns that my muddled mind barely comprehends. I nod along with faith that there are proper signs posted. When I stay unmoving in front of her, she quirks a brow. "Is there a problem, dear?"

I jolt out of my stupor. The troubles are stacking up against me. I don't bother sharing that. After a timid wave, I take off to the left wing. I follow the woman's instructions to the best of my ability. The dimly lit hallway on the third floor is something out of a horror film. Overhead lights flicker.

The drab walls are barren. My sandals squeak with every inch I cover. This trek is ominous as hell. As if hospitals need to be more creepy. 313 finally appears in front of me and a sob tickles my tongue. The door is slightly ajar. I push the gap wider and peek inside.

"Gray?"

I'm welcomed by stilted silence and darkness. The square space is almost pitch-black, only a single strand of sunshine breaks through the blinds. My feet carry me across the room without pause. There's a slim figure tucked in bed, tranquil and sleeping. Stark white sheets cover most of Camilla's petite form. If I didn't know better, I'd assume she's enjoying a midday nap.

Grady is there, hunched over the mattress, motionless and waiting. The torrent of sorrow in his green eyes is a punch to my sternum. I choke out a garbled breath. His raw expression showers me with a downpour of emotions. Remaining upright is no longer an option.

I collapse onto the empty chair beside him. My forehead kisses his. "I'm so damn sorry, Gray."

He folds into me, a tremor wracking his entire body. "Thank you for coming. I can't do this by myself. Not anymore."

"Of course, baby. You never have to be alone again. I'll always be by your side."

His arms cinch around me in an unrelenting hold, as if I'll vanish at any moment. "I don't know what to do, Sutt."

I stroke a palm down his bowed back. "Are there options?"

A cutting jerk of his head. "Only one. I c-can't even say it."

Sweat prickles along my hairline. "Nothing needs to be decided right away."

"Why delay the inevitable?" His haunted tone vibrates my bones.

"Who found her?" I study Camilla in front of us. "What happened?"

The heat of his mouth is a puff across my neck. "For whatever reason, the landlord dropped in to see her. She was already unconscious and barely breathing. The doctor listed off all sorts of failures with her body. He thinks the stroke is what caused the most damage to her brain. But she's been in a perpetual nosedive my entire life. I guess she finally crashed."

My chest jerks with a shuddering wheeze. "That's so sad. I can't believe it. We were just with her, alive and seemingly well."

Grady straightens, those piercing green eyes lasering into me. "Did you know she was sick?"

I baulk at that. "How could I?"

He scrubs a palm down his face. "Maybe she mentioned it during your private chat."

I allow the edges of my lips to tip up with the slightest hint of a smile. The motion is shaky, but it holds. "All she did was talk about you, Gray. She asked me about your job. What your hobbies are. How long we've been dating. Where you live. Your dreams and goals and wishes. She wanted to know what you're passionate about. What makes you tick. We played a one-sided game of twenty questions. She was a sponge for any drop of information on you. I was also told to keep our conversation a secret."

"Damn. I can almost believe she meant well." He lets a few choice words loose. Moisture collects on his lashes when he blinks. "No mention of not feeling well?"

"She avoided answering anything about herself. I tried to engage deeper, but nope."

His posture deflates. "This is very surreal for me. I don't even know her. She birthed me, and gave me life. But what else? A bunch of bad blood and toxic memories."

I rest my head on his shoulder. "She's always going to be your mother."

Grady's throat bobs. "I know."

"There aren't many moments I can share about your mom. Before yesterday, I hadn't seen her since we were in high school. I wasn't sure what to expect when we pulled in. That trailer park leaves a lot to be desired. A graveyard of broken dreams. But your mom was kind to me, in her own way."

"I'm really glad you had that time with her."

"So am I. It's something I can carry with me. Doesn't hurt to know she approves of us being together."

Grady scoffs. "As if she would ever deny you. That trait runs in my family."

"Oh my gosh." If I wasn't already sitting, my knees would have given out. Fresh tears blur my vision. "I can't even. You're so damn sweet to me, Gray."

His thumb wipes at my wet cheeks. "I'd be a shell without you, Sutt. This situation would throw me over the edge. Because of you, I'm able to push past the bad. I'll be okay."

I lean into his touch. "We'll always make it through, Gray. I truly believe that. Today is going to be nearly impossible. Tell me what to do. Anything you need."

"Just you, baby. Having you with me for this means everything. My happy something in the pit of sorrow."

"I'd never be anywhere else."

His lips find mine, sealing us in an intimate bubble. I hug my arms around him and erase any sliver of distance between us. We get lost in one another, the ache ebbing ever so slightly.

A soft knock interrupts our tender moment. We sigh in unison and glance over to the sound. The door edges open and a nurse appears. "Is this an okay time?"

Grady glares at her. "For what?"

I startle at the harsh whip in his tone. "Easy, Gray."

His stare tracks her hesitant steps, as if she's an enemy about to pounce. She holds up her palms and moves toward us. "I didn't mean to disturb. This was my next stop. I'm Bianca, the nurse assigned to Camilla this evening." She gives an awkward wave. "I just need to check her vitals. It shouldn't take long."

Grady continues staring at her through narrow slits. "What could've changed?"

I nudge him in the ribs. "Stop it. She's just doing her job."

Bianca busies herself charting levels from the machines hooked up to Camilla. Grady rips his gaze off her and focuses those green depths on me. My stomach squeezes at the pure agony reflecting there.

"I'm the one"—he gulps in a breath—"in charge of telling them when to kill her."

I hiss out an exhale. Talk about morbid. No child should have to make that decision for their parent, or anyone really. What a horrible position to be in. "Now?"

Bianca drops her tablet and it clatters to the floor. She scoops up the device, darting across the room and out of sight.

Grady watches her scurry off. "Not necessarily. When I'm ready." His eyes roll. "Because that's a humane option to offer. They'll keep her heart beating and force air into her lungs until I'm willing to pull the plug. As if that makes it easier to let go."

"This will be the most difficult decision you'll ever make. But she's in your hands. Think about it as setting her free. We'll do it together. I'll be right here with you."

A single drop trickles down his cheek. "I'm not strong enough for this shit."

I grab his hand, linking our fingers in a tight web. My

eyes are hot and leaking in earnest. I don't bother wiping the salty tracks away. "You're a damn warrior, Grady Bowen. Life has been a constant battle. But you fight and never quit. Your mom is going to a better place, Gray. You have to trust in that."

His nod is a slow dip. "I do. She wasn't happy here. Hopefully her next stop is better."

"It will be." I barely recognize the croak of my voice.

The silence swoops in, dark and heavy. The weight of what needs to happen hangs in a thick curtain around us. I blink my swollen eyelids, her resting body a glow of white light. She's so calm and ethereal. Hopefully Grady sees that.

I lean forward to whisper in her ear. "We ran out of time. I wish we had more. Find peace. Look down on us. We'll look up for you." I press a palm to my mouth to trap a sob. "I promise to take good care of him for you. He's very well loved." I can't say more without choking over my words. The chair squeaks when I fall into it.

Grady kisses her forehead, his tears raining onto her pale skin. "Love you, mama."

I hiccup over the lump clogging my windpipe. My chest is caving in, a hurricane wreaking havoc inside of me. Grady has given up hiding his grief. The streaks flow freely down his face. I open my arms and he slumps into me. His entire body shakes in my hold. My mountain of a man is crumbling.

Seconds bleed into minutes as we share in this wrenching misery. We stay locked together until the tears dry and the clouds part. Grady picks up a remote attached to the bed, pressing the red button.

A flurry of activity ensues almost immediately. Three nurses stride in, followed by a doctor. He nods at Grady on his way to Camilla's side. "Mr. Bowen?"

He lifts his watery gaze to the doctor. "We've said goodbye."

The man's expression is polluted with sadness. "I'm very sorry."

I have a sinking feeling he'll be hearing a lot of that in the near future. Grady's features remain stoic. He doesn't respond. His grasp on my fingers borders on pain, but I don't wince. I tuck my face into his neck and breathe in a bit of good.

A nurse is flipping off switches on the cluster of equipment responsible for keeping Camilla alive. The screens go blank one after another. All alerts fall silent. Any movement ceases. There's just… nothing.

I don't focus on the sluggish rise and fall of her chest. There's no sense watching life leave her body. I keep my eyes trained to the ceiling. With a final whoosh of air, she's gone.

And we cry over a life lost too soon.

CHAPTER TWENTY–FIVE

Sutton

*Happy something #47: Receiving a spontaneous hug,
especially from Grady.*

THE FUNERAL IS A QUIET AFFAIR.

There's a small crowd gathering on the peak of Silo Ridge. Rumor has it that Camilla enjoyed hiking up this clifftop as a teenager. Seems as though this is the most appropriate place to set her free. The view is stunning. A direct shot of Spring Falls is in front of us. The lush trees of Wheaton Forest decorate the landscape on our left. Miles of wild flower meadows spread across the opposite side. I'm ashamed to admit this is my first visit. One glance at Grady and I know we'll be making the climb again soon.

It's nearly dusk, a warm burst of color is kissing the horizon. The dozen people in attendance are huddling near the rocky edge to watch the sunset. My parents are clutching each other tight. Their glittering eyes are focusing on the vibrant backdrop. Jace hovers nearby, his guarded expression blocking everyone out.

A floating sensation sweeps over me. There's serenity whisking within the pain. I wipe another set of tears off my sensitive cheeks. My skin is practically rubbed raw at this point. I can't get the swelling in my eyelids down. No amount of cucumber slices or mud masks alleviate the burn. Grady's features wear similar evidence of grief. I doubt anyone else can see beyond his fierce exterior. The neglected scruff lining his jaw and grooves crossing his forehead are badges of honor. That's all he's willing to display. His face is a blank mask. The purest proof of her impact is soul-deep.

Camilla Bowen wasn't a saint. The total opposite, in fact. Her choices were often dishonorable. She didn't treat her son the way a mother should. I hardly had the chance to know her. None of that counts after the dust clears. Her death has changed us. She's a reminder of how precious life is. As if we could so easily forget.

Grady shifts on restless feet beside me. His gaze is downcast, broad shoulders spanning wide even with the added pressure. The urn trembles in his hold. Camilla was cremated. She once mentioned that her body doesn't belong in the ground. Her destiny is to spend eternity soaring in the clouds. Grady believes she was high on more than fresh air when this plan was created. He followed through with her wishes all the same.

The blue ceramic matches her eyes, at least that's what my dad tells me. He knew a different side of her. His memories are full of smiles and joy. I wish Grady had more of those, along with the rest of Silo Springs. A quick glance across the cliff makes me queasy. Not many people in this town were interested or willing to pay their respects. Sympathy for the deceased has been lacking. We predicted this, and don't necessarily blame them. It makes the few distant friends and acquaintances that are filtering in more meaningful.

Grady's silence extends wider than usual. The load of

these decisions for his mom has been an undertaking. The strain rarely leaves his muscles. There's a constant war waging in his mind. But he doesn't push me away. Not sure what would happen if he did. I never stray far from his side. We've been relying on one another to share the burden.

I drift a palm over his forearm. "Hey, Gray."

His lips twitch. My heart leaps at the slight movement. "Hi, Sutt."

"Is it time?"

He scans the skyline and nods. "I think so."

A eulogy isn't in the cards for this affair. My dad spoke earlier, prior to our moment of quiet reflection. Further words aren't needed. Cicadas serenade us with a melancholy lullaby. Grady exhales a long stream of pent-up jitters. He loosens the lid and shuffles forward. With a slow tip, Camilla stretches her wings. Ashes scatter in dusty spirals and get carried by the wind. She sails in every direction—from meadows and forests and waterfalls. Her final resting place is the sky.

We step off the cliff once the final traces are welcomed up in a breeze. Grady loops an arm around my waist when I shiver. He's so intuitive when it comes to me. I never have to worry about a thing when he's within reach.

Our relationship has braved a bitter trial with his mother's passing. We're stronger because of it, but the road is littered with rocks. He's been broody and withdrawn this past week. I recognize the steely armor he slips behind. He resembles the man I found after moving back home. Not that anyone can blame him. But he lets that bulletproof guard off-duty when it's just the two of us. I crave that intimate connection after watching him stonewall everyone.

I brush against him with my hip, grinning with the flirty nudge. He buries his nose into my hair and drags in a deep breath. The rumble that follows has another shudder wracking my limbs.

"Missed you, Sutt."

"Right here, Gray. I'm never far," I murmur.

He kisses my temple. "You know what I mean."

And I do. Those cherished romantic moments that aren't tainted with darkness. "The night is young."

Grady flicks a glance at my parents and Jace. The other guests trickled out after the ceremony. "I want us to be alone. I don't give a shit if that's insensitive or selfish."

I nibble my bottom lip. "You're excused. Pretty sure you have a pass for just about anything."

His emerald gaze latches onto my mouth. Grady bends lower and groans in my ear. "Then it's time to collect."

I tug on his shirt. "Let's go home."

His eyes flash with molten fire. There's my Grady. "My girl knows just what I want to hear."

I almost yelp when my father suddenly appears in front of us. His chuckle suggests that he's been spying on us. I try not to wither while my stomach turns. Dammit.

My dad claps Grady on the back. "You hanging in there, son?"

His nod is delayed. "Doing my best. Sutton helps."

"I can see that."

The temperature spikes one-hundred degrees and my face goes up in flames. "Dad," I complain.

He winks at me. "You kids need each other. I'm not trying to intrude. You're adults. Be grown and live happy."

The corners of Grady's lips curl ever so slightly. "Thanks, Barry."

Jace nudges his friend. "I'm gonna get piss-ass drunk. Interested?"

Grady strokes his stubbled chin. "That's tempting, but nah. I need lowkey. We'll paint the town a different night."

"I'll hold you to that." My brother takes a step backward.

"Are you two interested in dinner at our house?" The

question comes from my mother. She's still wrapped in my father's arms. They're the epitome of a blissful marriage, even after thirty years.

One look at Grady's somber expression and I have my answer. "We're going to spend the evening alone."

Her smile is soft and kind. "I think that's best."

We part ways after a round of hugs. My palm is safely nestled inside of Grady's much bigger one. We took my car here, but I very willingly let him drive. Handing over the reins to Grady is strictly for my visual benefit. Giving him complete control is drool-worthy. He reclines low in the seat with his left arm hanging loose on top of the steering wheel. Swagger oozes from his massive frame. My inner muscles clench on nothingness. The missing piece is sitting a foot away. I want to straddle his lap and show him how hot he makes me. Not sure that would fly with traffic laws. I tamp down the wanton fantasy and stay planted on my side of the vehicle.

The trip home is quiet, but we find comfort in the silence. There's been too much suffering. I can sense a change in the cool evening air. Flakes of rust and rot chip away, fluttering out the open windows. We're releasing the toxins and leaving the pain behind us. All that's left is good and happy. The sparking electricity between us has me buzzing on a high voltage wire. Our heated stares don't quit. When we pull into the driveway, I'm rejuvenated and ready to combust.

Grady guides me inside with a searing palm at the small of my back. I lean into him, preparing to claw his clothes off.

"I'm depleted, Sutt."

His raspy tone is ice across my steaming skin. I release him and glance up. Those bottomless green eyes are shining. "I know, Gray. What can I do?"

His lips dust my forehead. "I need a dozen happy somethings to refill my stock."

I nod into his touch. "Should we take a bath? I bought more bubble bombs."

"We can do that after."

That last word hangs between us. "What comes first?"

"Hopefully both of us."

There's no hiding the quiver that ripples through me from top to bottom. I lift a shaky brow. "Oh?"

"Give yourself to me."

He says that as if I haven't already handed over my heart, along with everything else. "Always," I purr.

He crowds my personal space, backing me against the wall. "I need you, Sutt."

There's no protest from me. The escape we find within one another is better than a dream. I'll gladly get lost with him until the sun rises. "Then take me. I'm yours."

He buries his face into my neck, nipping at the sensitive flesh. "I love you so damn much, Sutt. You're oxygen in my lungs. The steady beat of my pulse. Sustenance to keep me strong and powerful. I couldn't survive without you."

"Love you to the stars, baby." I kiss across his angular jaw. "I'm getting the sweet Grady tonight."

"Only you."

"Good. That makes me feel special."

Grady scoops me up as if I'm his bride. "You are, Sutt. So damn special. I'll never quit showing you. Every second we have left in this world, you'll be treated as a queen." He climbs the stairs two at once. His feet pound into the wood with an urgency I feel in my core.

Our bedroom has become a sanctuary. Every inch is shared. The space is a blend of fresh pine and savory coconut. Symbols of our lives joining decorate any available surface. Soon the floor will be cluttered with more of us.

Grady undresses me with the utmost care. I return his devotion, removing every scrap with soft kisses and whispers of more. Each layer is peeling away to reveal new truths. There are a few more dents and nicks than before. Those blemishes meld our bond into something more imperfectly beautiful. The grit and grime distorting our appearance disappears with the fabric. I'm left naked and bare for him, just as he is for me.

We're desperate to erase the space between us. He lays me down in the middle of our bed. My soul sings with the promise of eternal pleasure. I dig my nails into his back and urge him to blanket me. When his body becomes one with mine, we're no longer alone. Nothing is broken. The sorrow of this last week melts off our entwining limbs. Together we become whole.

CHAPTER TWENTY-SIX

Grady

Happy something #33: Picturing a life where I'm accepted.
By everyone.

TIME DOESN'T PAUSE WHEN THE GOING GETS ROUGH. It's been nearly a month since my mom died. I've been busting ass cleaning up her countless loose ends. All the messes she left behind were suddenly mine. That type of inheritance should stay buried. I wanted to burn it all to the ground and be done. That wasn't an option—reality will never be so simple.

The bills didn't quit. A different unpaid notice appeared in my mailbox daily. The debts that woman owed twisted my gut into a pretzel. Sutton is by my side through it all. Her unwavering commitment has been my saving grace. She helps me sift through the piles of shit without complaint. Not sure what I did right to deserve her unyielding loyalty, but I'll never take that for granted.

I lose myself in her warmth every single night. She gives

so freely without hesitation. I probably take too much. But the desperation is imbedded in my roots. Everything inside of me craves her with a fierce hunger that has no limits. Her radiant light recharges me. I can only hope to give her a fraction of that boost in return.

That's how I find myself on a cushioned stool at Bronco Buck. My girl wanted to dance. I'll never refuse her wishes. Besides all that, an evening out to let loose is long overdue.

I take another swig of my beer without taking my stare off Sutton. She's shaking her ass, twirling around with Molly and Lacie. Only a few other girls are brave enough to join them. A horde of slobbering men form a half circle around them. The other women in this bar are probably scared off.

Music blasts from the speakers. The heavy bass pumps into my veins. Sutton dips low, pointing her ass in the air. A growl rips from my throat. What the fuck is she trying to prove? Especially in that sorry excuse for an outfit. Her bandana shirt is barely more than a triangle. Those shorts have more rips and holes than fabric. I'm shocked her thong isn't fully on display. If that happens, she's getting tossed over my shoulder and spanked before I haul her ass out of here. My palm tingles at the possibility. She didn't mind the light tap I gave her the other night.

A groan vibrates my chest when Sutton spins to face me. Her baby blues glitter from the colorful strobe lights turning this place into a chaotic rainbow. I palm my cock and squeeze the hard ridge. My jeans are restricting proper blood flow. Maybe that's why I'm dizzy just looking at her. The denim has become uncomfortably tight, strangling my junk in a chokehold.

A damn riot is about to ensue. Some dude with a death wish takes a step toward Sutton. Over my lifeless body will that shit fly. I prowl toward her with fire under my skin. Her responding smile tells me she finds this little act very entertaining. I tug her into me by the belt loops of those sinful cutoffs. The threadbare material nearly rips in my harsh grip.

I dip my face into the crook of her neck, nuzzling the soft skin there. "Are you trying to drive me crazy on purpose?"

She wiggles her ass into my dick. "Maybe."

"You're doing a damn good job. I want to kick the shit out of every guy staring at you."

She glances around the crowded space. It's hazy and difficult to see anything five feet away. But I'm sure she can feel their undivided attention. "They're harmless."

I nip the column of her throat. "Yeah? If I wasn't here, they'd be lining up for a shot at your panties."

"I'd like to see them try."

"They'd have broken wrists before getting a chance." I grind into her, following the smooth flow of her movements.

"No man has the right to roll his hips so well." I repeat the motion and she moans. "You're naughty."

"And you're mine, Sutt."

"I know."

"Say it."

She peeks up at me from over her shoulder. "I'm yours, Gray. Only yours."

"Come home with me."

Her painted lips lift with a wide grin. "Well, yeah."

"Now." My demand is a boom across the noisy space.

She gasps. "Now?"

"Did I stutter?"

"But I'm having fun." Sutton pouts, peeking up at me from under lowered lashes. "Thirty more minutes?"

I'm weak for this woman. She knows that indisputable fact, probably too well. I press a branding kiss to her mouth. "Fine. I'm gonna take a piss and step outside for some air.

You've wound me tighter than a fist. I'll be back in five. Don't steal any hearts while I'm gone."

She shoots me a wink. "I'll only break them."

"That's my girl." I fuse our lips together once more for good measure. She smiles into me and I grab a handful of her ass. When we split, I'm a tad breathless. Damn.

I stride backward through the crowd, keeping her locked in my sight until the swarm swallows her. The bathroom reeks like an outhouse. My boots stick to the rank floor as I rush to do my business. I don't want to spend longer than a minute in this pit. After I'm drained, I zip up and rinse my hands. The lack of soap and paper towels doesn't surprise me.

I shove through the backdoor into the alley, metal hitting brick with a resounding bang. The sound reminds me of when I dragged Sutton out here to get away from Deputy Dipshit. A chuckle rises off my chest. How much has changed. A quick glance in both directions shows I'm alone. I could suggest a quickie up against the wall. Her skimpy clothes would come in handy.

The evening air is crisp and biting. Normal functioning returns to my brain. Half hour. I can wait that long. The fire in my veins has cooled slightly. I'm about to head inside when a figure appears at the alley entrance. Lance Fucking Morris. Did my earlier thoughts summon him? I caught him hovering on the opposite side of the bar earlier. He's been here with Molly, but was smart enough to keep his distance. That break I was granted is apparently over.

The air shifts, sending rotten waves around us. Lance isn't in uniform. Off-duty is easier to deal with when it comes to this asshole. I straighten and widen my stance, staring at him straight on. He smiles at me, but I see right through it.

"Hey, Grady. Didn't expect to find you out here."

I grunt at his blatant bullshit. "No? Who are you looking for?"

He rocks on his heels. "A moment alone. Kinda loud in there."

"Well, I'll leave you to it." I take a step toward the door.

His question halts my retreat. "How's Sutton?"

I squint at him, getting a good look. "Great, as always."

"Isn't that nice for you."

"Sure is." Pinpricks creep along my neck. I belatedly realize that he's no longer smiling. At some point in our conversation, that grin collapsed into a sneer. His usually aloof mannerisms are absent. "You okay, Morris?"

Lance's tone is more of a snarl. "No, Grady. I'm not fucking all right."

And I couldn't care less. Something prods at the back of my brain. I should get out of this creepy alley. But this guy clearly sought me out for a reason. "Is there something I can do for you?"

"Get out of my way."

"What?" I glance over my shoulder. This dude has to be on something.

He cracks his neck. "I figured you'd skip town once that dumpster diving piece of trailer trash died. But no. You stuck around for Sutton."

I narrow my eyes into deadly thin slits. "My mother wasn't award-winning, but don't talk about her that way."

He swats the air. "Who fucking cares about her. You stole my girl. I want her back."

"She was never yours to begin with."

"Was so." Acting like a toddler must be one of his hobbies.

"I believe you're mistaken."

"She just doesn't know about us yet. That'll change soon."

Lance is talking about Sutton as if she's a toy or some possession to own. How is this clown an officer of the law? An idea occurs to me. "Aren't you dating Molly?"

He shrugs. "Not sure what she has to do with this."

Is this dude for real? "She's your girlfriend. Stop talking about Sutton and focus on Molly."

His snort echoes off the brick wall. "Please. As if that bossy loudmouth could replace true love. Molly is just a poor substitute while this Sutton situation gets sorted. She's the one I really want."

What a lunatic. "Too fucking bad that's never going to happen."

Lance steeples his fingers. "We'll see about that."

"You're delusional."

His laugh is maniacal. "I've been called worse."

"What's your problem?" I flex my muscles, the itch for a fight screaming at me.

He points a stubby finger at me. "You. You're my damn problem."

I swing my arms out and spread them wide. "I haven't done shit to you. If anyone has dirt on their hands, it's you."

"Sutton is supposed to be mine."

I let my hands drop, fists forming with his words. "Wrong, buddy. Try again."

He watches my every move. "Getting mad? Good. Wanna punch me?"

The answer is hell yes, I really do. But that'll get me locked up faster than his blood spilling. A heavy exhale breezes through my clenching jaw. I force myself to relax. Sutton comes to mind and I almost smirk. She gets me even when we're apart.

Our silence yawns and I'm more than ready to end this exchange. Before I can get gone, sirens begin wailing in the distance. Maybe Lance will get called in and leave me the fuck alone. He stays put, squaring off against me. There's an odd gleam in his eye. I wonder absently if he's high. Wouldn't that be a shit-kicker?

A warped grin curls his lips. Out of nowhere, Lance

punches himself in the nose. The crack is sickening. A river of red immediately pours down his face.

My stomach curdles. "What the fuck, man? Are you psycho?"

He smiles, showing off his bloody teeth. "Close, but the correct term is sociopath. The doctors would be proud to hear me finally admit it. But that's not important. You just assaulted an officer, Grady."

"The fuck I did. I haven't laid a finger on you."

"We'll see who they believe." Lance smashes a fist into his cheekbone.

The sirens drift closer. I can only gawk at him. Startling clarity smacks me in the face. Holy shit, he's setting me up. My heart gallops beyond reasonable rhythm. I stumble backward, already picturing how this will go.

His eyes flare with some sort of sick excitement. "Scared now? I dare you to run. That'll make this even better for me."

When a squad car screeches to a halt along the curb, Lance's entire persona changes. He begins whimpering, folding over and shying away from me. It's his word against mine. Fuck, I'm screwed. I'll always be the lowlife loser who makes an easy target. There's no escaping the stigma.

Two officers I don't recognize storm toward me. I hold up my palms, not bothering to fight. This will only end one way. They slam me to the filthy ground with a knee jabbing into my spine. I land with a jarring thud that radiates through my body and has me seeing stars. Cold metal slaps around my wrists, tighter than necessary. I feel my wallet get yanked out of my pocket. A set of hands hauls me off the pavement and I tilt from the force.

The required speech starts up once their hold on me is secure. "Grady Bowen, you're under arrest. You have the right to remain silent..." The officer's voice drones on, but I don't hear any of it. How the fuck did this happen? I look up and see another cop inspecting Lance's injuries. Mother fucker hurt himself. I want to shout and fight, but that won't help me. I'm more than aware how this goes. The echoing vibrations linger for a second or two. Dread for what's to come rests heavy on my shoulders.

We pass Lance, who's done sobbing like a little bitch. His expression is pure evil. "Don't worry, I'll take care of Sutton for you."

An animalistic roar rips from my throat. "Don't you fucking touch her. I'll kill you."

He cackles. "You're only proving my case, Bowen."

Piping hot rage fills my veins and I struggle against the cuffs. The officers clutching my arms grip me tighter. "Knock it off, kid. You're only making this worse."

How the fuck could this possibly get worse? A vision of Sutton's beautiful face appears in front of me. What the hell are we going to do? I try to hold onto images of her, but the shadows are already obscuring my view. They toss me into the back of a cruiser. Just as they're about to trap me inside, Lance appears.

He leans in so only I can hear. "Say hello to your dad for me."

CHAPTER TWENTY-SEVEN

Sutton

Happy something #126: Trusting against all odds.

GUZZLE SOME MORE WATER WHILE KEEPING MY GAZE TRAINED on the bathroom hallway. Grady hasn't emerged, regardless of my insistent staring. He's been gone for at least fifteen minutes. Am I being paranoid? There's little doubt. But he wouldn't leave me alone longer than absolutely necessary. The tether between us is straining and I feel the taut pull in my chest. Something isn't right.

My gut is yelling at me to investigate. I chomp on an ice cube and check the clock. We should be leaving soon. The blaring hip hop that's been playing fades into a muted whisper. My vision tunnels and blocks out anything that's beyond the dark alcove. Where is he? I'm about to send him a text when Lacie sits beside me.

She rubs my arm. "What's wrong, Sutt?"

I tap my nails on the table. "Grady isn't back yet."

Her eyes follow the unwavering line of mine. "Where'd he go?"

"To the bathroom. He was going to get some air after that."

"He's taking an extended breather. No big deal. This place is popping. I'm sure a lot of people are stepping outside for a break." Her placating touch continues and my skin crawls. I need his coarse palm to be reassuring me.

"No, that doesn't sound like Grady."

"Maybe he's dropping a deuce."

I wrinkle my nose. "Eww, no way. Not at the bar."

She huffs and rolls her eyes. "You're freaking for no reason. He'll be stomping through that door at any moment."

"That's what I'm waiting for." Each second ticks by slower than the last. The knot in my stomach yanks harder until I'm a ball of tension. I give into my earlier impulse and message him.

Me: Did you get lost? I'm starting to worry. Tell me you ran into an old friend so I can relax.

The three little dots don't appear. There's no sign of him opening the text. I force down the bubble in my throat that's doubling in size. He's fine. I'm overreacting. Everything is all good. There's no reason to lose my head over a few pesky minutes. I try to smooth the furrow from my features.

When I glance over, Lacie has a front row view to my mini-meltdown. She raises a slim brow. "Should we look for him?"

I'm not fooling anyone. I allow my expression to collapse. "I think so."

My ass is halfway off the stool when Molly appears in front of me. A frown is pinching her pretty face. "Have you seen Lance?"

I just shake my head.

"Is he missing? Seems like a common theme," Lacie muses.

I shoot her a glare. "Don't say that. I'm scared enough."

She has the decency to wince. "Sorry. I'm not trying to be insensitive. Think of me as staying on the bright side."

A slow rush of pressure eases off my lips. "Yeah, okay. Thanks."

"What's going on? Grady is gone?" Molly is still blocking my view.

Any semblance of calm shatters with her questions. I peek at my phone. The damn device is silent. Not a single notification wakes the black screen. "I refuse to believe he left me. He's around here somewhere."

Molly taps her chin. "Do you think they're together?"

A chill slithers through me. "I highly doubt that."

"Why not?" She fiddles with a perfectly coiffed curl.

"They don't really get along." I'm distracted, my brain scrambling over possibilities. Her gasp has me looking over. "What?"

"It looks like something big is going down." She points out the window.

The flashes of red and blue catch my attention first. At least three police cruisers are lined up along the curb. That sneaking suspicion in my gut rips wide open and swallows me. In the next beat, I'm off my seat and dashing out the door.

Lance is the first person I stumble across. He's sitting on the trunk of a squad car with an ice pack covering half his face. I slam to a skidding halt in front of him.

"Have you seen Grady?"

He removes the compress with a cringe. I gag at the sight of his busted nose. "I'm so sorry, Sutton. I tried to stop him."

A cannonball drops in my stomach. "What happened?"

"He attacked me."

I allow my jaw to fall open. "No way."

His head bobs with rapid nods. The jerky move must

bump a clot loose. Blood begins dribbling from his nostrils. "Yep, that's how it went. He was in the alley spouting off all this degrading stuff about you—"

I hold up a palm. "Wait a minute. Grady was bad mouthing me?"

Lance grinds his teeth. "Yes, that's what I'm trying to explain. He sucker punched me."

"I don't believe you. Where is he?" My tone is flatter than concrete.

He blinks and ignores my question. "What? Why not?"

This moron could've given me all types of explanations or motives as to why Grady socked him. I might've believed a select few. But to accuse him of talking shit about me? Yeah, that's a big pile of horse crap. I cross my arms and stare him down. "You're lying."

"I was protecting you." He wipes at his bloody nose. How attractive.

"From Grady? That's not possible, or necessary." I almost choke on a mouthful of bile from the thought alone. Lance lifts a hand as if to cup my cheek. I leap out of the way. "What are you doing?"

"Comforting you. I'm sure this is a huge shock."

I rub my throbbing temples. Am I having a nightmare? "I'll be fine once I see Grady. Where is he? I shouldn't have to repeat myself."

He coos at me as if I'm a simpering toddler. "You're safe now, Sutton. I understand this is hard to accept, but your boyfriend is a monster. Let me give you a hug." He holds his arms out and motions me in.

I shy away from his advances. "No, knock it off. Grady is the only one I need. He couldn't have done this. There's no way that's the true story. Please tell me where he is, Lance."

"You're defending him?"

"Of course, and I always will."

The sympathy in his expression melts into something far more sinister. "You'll see the truth soon enough."

I shiver at his frosty tone. "How about you just tell me."

His sneer is nasty. "That asshole tried to kill me and all you care about is him. Great sense of empathy, Sutton. They're taking him to county where he belongs."

Ice fills my veins. "Why would they do that?"

Lance gestures at his injuries. "Are you blind? He pummeled me."

I purse my lips. "Nope, no way. Grady wouldn't do that."

He stabs a thumb at his chest. "I was there, Sutton."

"Yeah, and who else? We need more witnesses."

Another trickle of blood drips out of his nose. "Too bad no one else was around. It's me against him."

Waves of nausea flip my stomach. "I need to see him."

"Good luck." He snorts, a wince following immediately. "Shit, that hurts."

I want to tell him he probably deserves it. I know Grady. He wouldn't attack without a damn good reason. "What's the procedure after getting arrested?"

"I'm not helping you see that criminal." If looks could kill, I'd be six feet under.

"Stop being a jerk, Lance."

"Name calling will get you nowhere. Go ask someone else."

I ball my hands into fists. "Fine. Thanks for absolutely nothing."

A familiar face lingers by the next cruiser in line. I recognize this officer more than the others. Kyler played football with Jace and Grady in high school. He looks nice enough. Maybe he'll be more willing to answer me.

I attempt to gulp down the desperation clawing at my throat. "Hey there. You're Kyler, right?"

He lifts his gaze at my greeting, a smile firmly in place.

"Hi, Sutton. I remember you sitting in the bleachers at our games. Wondering about Grady?"

Heat springs to my eyes and I sniff. "Yes. Can you tell me what happened?"

Kyler scratches the back of his neck. "I'm not supposed to share that. Need to know basis and all that."

"Please." The beg wobbles my lips.

He glances around and sighs. "There was a brawl in the alley. Report states that Grady got angry and struck Lance twice."

I press a palm to my forehead. "What if that isn't true?"

Kyler squints at me. "Uh, well, the case is pretty much set."

"How? Grady wouldn't do this."

"How much did he have to drink? Alcohol can cause extreme reactions."

I swipe at my wet cheeks. "He only had one beer. Two at the most."

He strokes his jaw. "That's not much. Must've been something else driving him."

A scream tickles my tongue. "He's innocent. Please believe me."

"Sutton." Kyler's tone is soft and probably meant to be pacifying. "I'm sure you want to believe that, but we have no evidence proving otherwise."

I'm unraveling, a spool spinning out of control. There's no hope of winding my brain around this new reality. "W-what happens next for him?"

He offers a limp shrug. "Protocol is for him to be booked with preliminary charges, especially for an assault of this degree."

"Assault?" My voice is hollow.

Kyler almost seems shocked by my reactions. "Well, yeah. Battery at best. Didn't you see Lance's face?"

A fresh wash of tears blurs my vision. "This can't be happening."

"I was a bit surprised myself. Never took Grady as the type to be brutal."

"Because he's not," I whisper. "You have to believe in him."

"The proof against him is pretty damning. Not much can change his fate."

"Have you heard Grady's side? Doesn't that count for anything?"

He scratches his jaw. "It does, but he's refusing to speak to anyone."

That makes this entire shit-storm even worse. My heartbeat ratchets up, creating an erratic thumping I feel everywhere. "There has to be something we can do. Where are they taking him?"

Kyler averts his gaze. "He'll be pent up at county for a week or two, maybe more. You never know how long it takes for trial to be set."

"Can we get him out on bail?"

He snorts out a laugh. "That's way down the road. He's assumed guilty and stuck for now."

I clap my palms over my ears. I refuse to hear these lies. My knees buckle and I almost face plant onto the sidewalk. "Why is this happening to him?"

Kyler glances over my shoulder. "Lance told us this was a lover's quarrel. Whatever that means."

"They weren't fighting over me." I force my tone to remain level. On the inside, I'm bordering on hysteria.

"The official statement suggests otherwise."

I let my jaw pop. Enough of the lies. Boiling fury rises inside of me and the need to attack flexes my muscles. I swing my gaze to Lance. A steady finger gets pointed directly at his chest.

"You did this." I don't even recognize my own voice. "You staged this entire thing."

Lance shoots a scathing glare at me. "You have no clue what you're implying."

I lunge forward but an arm flings out to hold me off. "Sutton, stop. You'll be no good to Grady behind bars."

The warm voice cuts through the bleak darkness. I glance over at my friend. "I can't do this without him."

Lacie tucks a few locks of hair behind my ear. "You have to. There's no choice. He needs you, Sutt. Be strong and rise up for the good."

That snuffs out the fight roaring in my veins. I sag against my friend. "You're right. I need to start planning ahead."

She gives me a small grin. "Yes, exactly. That's what he would do."

I cast a quick glance at the activity buzzing along the street. A twitch curls my upper lip. "Let's get out of here. Can I catch a ride with you? I need to get thinking smart and strategize."

"Wanna sleep at my place?"

"I need to go home."

Lacie begins leading me toward the parking lot. "To your parents' house?"

"No, my house with Grady." Except he won't be there. The bed will be cold. I can't even picture where he's resting his head tonight. Pressure threatens to burst my blood vessels. And the tears don't quit.

The list of things to do begins piling up in my mind. I should call my brother. Probably my parents while I'm at it. But that can wait another moment. For now, I need Grady. I need a hug. I need woodsy pine and campfire and spicy cologne to soothe me. I need the comfort from a very specific pair of bulky arms wrapping around me. Too bad he's far out of reach until Lord only knows when. The bite of defeat is already nipping at my heels. They might win this round, but the war is just beginning.

I hang my head and continue trekking forward. "Please just take me home."

CHAPTER TWENTY-EIGHT

Grady

THE STILTED CLIP OF BOOTS ON CONCRETE IS A SOLO SOUNDTRACK for this edition of hell. Hours of the guards prowling back and forth play on repeat. I try to block out the droning noise, but there's nothing else beyond cement and manipulation. Not even the drip of a leaky faucet can be heard. This is one more way of slowly steering us toward the breaking point.

I always figured the documentaries were full of shit. This dose of reality is already proving just how wrong I was. They toy with us on purpose. Anything to strip away dignity and humanity. I'm already feeling the spiraling effects, their influence messing with my mind. The footsteps move closer and stop just outside my cell. A knife twists in my gut. Over this past week, I've learned these visits are never pleasant.

With a low buzz, the door to my cage opens and a guard appears. "Bowen."

I raise my head off the moldy pillow to get a better view. He stands in the threshold with his arms folded. I don't recognize this guy. His face is almost kind, which is some sort of trick. There are no niceties to be found within these four walls. Any semblance of good is a disguise. I'm bound to get the hidden pieces beaten out of me.

My mouth remains sealed. I refuse to give them any ammunition against me.

He rolls his eyes. "Someone's here to speak with your stubborn ass. Maybe you'll actually talk to her."

Her.

The suggestion is enough to get me moving. I heave myself off the lumpy mattress. I've been trapped in this box for seven long days. Any excuse to leave, even for a moment, is a blessing I won't refuse. The possibility of seeing Sutton would almost be too good.

He cuffs my wrists in front of me and motions to the left. "After you, inmate."

The guard escorts me down a dank hallway that reeks of mildew. The visitation room is straight ahead, a beacon of light in the sea of darkness. Will she be in there? I propel forward at a fast stride. The guard snorts while hustling to catch up. When he unlocks the door, I'm graced by the vision of my single best happy something.

Just the sight of Sutton has my blood pumping hotter. She's a splash of vibrant color against the dingy gray walls. Having her separated from me by plexiglass should be a crime. But she doesn't belong here at all. This type of ugly is far worse than anything we came across at the trailer park.

Her smile could flip the blackest of moods. I nearly trip in my haste to reach the sectioned off portion. The plastic chair creaks with my weight. When I pick up the phone, a tremor rattles the receiver.

"Gray." Her small palm rests on the bulletproof barrier. I lift my hand and align our fingers together.

"Damn, you're a fine sight."

"I miss you so much." Her bottom lip wobbles when she bites the corner. Tears already shine in her eyes.

I almost close mine to absorb her whimsical voice. Pretending we're secluded in our meadow is far more appealing. But I don't risk removing my gaze from her. "Don't cry, baby."

Sutton sniffs. "How can I not? You're stuck in here."

I want to comfort her, spout off half-truths that will provide a false sense of hope. Hell, I need to believe in something to survive this torture. This entire situation has been a cruel awakening. Having her near is already clearing the toxins being forced into me. She purges the venom of their lethal bite.

With a deep inhale, I dream of strawberries and freedom. What I wouldn't give to devour her fresh scent. All I get is stale smoke and foul sweat and crumbling sanity. My stomach lurches and I gag.

She leans forward. "Are you sick? What's wrong?"

Everything, I want to admit. What I really say is, "Just doing my best."

"I can't even fathom what you're dealing with. I'm so sorry."

I jerk backward in my seat. "What're you apologizing for?"

Her breathing is choppy. "They wouldn't let me see you until now. I tried, Gray. They forced me to wait until you were cleared for visitors. Whatever that means."

I smirk at her. "I had to earn this with good behavior. They hold everything against us."

"That sounds terrible."

I don't want to lie to her. "It's an adjustment. They study

us. New inmates are under observation. Gotta make sure I'm not a danger or liable to go off the rails. Guess this means I'm good to go."

"Are you suffering?" Her voice cracks and more rivulets drift down those smooth cheeks. I curl my fingers, wanting nothing more than to feel the heat of her skin beneath me.

"I'll adapt to this latest version of torment. Don't worry about me, Sutt."

She huffs into the phone. "That's impossible, especially when they're keeping us apart. Hopefully we're past all those hurdles. I was the squeakiest damn wheel. Pretty sure their front desk phone didn't stop ringing until they granted me permission. I'd camp out in the parking lot if that did us any good."

I crack a grin at her tenacity. "You're too much, beautiful. They're gonna kick you out."

Her gasp pierces my eardrum. "I dare them to try."

"So feisty," I growl.

Sutton gives me a long once-over. "I want to kiss you."

"I want a lot more than that."

"Is it weird that I find you ridiculously attractive right now? You're so hot, Gray."

I rub over my newly acquired beard. "You like the convict vibe? I wasn't sure if orange is my color."

Her forehead bunches, the flirty undertone between us vanishing in a snap. "Stop it."

"I'm being real, Sutt. This is my new normal."

"I refuse to accept that. Did you talk to a lawyer? My parents said they hired the best one for you. They wanted to come with me, but you were only approved for one visitor."

I drag a hand through my shaggy hair. "Yeah, he met with me after initial intake. He'll be back next week."

"Have you heard about a court date?"

"The attorney says it's best to drag out this limbo period

for the maximum allotted time. That way we build the strongest case for a plea deal. Thanks to Lance and his persuasion, there's no chance for bail. I could be a hazard to society." I hitch a thumb over my shoulder. "I'm trapped in the holding pen until trial."

"They don't care about your side of the story?"

I offer a shrug. "It's his word against mine. Who are they gonna believe?"

"How is that justice?"

"Flawed system, Sutt."

She flicks her gaze to the stained ceiling. "What happens to you after the official judge's hearing?"

"I'll stay in county jail until getting hauled off to state prison." I clench my jaw at those daunting options.

She flinches. "They can't send you there."

"They probably will, Sutt. That's a reality we need to discuss. I don't expect you to wait around—"

"You better stop that train of thought right now, Grady Bowen. We're going to fight this. You'll be free to go in a few days. You're getting out of here. We're getting you out, Gray," she repeats.

She shouldn't bother trying. None of them should. Why waste money and effort on me? But I know Sutton won't quit. Deep down in the pit of my sour gut I can admit I don't want her to. That doesn't mean I'm going to let her be shackled to me.

I breathe deep and get another punch of rotten odor. "What the fuck do you think I can offer after this? I have no damn free will. There's less than a thousand dollars in my bank account. I live in a money pit. What the hell kind of life will I lead for us, huh? A dead end, Sutt. I'm giving you an out. Be smart and take it."

"No."

"Wasn't a choice, baby."

"I'm not asking for one. There's never been one. I've never needed one. I certainly don't want one now."

"You need to be the one to walk away. I'm not strong enough, Sutt."

Her baby blues flash, all traces of sorrow gone. My girl is digging her heels in. "I'm not going anywhere."

I let my shoulders drop with a mixture of relief and shame. "All right, beautiful. Hang on for a long haul."

"I plan on it."

We exchange a silent stare for a moment. I can feel my reprieve with her running out. "Tell me a happy something, Sutt."

Her lashes flutter and she sucks in a quick breath. "That's kind of difficult at the moment."

"Please try for me," I murmur into the phone.

She swipes at a fat tear trailing down her cheek. "There was a meteor shower last night. I wished upon a shooting star."

Warmth spreads through my veins. "I bet it was a good one. Tell me another."

Sutton wrinkles her nose. "Bear has been very attached to me. I let him sleep on your side of the bed. But he drools."

A dry chuckle grates from me. "Lucky bastard. One more," I urge.

"I wrote you a letter. They wouldn't let me give it to you directly. Make sure a guard passes it along. There's plenty of happy in there." A flush rushes up her slender neck.

The prospect of her scrawled words gives me a little light in this black hole. "I will, baby."

"Not a moment goes by that I don't think of you. I'll love you forever plus infinity." She makes a sideways figure-eight with her fingers.

I trace the pattern through the air. "Even though I'm a convicted criminal?"

Her finger jabs at the clear divider. "You're not, Gray. This is all a huge mistake."

"What makes you so sure?"

"Because I know what's in your soul. Lance is a snake, but you wouldn't hurt him. Not without a damn good reason, like attacking me. I was safely inside."

I scrub over my weary eyes. "Yeah, that's a pretty big fucking issue."

She tucks the receiver tighter to her ear and lowers her voice. "Lance is accusing you of assault, Gray. Can you tell me what happened?"

I shake my head. "Nah, not like this. It's not safe. But make me a promise?"

"Anything."

A murky shadow falls over me. "Stay away from Morris. He's bad news. It drives me half-mad knowing he's on the loose and I'm not around to protect you. Be safe and smart, okay?"

"That goes without saying."

"I'm serious, Sutt. Don't put yourself in harm's way to defend my honor. Lance has zero limits. Don't test them by being a vigilante." I want to spill everything, but not in this public space. There are far too many prying ears who will put a bigger target on my back.

Sutton twists her mouth into an adorable pout. "You know me too well. But I can't just sit by and do nothing. You can't expect me to, Gray."

I'm about to respond when a guard approaches from behind me. This guy is one I try to avoid by all means necessary. He makes it his mission to ensure we're kept in line. His specialty is unethical punishments. "Time's up, Bowen. Let's go."

She yelps at his harsh tone. I glare up at him before stealing another slice of happy from her. "Love you, beautiful. Don't worry about me. Everything is gonna be okay."

"I love you—"

The guard clamps a meaty hand on my shirt and jerks me off the chair. The phone clatters out of my grip. "You're done, inmate."

Sutton bangs on the glass and my heart cracks from the impact. When I swing my gaze to her, everything goes dark. Streams of fresh tears pour down her face. She's on the verge of shouting at the man ripping me away.

"Leave him alone. He's innocent."

He laughs in my ear. "Quite the spitfire you've got there. I bet she's a tiger in the sack. Maybe I'll take her for a spin since you're out of commission."

Everything inside of me roars at his crude filth. A bellow rips from my throat. I want to smash my elbow into his nose. Instead of getting another sentence tacked on, I focus on my girl. She's sobbing and alone and I need to be better for her. I mouth the three little words she needs. Sutton returns my sentiment with a watery smile. She draws a line of X's and O's on the glass.

"How fucking cute," the guard spits. "Hold onto that image to get you off later."

I wrench out of his hold and continue stomping toward my dungeon.

His laugh bounces off the chipping walls. "Better watch yourself, inmate. I can make your stay here far more painful."

There isn't a single doubt in my mind that he'd follow through on his threat. That doesn't mean I'm going to kiss his degrading ass. I pause in the doorway and hold out my bound wrists.

"Maybe I should leave you cuffed. I have plenty of reason after that stunt. It's a precautionary measure, right?"

What I really want to do is demand Sutton's letter. But this asshole will only use that weakness against me. I remain silent, narrowing my eyes into thin slits.

The guard reflects my glare, adding a predatory snarl. "Maybe that lenient bitch Matthews has been too soft on you. Breaking you down will be fun, inmate. We'll start tomorrow so rest up." His rancid breath burns my nostril. "Get the fuck outta my sight."

He shoves me backwards into my cell and slams the door. The heavy steel slides shut with a whisper of dusty wind. There's no resounding clang of metal. No satisfying bang. Technology takes the fun out of it, unlike the movies. Maybe that's a win in my column. I certainly could use one.

That quiet hum of the lock system initiating is a nail in my coffin. I'm trapped with my hands securely fastened in front of me. Looks like I'm shit out of luck once again.

CHAPTER TWENTY-NINE

Sutton

*Happy something #187: Having a shoulder to
sob on uncontrollably.*

THE PORCH SWING TILTS UPWARD WITH A CREAK WHEN JACE straightens his knee. We hover at an angle on the bench before he lifts his foot. Our bodies rock on the wooden seat from the forward motion. Forth and back in a repeated glide. This is reminiscent of our youth, but there's no joy between us now. The usually comforting sway is flat and dull. Much like my mood.

I've lost count of how many monotonous cycles we've completed. Other than the squeak of rusting springs, our surroundings are quiet. Under different circumstances I could probably doze off. My parents' farm has a somber lull from missing a vital member. Not even the endlessly rolling acres or stunning cloudless sky holds appeal.

Another metallic grind interrupts the silence. Neither one of us seems to care about time ticking by without subsequent meaning. My mom and dad left for dinner an hour ago. They tried convincing us to join them. According to them, getting out of the house would be good for us. We had a different opinion. Jace and I pretended to be content eating cold turkey sandwiches. The truth is that we didn't bother making any. We're caught in a damn rut that only gets wider with no way out.

The cling of humidity is still sticky in the air. I have my legs tucked underneath me to ward off an internal chill. That cloying heat doesn't penetrate the frost that's burrowing into my bones. I better get used to the cold.

A shuddering sigh whisks from my lungs. I'm metaphorically teetering on the ledge of a steep cliff. One wrong move and I'll go tumbling down. It's impossible to focus on keeping myself stable. My mind is miles away in the county jail. There's no forgetting that specific type of horror.

I tried to force a brave face for Grady yesterday. On the inside I was crumbling faster than a tissue in the rain. He looked so defeated. The dark cavern in his green eyes made me shiver. I can't let him rot in that disgusting place. Our lack of options are making me sicker by the day. My wheels are spinning to the point of failure.

I can't take the silence another moment. "What're we gonna do, Ace?"

My brother drags his foot on the deck to pause our endless loop. "I dunno, Sutt."

I've asked a similar version of this question an infinite amount over the last eight days. Jace always gives a nearly identical response. Just one more way we're stuck. I press two fingers over my puffy eyes. "He's already changing from being in that awful place. We have to help him."

"I'm well aware. Too bad our hands are mostly tied."

"We need to try harder."

My brother groans and thumps the back of his head on the seat. "Don't you think I know that? We've been over this."

I tug on a snarl in my hair. "There has to be something we've missed. Can't we uncover a piece of clear evidence in his favor? Grady didn't have any blood under his nails or traces of Lance on him. How can they prove he hit him?"

His gives me a pitiful shrug. "They really can't. But no one else was around. It goes both ways. Assault is a fine line like that. All signs point to Grady being the guilty party."

A groan barrels out of me. "That's bullshit. There should be a more in-depth investigation before tossing someone in jail."

"I'm not disagreeing with you, Sutt. But think about how it looks to everyone from the outer edge. Lance comes across as an innocent police officer trying to keep the peace. This was another bar fight gone to the extreme. Grady is the brute bully throwing fists."

"Well, they're all morons with a skewed view. He's the greatest kind of man."

Jace nods and nudges my arm. "He truly is. It's a shame more don't see him that way." He clears his throat, avoiding eye contact. "I owe you an apology."

My thoughts reel on a zipline while I gape at him. My brother rarely admits to any sort of wrongdoing. "For what?"

"I've given you a lot of shit for dating Grady. That isn't fair. I should be more supportive. You're clearly meant to be with one another. So, I'm sorry for my shitty attitude."

My lashes stick together when I blink at him. I find myself at a loss for words. "O-okay."

His lips twitch ever so slightly. "I also need to say thanks."

A wrinkle pinches my brow. "For what?"

"Bringing my best friend back to life. He was lost without you. I didn't realize just how much until you came home. That dude brightens up whenever you're nearby." His smile tips a bit higher. "Grady really loves you, Sutt."

I feel the tremble start in my chin. The heat pinches my

eyes shortly after. Soon tears zigzag down my cheeks. I press a hand to my chest and check for a Grady-sized hole.

Jace's gaze snaps wide open. "Ah, hell. I didn't mean to make you cry."

I wrap my arms around him and sputter into his shoulder. "T-that is s-so sweet. Thank y-you, Jace. I needed to hear that."

"As if you didn't know," he murmurs into my hair.

"It's so hard being apart from him," I sob. "Everything seems so hopeless lately. I miss him so much."

"I guarantee he misses you more."

"We're supposed to be carrying out our happy something and making new ones. But he isn't here." I hiccup over a shuddering exhale.

He hugs me tighter. "A happy what?"

"It's special between us. Joyful moments."

"You're still doing those? I remember hearing a few when we were young."

"We never really stopped." At least our hearts didn't.

Jace forces out a dry chuckle. "Damn, you two are perfect."

"Thank you," I whisper.

"It's gonna be okay, Sutt. Life can't be this unjust."

I pull away from him, catching his stare. "You sure about that?"

His body deflates with a long sigh. "No, but I have faith. Something will give."

"Have you dug up any new info on Lance?"

He reclines on the swing, pushing off the ground so we begin rocking again. "Nah. The guy is definitely shady, but he covers his tracks well. A few friends on the force tell me he's an oddball and hard to work with. No one wants to patrol with him."

"Isn't that a red flag?"

"Not a big enough one. Do you recall anything else about when he was in school with you?"

I lay my cheek on an open palm. "It's tough to remember more and I don't know who to ask. All I'm certain of is his family moved to Silo Springs our freshman year. He didn't stand out in the crowd. I never noticed him."

"Maybe that's part of the problem," he mutters.

"What do you mean?"

"I've been hearing he's rather obsessed with you, Sutt."

I glare across the yard at a wide expanse of nothing. "That's what people keep telling me."

Jace grunts. "Yeah, exactly. It probably didn't help his delusions when you wouldn't give him the time of day. Who the hell knows. That's a wild assumption."

Blame rests heavy on my shoulders. "This is probably all my fault. Grady was on his radar because of me."

He shakes his head. "No, that's not true. Lance was picking on Grady when you were off at college."

"Yeah, after I ignored him all four years of high school. What can I do about it now?"

"Have you talked to Molly? Maybe she's privy to something useful."

I yank at the collar of my shirt, a creeping sensation prodding at me. "They broke up. I think it was his doing. She doesn't seem too bent out of shape, but also didn't want to discuss it."

He blows out all the air trapped in his cheeks. "Damn. There goes that lead."

"Should I try talking to him?"

Jace jerks his startled gaze to mine. "No. Absolutely not. It's too dangerous."

"But what if he tells me the truth? I can save Grady."

"At what cost, Sutt? I can't let you dive into this shitfest headfirst. We'll think of something else. Be smart and safe."

Grady's warnings come screeching to the surface. Another bout of searing pressure squeezes my eyes and I look away. My brother notices.

"What's wrong?"

I wipe my face against my bent knees. "Grady told me the same thing."

He smirks. "Because he's looking out for you. I'm not surprised in the slightest. Even locked up, he's watching your back."

"I want to return the favor."

"Then stay out of trouble. For all our sakes."

My empty stomach gurgles, choking on acid and cracking dreams. "Easier said than done, Ace."

He bumps into me. "I mean it, little sister. We all want Grady to be set free. Don't do anything to jeopardize yourself for when that happens."

I hunch lower in the seat and roll my eyes. "Fine, I'll just sit idly by and wait for my boyfriend to get magically released."

Jace snorts over a laugh. "And I almost believe you. Listen, I'm going to trap that bastard in his lie. He's bound to squeal at some point, right?"

"Who knows how long that could take. Grady might be serving a twelve-month sentence by then."

"It would be a lot easier to wring Lance's neck until he spills the truth. But we know how that'll end."

"Unfortunately. Please don't get yourself arrested. I can't fight this without you."

He ruffles my hair. "Likewise, Sutt. Let's leave physical violence out of the equation. When can you visit Grady again? We need to get his full story."

Ash forms on my tongue. "Next Sunday."

My brother whistles. "Damn, that's ruthless. He only gets to see you once a week?"

"Don't remind me."

We settle into a beat of silence and a blanket of numb envelops me. I welcome the reprieve for a few moments. It doesn't last more than a handful of seconds. Thankfully I'm distracted by a flurry of movement in front of us.

Bear scampers across the yard, probably chasing a stray cat. It's good to see him running around instead of staring down the empty driveway, waiting for his best friend to come home. I brought him along so he wasn't alone. He makes me feel like a piece of Grady is with us.

"He's a really great dog." Jace leans forward and calls to him. Bear bounds over with a trail of drool dangling from his mouth. I cringe and cross my fingers that the slobber disappears. My brother doesn't seem to mind, scratching under his jaw and ears. Bear shuffles closer and practically climbs into his lap.

Jace chuckles. "Grady isn't the only one you're changing."

"What do you mean?"

"This pooch had a serious vendetta against me. He's never been my biggest fan, but you're softening him up."

A twinge of glee tickles my gut. "That's a nice sentiment. Pretty sure he's just lonely."

"Nah, he's becoming a lover. Just like his owner."

I fan at my eyes, refusing to cry for a third time. "Dammit, Jace. Stop being so sweet."

"Quit being so emotional," he shoots back.

"I have a decent excuse."

"Yeah, you're off the hook. Sob away. I'll loan you my shoulder." He continues petting Bear, who rolls over and offers his belly for a rub. My brother doesn't hesitate and lavishes the dog with attention. We're all a bunch of blubbering softies.

And on that note.

I reach for my favorite uplifting romance that's reliably

waiting on an end table. Best Laid Plans by LK Farlow always hits me right in the feels. Even on my lowest days, I can count on her words to bring me back to the surface. Maybe getting lost in the pages will help me figure out a stellar plan of my own.

Lord only knows what kind of miracle we need to get Grady out of this mess.

CHAPTER THIRTY

Grady

Happy something #97: Waking up with the sunshine warming my face.

I PACE THE SHORT LENGTH OF MY CELL, A CAGED LION PREPARING for an attack. Seconds bleed into minutes with the pounding of my shoes. Only silence greets me. Slapping footsteps along the linoleum hall never come. Doors remain firmly locked. No one travels in or out of this wing. The guards are avoiding me on purpose. Their new game is to keep me waiting until I snap. That fragile hold I maintain on my control is beginning to fray.

The forced isolation is getting to me, chipping away at my sanity. I can't fucking handle this version of persecution. Keeping my wrists cuffed for over twelve hours was only the beginning. The skin is still raw days later, but I barely notice. Not while they ramp up the cruelty when I refuse to bend. I'm not a docile inmate they can boss around. That doesn't stop them from trying.

Life wasn't supposed to smash against rock bottom after Sutton returned from college. We were doing everything right, and finally starting our forever together. But she's being kept away from me on purpose. It's not too shocking considering the shit I'm always being dealt. I'm capable of handling their hate. Dragging Sutton into the depths of hell is what fractures the reconstructed fissures in my heart.

I've never needed a happy something more than this moment. She graciously penned me one, but these bastards are still holding it as ransom for my soul. The guards must take courses on doling out torture in its most wicked form.

They've already taunted me this morning. Grousse—the worst of them all—waved my salvation in front of the window as he strolled by. My name printed in her neat script was barely legible through the grimy glass. All I'm able to imagine is their greasy fingerprints tainting her pristine intentions. I'd felt the shift inside of me. They stole another piece of my soul. My spirit is tainted. My ego is battered. I'm whipped and beaten, but not broken. There's still some pride left in me. The black abyss is beckoning me in with open arms. My defenses are splintering further with every nasty word spat at me.

It's been three damn days. Seventy-two hours they've held her words from me. They've tried to make me surrender. The letter is a reward only a trained puppet shall receive. But those pages belong to me. Sutton is mine, dammit.

I'm almost convinced my ears are playing tricks when a low whistle kicks up beyond my walls. The shallow clip of steel-toed boots soon follows. In the next instant, I'm at the door with my palms pressed flat against the metal. My desperation is pitiful, but I could give half a shit. Let them laugh at my barking demands. It won't change the outcome. That doesn't stop me from trying.

When Matthews comes into view, I almost crash to my knees. He's my best chance. "Hey, Lush."

His feet stumble to a halt. He pins me with a glare. "You know better than to use that nickname."

I swallow a humble dose of defeat and try again. "Sorry, C.O. My bad."

Matthews turns to face me straight on. "That's more like it. How's the afternoon treating you?"

Good to know it's past lunch. They haven't given me anything to eat since that moldy bagel earlier. "Like shit. Haven't seen the sun in over a week."

His expression remains flat. "Should've thought things through before breaking the law."

I snap my fingers. "Aww, shucks. Guess it sucks to be me since I'm innocent."

Matthews cocks his head back and belts out a hoot. "Yeah, haven't heard that a time or two. Oh, wait. I have. You and every other con on this block babble the same bullshit. Save it, Bowen."

"I don't fucking belong here," I spit against the scratched window between us.

"You think being holed up at county is bad? Just wait until you're shipped off to state. Then you'll be wishing things were different."

Was he for real right now? None of this was okay. I'm falsely accused of bogus charges. "They have no evidence," I argue.

He salutes at me. "Keep telling yourself that. There's no disputing your crime. Take a plea. Serve your time. Walk away a free man."

As if it's that easy. I grunt, done with this pointless conversation. "You have something for me?"

He makes a show of patting his pockets. "Nope. Grousse is still whacking off to your girl's dirty mouth. She's a keeper, Bowen."

A prisoner isn't afforded privacy. There's no such thing

as violating my rights because I don't have any. Even the most basic and bare have been stripped from me. I didn't do a damn thing wrong. There was no crime committed to land my ass in here. Not by my hand, at least. It would be easy to lose my shit and go nuclear. But it won't change my fate. I won't stoop to their level.

I grind my molars until a filling threatens to crack. "Give me my damn letter."

He chokes out a laugh. "Excuse me?"

"You heard me."

"Wanna spend a night in solitary, inmate?"

His threat of the SHU doesn't scare me. Anyone else touching Sutton's words is enough to release a savage beast inside of me. But ripping his throat out won't grant me any favors. I choose to stay silent.

He raises a brow at me. "Good choice. Being a nasty fuck to the guards in this joint won't grant you any favors."

I sneer at him. "What the fuck does it matter? I'm already considered guilty before my trial has been set."

"You wanna be locked up longer? Fine, be my guest. Cock off to whoever the hell you want."

Was he helping me? Or setting a trap? I couldn't be too sure anymore. My head has been in a fog since Lance cornered me and punched himself. I'm snapped out of it by the sweetest sound this place offers.

That creaking slide of metal usually signals chow time. I couldn't care less about food. Pavlov and his dog would be salivating. He tosses my lifeline through the narrow slot. "It's your lucky day, inmate. Turns out someone on the outside is pulling strings for your ass. The warden gave us strict instructions to quit dicking you around."

I snag the envelope before it drops to the filthy floor. The seal has been torn open, but that doesn't surprise me. I doubt any mail passes through here without a thorough inspection.

"You're welcome," he mutters.

All I offer him is a flick of my injured wrist. His poison can't touch me now. It's not like he gained a sudden soft spot and decided to throw me a bone. He can piss off. After a couple of colorful curses, Matthews leaves me alone.

I trace my name in Sutton's bold writing, getting a direct hit of warmth injected into my veins. The urgency to be near her trembles my fingers. I almost rip the thin sheets in my haste. A burst of sweet summer flowers and a mixture of my favorite fruits waft off the paper. I almost groan while burying my nose in the open pages. Damn, I miss her.

A pang reverberates across my ribs with a shallow breath. She scrawled my name in a ridiculous loopy style along the top. The sight makes me grin. My girl put some effort into this note. I enjoy another deep inhale and let her voice play in my head.

Hey, Gray.

I wish my first officially delivered love letter to you arrived under different circumstances. Yeah, that's right. There's been at least a hundred scribbled confessions of my undying devotion prior to this. I think they're all stored in a box at my parents' place if you're ever interested. I was too chicken to admit that until now. No more secrets. I've always been crazy in love with you, Grady Bowen.

But I digress.

Remember when we first met? I'll never forget a single second of that night. You looked so lost and sad. All I wanted was to hug you. That's all I want to do now, Gray. I want to wrap my arms around you and say everything will be okay. It has to be. I refuse to believe otherwise.

I'd love to wave a magic wand and make all of this disappear. You could never do what they're accusing you of. It isn't fair that you're paying a price for nothing. I guess life isn't really fair. All of the hardships you've faced are proof of that. I'd take it all away for you. That could be one of my greatest wishes. You could live a life full of flowers and rainbows and peace without an ounce of suffering. Can you imagine the beauty?

Maybe we wouldn't have crossed paths then. You wouldn't have needed me, or my family. I guess we weren't meant to have it so simple.

I can only hope you aren't being treated poorly. But it's jail. How good can I expect it to be? Should I assume the worst? That hurts my soul. I can't picture you behind bars. Let's pretend you're lying next to me, okay? Close your eyes right now and reach for me across the mattress. Do you feel me?

I wish that were real.

I'm missing you like crazy.

Oh, Gray. You've saved me so many times. I need to do the same for you. Think of our happy somethings. That first one all those years ago. We were going to count stars until falling asleep and dreaming of flying. You always soar, Grady. And that's not all. I've been spreading dandelion seeds with so many wishes. My dad is going to be so mad next year when a fresh round of weeds sprout up. I've lost count of how many. And I'm far from done because you know what? We're only just beginning. Our hope and love will be blanketing the meadow more than ever.

I'm trying to stay positive. I'm still trying to figure out how this happened. You must feel so betrayed. It's hard to imagine someone being so vindictive. Maybe it's better that I don't.

This won't beat you, Gray. Don't let them shove you down. Keep your head up. I'm in your heart and mind, baby. Don't lose the light. The darkest days cannot keep us apart. Remember the love we create. Hold onto the warmth. Never lose sight of what's just beyond reach.

I feel like I've just rambled on for three pages without any structure. But that's my new normal. I'm wandering around without any sense of where to go. You're my compass, a lighthouse in the dark sea, the only correct turn while speeding in the opposite direction. I truly am lost without you.

Come back to me, okay? In a day or two weeks or three months. Just please come back. I can't smile without you. Breathing is a chore. Forget about sleeping. See? I'm a mess. But I'll be strong for you. That's a promise.

I love you, Grady Bowen.

I. Love. You.

Then, now, and tomorrow. Never without a moment.

Until I see you in my dreams.

XOXOXOXO

Sutt

P.S. This is a little something just between us. Use your imagination.

Her kiss is a bright red stamp in the bottom corner. The imprint is sticky to the touch. I can clearly picture her lips on mine. Just like her words are whispering in my ear. The second read through is better than the first. But after a third and fourth round, the darkness creeps into the edges of my vision. When will I see her again? It will be months before I can even hold her hand. The thought is enough to drown Sutton's message down the drain.

I crumple onto the dingy floor, slamming my back against the wall. Tears erupt from the very depths of me. I can't dredge up the sheer might to stop. Crying in jail is a death sentence, but I'm already dying.

CHAPTER THIRTY-ONE

Sutton

Happy something #139: Dancing as if no one is watching.

NEED TO GET OUT OF SILO SPRINGS FOR THE NIGHT, OR AT LEAST a few hours. Harlyn agreed to meet me at some sports pub off the freeway. Foster told us they have great burgers. I couldn't care less about dinner. The escape is what I need. Almost an hour from home should do the trick.

That's how I find myself pulling into Mad Jax on a Thursday night. The parking lot is mostly packed, but I find a spot in the middle row. I slink out of the low seater with a stretch. The long drive rammed a kink in the center of my neck. A quick roll of my shoulders alleviates a bit of the pinch.

The sun is just beginning to set, casting off shades of purple and pink across the sky. I strut across the pavement in my favorite wedge sandals. My simple tee and shorts will blend into any background. I'll be another face in the crowd. Not the sad girl whose boyfriend got locked up. Tonight I can pretend everything is back to normal, especially with my bestie in tow.

I walk into the entrance with my chin tipped high. This will be a fun night out of the house. If I keep repeating that, maybe it will come true. I'm looking around for a place to sit when I hear him. My startled gaze snaps toward the muffled tone.

Lance Fucking Morris.

What the hell is he doing out here? And what are the damn chances? Pretty effing slim on a bad day. This must be the bottom of luck barrel. I drag in a slow breath, fried food and popcorn heavy in the air. Jace and Grady simultaneously scold me—in my mind.

Smart and safe.

I whip out my phone and search for other bars in the area. After a quick scan, I click on the closest one. Looks decent enough. I open my messages and get typing.

Me: Last second change of plans. Let's meet at Hal's off Exit 54.

I tap my shoe on the sticky floor while waiting for the three little dots to appear. Thirty seconds later and nothing. I belatedly realize she's probably well on her way. Calling her from the car will be far more effective.

I'm preparing to turn and leave, but Lance's slurring words stop me in my tracks. The sight of him makes putrid acid roil in my belly. He's propped up on a corner stool and appears seven sheets to the wind. No one else is sitting nearby. Even strangers can sniff out a wolf in sheep's clothing.

He holds up a bottle, swinging the beer in a wide arc. "Sutton is meant for me. That girl might as well have my last name tattooed on her ass." His shoulders shake with a silent laugh. "Wouldn't that be a sight? I'd love to see the look on her precious boyfriend's face. He'd deserve to witness that permanent display."

My thoughts are a catastrophic hurricane swooping down to wreak havoc. I want to storm over and rain a wrath of fury upon him. But he seems to be brewing up his side of the travesty without my intervention.

Lance squints into the distance, or maybe he's attempting to focus on something specific. It's almost impossible to tell. "That asshole was supposed to skip town after his mother died. He hates Silo Springs and all the people in it. Well, almost everyone. I was certain he'd be long gone before she moved home. He could've avoided jail, but no."

Who the hell is he talking to?

I inch toward a booth across from him, remaining hidden in the shadows. Lance doesn't notice me in his inebriated state. I hunch low in the seat and settle in for his production.

He guzzles half his drink, not that he needs more booze. "I'd been planning it for a month. Just needed the right moment, you know? The opportunity fell right into my lap."

Holy shit, he's bragging. Is this actually happening? It might be worthless, but I'm not taking any chances.

I scramble to reach my phone. After opening the camera app, I set it to record. I hold the screen out and up until his sloppy face comes into view.

Lance burps and almost falls off his stool. "It's one of my best ideas yet. I watched him all night. The bastard barely left her side. But he finally did and I followed him into the alley."

Oh my gosh, poor Grady. He had no warning that Lance was coming for him. None of us would've pegged this drunk doofus as a conniving villain. I glance around the buzzing space with wide eyes. My pulse rivals a raging thunderstorm. Even now, no one is suspecting a thing.

He slams the empty bottle down and signals for another. The bartender shakes his head. Lance spreads his arms out wide. "What's the problem? Are you taking his side? Everyone loves that cocky asshole. Did he tell you to cut me off?" He wags a sloppy finger at his newfound audience. "That's not possible. He can't tattletale from where I sent him."

The other guy rolls his eyes and walks away. Smart man.

It's nearly impossible to sit back and listen to him rave about this horrific accomplishment. I scratch at my crawling skin. The urge to vomit tickles my tonsils. I wrestle with instinct and exhale through the nausea.

What is Lance doing unloading all this? The possibility that he's feeling guilty is more insane than the man himself. His confession is purely selfish boasting. He's probably scouting out his next victim. An eerie chill prickles at me. This is the end of all that.

"What makes him so damn special? He's trailer park trash. His entire life has been one disaster after another. She should be with someone on her level. That's how it always should've been. But she looks at him like he hung all the stars in the universe just for her."

I want to smack his forehead and yell, *"News flash, Lance. Get a damn clue."* He'll never be able to see the truth. His vision is clouded by his own ego. Grady is a million times better than any man he could hope to be.

"So, yeah, he had to go. And I finally got my chance to make it happen." He makes a walking motion with his fingers.

If I didn't know how this ends, his story would be a huge clusterfuck. Maybe that's why it appears no one is listening to his belligerent confession. That probably gives him a false sense of security. Is he stupid? I snort at that. The answer is directly in front of me, swaying on his seat. I suppose it's hard keeping this type of fool-proof plan to himself. Such a moron.

Too bad, Lance. I stumbled into the same bar.

He continues prattling on without a care in the world. "I struck up a pleasant conversation with him at first. Didn't want to seem suspicious right off the bat, you know? But then I provoked him. Talking about her really pissed him off. He still held back, though. The noble guy didn't take my bait. I prepared for that."

Lance makes a spectacle of pretending to punch himself in the nose. I slap a palm over my mouth to trap my scream. This dude is straight up crazy. I gag when a loud belch rips from his throat.

"Poor bastard never saw it coming. He just stood there with his life vanishing in front of him. I stole at least a year from him. Maybe more. I did hit myself twice just to make it look extra bad. It's almost a guarantee they'll be putting him away longer."

He sighs and slumps lower in his seat. "The entire reason I needed him gone was for a girl. She won't even talk to me. But she'll come around. I love her. Doesn't she want to be happy with me? Doesn't matter. We're gonna get married."

Over my dead body.

I cough into my fist as tears begin welling. Grady is locked up while this man is roaming free. Talk about abusing the system. But justice is about to be served.

The phone trembles in my hand as I switch off the camera. I've seen plenty to put him away and clear Grady's name. My sandals thud on the tile floor as I haul ass out of this joint. I'm not running the risk of that lunatic catching me.

Once I'm outside, the realization of what this means really dawns on me. My knees knock together and I stumble over the curb. Grady will get to prove his innocence. He'll be released. His redemption will be the sweetest reward.

I almost drop my cell in the bubbling rush to find our police station's number. The line rings twice before he answers.

"This is Chief Wilson speaking."

"Hi, uh, sir. This is Sutton Olsen." I grind the tremor from my voice. "I have something you need to see. Immediately."

CHAPTER THIRTY-TWO

Grady

Happy something #60: Unexplainable miracles.

THE ELECTRIC HUM OF THE LOCKS DISENGAGING WAKE ME from a fitful doze. I'd finally managed to drift off, but that sound is more effective than any alarm. My system reboots and snaps alert as if a cold bucket of water has been dumped all over me. This is most likely one of their non-mandatory cell inspections. I don't bother lifting my head off the disintegrating pillow.

Matthews strides in and kicks the bed frame. "Get up, inmate."

Pretty sure it's barely morning. This has to violate some sort of protocol. I remain slack on the mattress. "I'm sleeping."

He makes the sound of a buzzard. "Wrong. You're leaving."

That gets a rise out of me. I sit up and nearly knock my skull on the top bunk. "What the hell do you mean? Trial isn't for another two weeks."

Matthews hitches a thumb over his shoulder. "You're getting out, dumbass. Get your ass up and get a move on. You're burning daylight."

I glare at him. "Is this some sort of sick joke?"

"Even we don't stoop that low, Bowen. New evidence came in and cleared your name. You're a free man."

I want to holler and scream, thank whatever lucky stars graced me with the light. But the thing I want most is a hug from my girl. My legs are unsteady when I stand. The relief is sinking straight to my marrow.

"Grab your shit."

"Don't have any." Except Sutton's letter, which is securely tucked into my waistband. This asshole will never get his paws on what's mine again.

"Even better." He moves out of the doorway and motions me forward.

I've never sprinted so fast in my adult life.

"Damn fool," Matthews mutters behind me. "Walk, don't run."

All I do is wave and keep moving toward the first checkpoint.

Being released from county jail is a zero frills affair. I'm shuffled from one station to the next as guards review different procedures and discharge orders. They hand over the clothes I was wearing when arrested. A pair of faded jeans and a white T-shirt has never looked so inviting. I strip off the orange jumpsuit, shedding that disgusting layer of skin never to be seen again. A glance in the smudged mirror shows a man I almost recognize.

Maybe this version will be better than the last.

I'm bouncing on my toes while waiting to pass through the security scanner. A guard manning the entrance gives me a bag of my personal belongings. I palm my phone, powering the device on. Score for me when the screen flashes to life.

"Is someone picking you up?"

I lift my gaze to the guard. A furrow dents my brow. "Not sure. This wasn't planned."

She scoffs. "Is it ever?"

"Good point." I check the time. It's just past seven. "There's someone I can call."

I dial Sutton's number. After five rings, her voicemail picks up. I try again and get the same result. Might as well add a text to my plea.

Me: You're never going to believe this, Sutt. They let me go. I'm free. Are you around?

The plastic rattles in my hand while I wait for a response. Nothing pops up.

The guard must notice a frown drooping my expression. "No answer?"

"Nah, but I'll keep trying."

"You can always get an Uber."

My gut tightens. How low have I dropped? That sounds miserable, but it might be my fastest option. "I'll give her a few more minutes."

"Suit yourself. Exit is dead ahead. Can't miss the sign." She points forward. "And make sure we don't see you back."

I almost chuckle. "Definitely not."

An invisible barrier appears in front of me. Less than fifty yards to freedom. The urge to pinch myself suddenly prods at me. The possibility of this rescue being real hasn't quite settled in. I flick my eyes around the room, waiting for someone to drag me under. Only a few random visitors speckle the space.

"What are you waiting for? Off you go," the guard mutters.

There's no escort in sight as I shuffle toward the door.

Pounding footsteps don't follow me. The strain that's been holding my muscles hostage evaporates. I stride out of the front gate with a clear conscience.

The harsh morning sun stings my eyes. I revel in the burn. A splash of vibrant color rushes toward me from the side, a high-pitched whine hammering into my ears. I pivot on my heel just in time to watch Sutton racing at full speed. In the next instant, she launches herself into the air with me as her direct target.

I catch her easily in my arms, gripping with every fiber inside of me. She latches on with an equal amount of force, my missing piece sliding into place.

I breathe her in, filling my lungs with a fresh dose of everything good. A moan vibrates off me and swirls around her. We're a spinning mass of clasping fingers and desperate babbling.

Sutton clings to me with the strength of a world champion wrestler. I wheeze, her hold bordering on choking, but press further into the embrace. A furnace of heat spreads throughout my chest. The massive knot in my throat follows right behind.

She peppers kisses all over my face. Eventually she finds my lips, locking us together with a searing brand of passion. Once again, we're bonded for life. Sutton begins sobbing, her body trembling against mine. Her tears soak into my shirt. I absorb the moisture into my neglected soul.

I spear into her hair, the silky strands sliding through my fingers. "Hey, hey. It's all right now."

She shakes her head. "Oh my gosh, Gray. I can't believe it. You're out. We're together."

I tilt her chin up until she's looking at me. "How'd you know?"

A wobble twitches the corners of her mouth. "Lance confessed. Not on purpose, or willingly. But that doesn't matter. I caught his lying ass on camera."

My grip on her tightens several more degrees. "When?"

"Last night. I caught the whole thing on video."

I flare my nostrils. "That sounds dangerous and reckless, Sutt."

"But it wasn't."

A vein in my temple throbs. "Sutton Rose, how is that staying smart and safe?"

She rolls those stunning baby blues. "It wasn't on purpose. I didn't follow him there or anything. Although he accused me of that after the fact." She huffs. "That's beside the point."

"You're gonna need to be far more specific."

"Don't worry, okay? I was very safe and smart. Lance was at a bar in Acklyn—"

"What were you doing way out there?"

Sutton presses a finger to my lips. "Shh, let me finish. I needed out of Silo Springs for a night. A little space from the shadowed stares and forced condolences. Bumping into Lance was a total accident. He was the last person I ever wanted to see. But it turned out to be a seriously crazy amazing coincidence. He blabbed his entire diabolical plan, from start to finish. I heard the entire thing."

I swallow the bellow clawing up my windpipe and focus on the good. "I want to hear everything, beautiful. Keep talking to me. Your voice is a choir of singing angels. This is like walking through the gates of heaven."

She giggles. "I think you're delusional."

"Wouldn't surprise me." I stroke a thumb across her damp cheek. "Tell me all of it."

And she does. Sutton pours out every disturbing detail. I do my best to tame the rage roaring inside of me while she recounts his purge. She finishes with a massive exhale, as if the weight has vanished off her chest. I know the feeling well.

I press my lips to her forehead. "Damn. Where is he now?"

She shrugs into me. "Hell if I care. Chief Wilson assured me Lance would no longer be a concern. He's supposed to call you later."

"Me?"

"Yup. Clear the air and all that."

I scrub the back of my neck. "Wow, that's heavy."

Sutton nuzzles against my throat. "You were wrongfully accused, Gray. The city has some apologizing to do."

"It's not their fault Lance is insane."

"True, but they hired him."

"Speaking of, how'd that fly?"

"Turns out Lance's parents have been hiding his illness for over a decade. He's very mentally unstable. The records are sealed tight and buried deep. That's why he had no trouble becoming a cop. He appeared squeaky clean."

Another load of kindling doused in gasoline gets thrown on the fire in my gut. "What a rat."

She nods. "The worst kind."

I cool the flames in my blood with a quick drink off her lips. "I'm so thankful for you, Sutt."

She blinks up at me. "So, you're not upset?"

I lift a brow. "How could I be?"

"Maybe I stepped a tad out of bounds?"

That earns her a chuckle, the first genuine one in almost two weeks. "I love you so damn much, Sutt."

Her sigh says it all. "Love you, Gray. I can't even describe how much. It's beyond reason."

"Marry me," I blurt. The question has been on my mind, but I didn't plan to ask in this moment. Maybe it was meant to happen here, releasing inhibitions and setting my intention free. Nothing has ever felt so... us.

Sutton's blue gaze snaps wide open. "W-what?"

I kiss her parted mouth and smile against my greatest gift. My words are shared between us. "I just survived ten days in the bowels of hell. That place is meant to break a man. But I'm looking forward, at you and us and everything we're meant for. We're destined for only good so long as we're one."

Her lashes flutter against my cheek. I release a groan at the slightest touch from her. Our future carves a path in my mind, certain and sure. "Be my wife. Agree to be my one and only happy something, forever plus a day. Life has taught me some harsh as fuck lessons, Sutt. Reality is unpredictable and fickle and cruel. I want us to live in the stars. You're my dream. Be my fantasy for always. I'm not taking more risks where we're concerned. I want you tied to me, irrevocably and always. Promise to be mine for the rest of our lives. Please make me the luckiest man to walk this jaded earth."

Her eyes mist with a fresh wave of tears. "Y-yes. Of course, I'll marry you."

I rub over the third finger on her left hand, bare and missing an essential symbol. "I don't have your ring with me."

She lets her jaw hang open. "You bought me a ring?"

"Course, baby. Remember the day I woke up with you lying next to me?"

"How could I forget?"

I brush my nose along hers. "Now you really won't."

Sutton nods in the general direction of her car. "Let's go home."

"Someone's in a sudden hurry," I laugh. "Are you aching?"

She rocks her hips into mine. "Yes, so much. Aren't you?"

"Hell yes. I need to shower and make love to my fiancée, not necessarily in that order."

"Well," she bites her lip, "good thing we discovered both of those can be done at once."

I kiss her again, longer this time. My tongue drags across

the seam of her mouth until she opens for me. We share a groan, hands fisting any fabric within reach. I pull away before things get out of control in the jail parking lot.

"Damn, I missed you," I whisper.

Her eyes are bedroom heavy and reflect the desire burning through me. "Show me how much?"

"I gladly will. Each day for the rest of mine."

CHAPTER THIRTY—THREE

Grady

Happy something #2: Sutton Rose Olsen.

I SCRUB A TOWEL OVER MY WET HAIR AND TURN TOWARD SUTTON. There's pure fire in her tropical blue eyes. I've missed that fierce desire over the last ten days. But I'm home and we're together. We'll never be apart that long again.

She's perched so pretty on the edge of our bed. A slinky white dress covers her slim figure, but I'm acutely aware of the seductive curves hidden underneath. I lick my lips with a slow glide. Her taste still lingers there. My mouth waters for another shot of that tangy flavor.

I prowl closer, wearing nothing except a pair of black boxer briefs. "Why'd you bother getting dressed?"

Sutton's gaze devours me. She doesn't bother hiding the appraisal. I flex my muscles for her benefit. My upper body is more defined due to vigorous hours in the county gym. Jail only offers a few options for recreation. At least this gets my girl more hot and bothered, if that's even possible.

When only a mere foot separates us, she walks her toes

up my bare legs. Her voice is all smoke and filthy promises about to be fulfilled. "What should we do today?"

I grab her ankle and kiss along the delicate bone. "I have several ideas. All of them involve you and this bed."

Sutton scoots closer to the edge of our mattress. "Oh? Just this room?"

"For starters." I ghost my lips up her smooth calf.

"Well, I have something in mind."

I reach the sensitive skin behind her knee. "Whatever it is can wait."

"This is a surprise."

Every part of my body visibly tenses. "Sutt, I've had my fill of the unexpected."

"This is a good one. I promise. Think of it as a celebration." She holds up her left hand. Her engagement ring catches the light, nearly blinding me with all that sparkle.

Good. I smirk at her showing off the bling. It'll be easy for everyone to see.

She wiggles her finger. The sapphire and diamonds glitter with her waving motion.

"Damn, you're a sexy fiancée."

She snaps the elastic at my waist. "And all yours."

I tower over her. "Remind me why we aren't naked?"

A sigh eases off her thoroughly-kissed pout. "I'm beginning to regret my other plans."

"Can we reschedule?"

She gives a slow toss of her hair. "Nope, not a chance. We'll return to this exact position in a few hours."

"And naked?"

Sutton laughs. "Very much so."

"Okay," I grumble. "I guess we have a deal."

"You'll enjoy this. It might take your mind off stripping me bare."

"I highly doubt that, but if you say so." I stride to my

closet, throwing on the first pair of jeans from my shelf. A white tee gets tugged over my head and I'm set.

I follow Sutton down the stairs, enjoying the view of her ass swaying in the slinky fabric. She switches off lights along the way, locking the door behind us. Next she releases Bear into his outdoor kennel.

"You've established a routine in my absence."

Her smile is a bit sad and I want to punch myself for bringing it up. "Kind of had to."

I thread our fingers together, kissing each of her knuckles. "I'm sorry, baby."

"There is absolutely nothing for you to apologize for. And we're all good now. Let's never go back to being apart."

"Couldn't agree more." I guide her toward the garage to get my bike. Sutton begins tugging me in the opposite direction. I pause my route and glance over at her. "Uh, what's up, Sutt? What are you doing?"

"Walking to my car. How about you?"

"Figured we could take the Harley."

She quirks a brow at me. "But it won't be a very good surprise if you know where we are going."

I already agreed to this so she's got me there. Relenting is inevitable. I allow her to drag me to the small coupe, squeezing my tall frame into the passenger seat. My knees bang into the dashboard and I bite off a curse.

Sutton cringes. "Sorry. We'll take the bike next time. And from then on if you want."

I wink at her. "Freedom on the road."

"And this is the opposite. You probably need the feeling of no barriers right now."

"Worth it, baby. I don't mind being cramped into a small space with you."

Her whimsy sigh soothes my hard edges, securing me around her pinkie. "You always say the perfect thing, Gray."

"Only the best for my girl. No bounds on our love, baby."

She fans herself with an open palm. "Swoon alert. You're straight out of a romance novel."

"But better?"

"So much."

Ten minutes is all it takes for us to reach the main drag of Silo Springs. My eyes are focusing out the window, watching the buildings pass. I assume we're having dinner at one of the few restaurants in town. But Sutton pulls over and parks in front of the very last place I ever imagined.

I do a double-take at the name, not computing how this adds up. A row of motorcycles decorate the designated area out front. I blink at the yellow and blue neon sign. Howlers is blinking bold and proud. I peer at Sutton from the corner of my eye. She's beaming at me, her expression about to burst with joy.

"Uh, is this my surprise?" I point to my old stomping ground.

She nods and steeples two fingers under her chin. "Yep. Let's go inside."

When we step through the entrance, an eruption of cheers and applause rings out. I almost topple backwards onto my ass. It appears more than half the residents of Silo Springs are packed inside this dingy space.

"What's everyone doing here?" I can hardly hear over the pounding parade of my pulse.

Sutton bumps her hip into me. "To celebrate, of course."

I scrub over rae prickle on my scalp. "How could they already know about our engagement?"

"They're here for you, silly. We all wanted to celebrate *you*."

"All of this is... for me?" I almost don't get the question out of my clogging throat.

She loops an arm around me, leaning her head on my arm. "Yes, baby. Everyone wanted to see you."

Barry, Alice, and Jace are the first to approach us. They don't bother asking before wrapping me up in a group hug. I return the affection without hesitation. These are my people. They're always here for me.

We find an open spot at the bar and settle in. The stools are more uncomfortable than ever. Familiar groans from worn leather paired with squeaks of rusting metal greet me.

Alice hugs me again. "I'm so glad we caught him. That man needs to pay for framing you."

A black shadow passes over my vision thinking of Lance and his attempt at ruining my life. I crack my neck, grinding all consideration of him into the stained ground. "Sounds like he will," I mutter.

"Mom," Sutton interrupts. She shoves her left hand under Alice's nose. Her mother gasps.

"Is that what—"

"Yes! We're getting married. Let's focus on that happy and leave the poison buried in the past."

"Oh, sweetie," Alice coos. "This is wonderful news. The absolute best." She lifts her watery features to me. "I can't wait for you to officially be part of our family."

Jace nudges his mom over a step. "He already is. Always has been."

She huffs. "You know what I mean."

Barry pats me on the back. "Damn proud of you son. Couldn't ask for a better man to make an honest woman of my daughter."

"Dad!" Sutton scolds.

He chuckles. "Just kidding, sweetheart. You've always been a catch."

She folds her arms. "Uh-huh, yeah."

I lean into her. "For me. That's what matters."

"So," Alice chirps. "When's the wedding?"

"Oh, mom. Stop." Sutton's wide gaze slides to me. "We just got engaged this morning. Maybe we'll plan for next—"

"Month?" I finish for her. She chokes on that little bomb I dropped. "Problem?"

Sutton whips her head back and forth. "Nope. That's great. Perfect, really."

I kiss her temple. "That's what I thought, beautiful."

She sags into me. "Love you, fiancé."

"Damn, I really like the sound of that. I'm gonna love calling you wife."

A collective sigh comes from her parents. Alice is practically glowing. "We better start planning."

I just laugh. Sutton holds up her left hand again, showing off the goods. "Not yet. I want to appreciate having my fiancé home. How about we spend today enjoying each other's company? Tomorrow we can discuss the future."

I cup her ass against the seat. "You're reading my mind, Sutt."

"Because we're one." There's awe in her voice.

We order a round of drinks and toast to this happy something. Family bonding. There's nothing quite like it.

Others begin trickling over to give me a clap on the back or offer to buy me a beer. Everyone has a smile and kind words reserved for me. My heart is bursting and threatening to overflow. I've never felt this level of acceptance. It's almost unbelievable, but my eyes don't deceive me.

One hour feeds into two. The third ticks over and my skin is getting itchy. I glance over at my girl. Her baby blues are already latched onto me. She gives me a little wave of her fingers. I nod toward the exit. Her eyebrows wag at me in return.

Well, damn. It looks like I'm getting all sorts of lucky today.

CHAPTER THIRTY—FOUR

Sutton

Happy something #199: Getting so caught up in something, or a certain someone, that I forget to breathe.

WAKE WITH A LAZY STRETCH. ALL OF MY MUSCLES, ESPECIALLY IN the lower half, are deliciously sore. I revel in the lingering burn. Aftershocks zap at my nerve endings and I smile into the pillow. That last orgasm is one for the books.

Grady stirs next to me, reaching over in his drowsy state. "Morning, baby."

I roll over and flop onto his bare chest. "Hey, Gray."

"Sleep well?"

"So good."

His lips find my forehead and I shiver. Grady got his wish about being naked. Not a single stitch of clothing has touched my body for almost seventy-two hours. We've barely separated for air since he was released. It's safe to say our codependency has reached record highs. Not that I'm complaining, and no one would blame us.

"Coffee?" The question is a murmur against my temple.

I brush my lips over his nipple. "Maybe in a bit."

"That's my girl." His fingers roam over the base of my spine, and drift lower.

We haven't left the bedroom for more than basic essentials. I'm perfectly pleased to survive on Grady and his very capable body. But alas, my pesky stomach growls intermittently with different demands.

In this moment, my lower belly is in charge and craving the naked man beside me. He seems to be having the same bout of hunger.

Grady presses his nose into the crook of my neck. A whisper of heat pebbles my skin when he growls against me. "You smell like a freshly showered dude."

I giggle and squirm closer. "I ran out of body wash. I've been more than happy to bathe in your manly aroma."

He treats himself to another whiff. "I'd rather put my scent on you the old fashioned way."

"Be my guest," I purr.

Grady flips our position in a single beat. He crawls over and lowers on top of me with a groan. Our naked limbs twine together within seconds. An idea strikes me just as he's about to slide in.

I push on his chest. "Wait."

He startles and props up on an elbow. "Care to repeat that? Pretty sure I misheard you."

"I have an idea."

"Does this involve simultaneous orgasms?"

"Yes."

"All right then." His dick twitches against my core as he lines us up again.

"Wait!" I giggle.

His forehead hits my shoulder. "Killing me, Sutt. I'm no longer familiar with that word when it comes to you and sex."

"My parents are out of town. I told them I'd feed the horses."

"You choose to bring this up now?"

I sweep some stray strands out of his eyes. "Wanna join me?"

"Afraid of a big, bad wolf?"

I dance my toes along his calf. "I might need your help."

"That involves us getting dressed." He nudges his eager insistence into me, steely hard against velvet soft. "Staying right here is much more promising."

I wiggle out of his intended target zone. "I have something else in mind while we're there."

"Another surprise?"

I nod. "Yes. The last one turned out well, right?"

"It did."

"And this one has been a long time coming."

A quiver skates over my body. "Those words from your mouth ruin me, Sutt."

"Is that a yes?"

Grady kisses me, a slow slide of lips that delves deeper. I loop my arms around him while brushing our tongues together. We share a groan and I'm almost regretting hitting the pause button.

He's the one to pull away. "Never can deny you."

I've never been more thankful that Grady bought a house within five miles of my family farm. We're pulling up in front of the barn before the desire has cooled from my blood. I drag him toward the door, his hands already wandering up the exposed skin of my thighs. The skirt I'm wearing is definitely on purpose.

The smell of sawdust and leather are hanging heavy in the air. I lead him toward the ladder, making my intentions clear.

Grady's cheek dents with a smile. "We haven't been up there in years."

"I loved those nights." I peek down at him once I've cleared the landing.

His gaze is latched onto my bare center. "No panties?"

"Makes this more exciting."

Grady meets me in the loft. "Sneaking off with your forbidden crush?"

"You were never a secret for me."

He tucks some hair behind my ear. "I wouldn't blame you."

"But I could never do that. You were always the one for me, Grady Bowen." My engagement ring catches a ray of early morning sun.

"So," he tucks a hand in his front pocket. "You got me up here. Now what will you do with me?"

I point to a short tower of bales. "Sit down, Gray."

He follows my orders without pause. His ass hits the nearest square and he reclines against the stack behind him. My sandals shuffle in the loose hay scattered across the ground. When I'm between his spread legs, I kneel onto the wood floor.

"Whatcha doing, Sutt?" His voice dips into gravel with the question.

"You'll see." I smooth my palms up his denim-clad thighs, palming the rigid length straining toward me. I unbuckle his belt with a quick yank. The button pops open almost on its own. Grady groans as the confines of his jeans gape.

I ease the zipper down at a tortuous pace meant to tease, the metal teeth tick with each pass. He lifts his hips to make my job easier. I lower the material until the vital part of him springs out for my taking. When I stop the stripping descent, he raises a brow.

"Wanna take them all the way off?"

I shake my head. "Less risk of getting caught."

A rumble rolls out of him. "Oh, we're playing like that?"

My eyes stay glued on the hard column of his penis. "Uh-huh."

"Well, we better hurry. Someone could come home at any minute." He fists himself, giving a few cursory pumps. The cords and ropes of muscle in his forearm make me drool. I'm totally transfixed on his steady movement.

"Yeah, uh-huh," I repeat.

"Ride me, baby."

I clamber on top of him. "I always pictured us like this."

"Sprawled out in the hay?" His hands travel up and under my skirt. He shoves the fabric around my waist with a rough rasp. The cool air breezes across my nude center. My responding shiver has nothing to do with the cold.

I straddle his lap, ignoring the scratch of hay against my bare skin. "Yeah, Gray. Just like this."

He cups my ass. "You have a dirty imagination."

I lean down and over him, my lips brushing his ear. "When it comes to you, I'm positively filthy."

My dark waves form a curtain around us, or maybe a veil. I hover over his length, the tip kissing my entrance. Grady's grip on me is punishing and will surely leave bruises. Nothing turns me on faster than the evidence of our passion. Another shot of piping hot arousal spreads in my veins. I'm already tripping toward that blissful edge from this position alone.

Grady plows forward without warning. The harsh thrust drives my upper body off his chest. His powerful glide into me is a surge of high-voltage electricity. I'm stunned still for a second, floating on static. A fiery zap shocks my limbs back to life. I flail and blindly reach for something solid to regain my balance. My hands find purchase on the sculpted rocks of his shoulders.

"The way we fit together, Sutt. Damn. Just like the first time. I'll never get used to having you this way."

I drift my palms down and settle on his wide pecs. "This is everything, Gray. You make me feel so good."

I'm fully seated on his lap and he's buried to the hilt. My

body welcomes him with a warm sigh, whispering for more. Soon those soft pleas will be deafening screams.

Grady clutches my hips and presses me deeper onto him. Only the slapping of skin accompanies us in this space. His length strikes that sensitive spot hidden inside of me. I toss my head back, the tips of my hair tickling my lower back. He repeats the motion and I collapse against him. To any unsuspecting onlookers, it appears we're just cuddling. But this is far more than a simple embrace.

"This is so much better than my teenage dreams."

He cups my nape, applying just the right amount of pressure to send a zing to the soles of my feet. "Bringing the images to life always comes out ahead."

And we do.

He punches in and out at a fierce rhythm. I grind down onto him, seeking more. We're propelling faster toward the stratosphere with each ruthless stroke. Our pace is rabid, the need for release chasing us. We have to hurry before someone catches us.

With a mutual groan, we hurdle off the cliff. The tumble wraps me up in blistering heat and rockets me skyward. I clack my teeth together and let go, releasing the pent-up lust with a muffled scream. Higher and hotter, the spiral swirling me tighter and faster.

I flop over, out of breath with stars sparkling in my vision. "Wow, that was, just really wow," I pant. "Thank you, Gray."

His chest rises and falls. He turns his head to face me. "For the orgasm?"

I roll my eyes. "Well, yeah. But mostly for making all of my fantasies come true."

He slaps a palm to his chest. "Delivering happy somethings for life."

I curl into his side, temporarily sated and wholly satisfied. "Just like I always knew you would."

EPILOGUE

Grady

Happy something #300: Dancing with my wife.

"**B**Y THE POWER VESTED IN ME BY THE STATE OF WYOMING, I'm proud to pronounce you as husband and wife. Grady," my best friend stares me down with a twitch in his smirk, "you may now kiss your bride."

The final portions of Jace's officiant speech are a shotgun blast. I spear my fingers into Sutton's perfectly styled hair and crash our lips together. With an arm banded around her waist, I bend my wife into a deep dip. Her lips are a flavorful burst of the juiciest strawberries picked right off the vine. I'm ravenous, dragging that plump pout between my teeth and going in for seconds. Her professionally painted nails dig into my suit jacket while she whimpers for more. We're so damn gone.

I smile against her glossy mouth. "Can we skip out of the reception?"

She giggles. "At our own wedding?"

I shrug a shoulder. "I made it through the entire ceremony."

"And you want a reward?"

"So long as you're my prize."

She gestures between us. "We just vowed forever and always."

"Didn't need rings and a license to tell me that, Sutt."

"Oh my gosh, we're actually married," she whispers.

Sutton's eyes resemble blue glass when she blinks up at me. I press another kiss to her painted lips. "I love you, wife."

She links the fingers of our left hands together. "And I love you, husband."

"Hey, love birds," Jace cuts in. "We're not done yet."

I chuckle. "Sorry, brother. Do your thing."

He clears his throat and addresses the crowd in front of us. "Please help me introduce, for the very first time, Mr. and Mrs. Bowen!"

Our guests erupt in cheers while we hold up our connected palms. Our meadow has been transformed for the event. Two modest rows are arranged near the trellis I built. Dandelions still blanket the grass, even though it's late in the season. Everyone holds a floppy stem in their hand. When we pass through the middle, they take turns blowing the puffy seeds at us. Wishes swirl up into the air along with our promise of eternity.

I scoop Sutton into my arms and she squeals. "I can walk."

"I'll be your chariot," I growl into her neck.

She cups my freshly shaved cheek. "Spoiling me already?"

"I'll never quit."

The overgrown weeds wisp against my black slacks as I stride ahead to the massive tent. Sutton and I wanted our celebration of love to take place in the spot we shared our first happy something. I can guarantee this day is earning a top spot on our list. From start to finish, our wedding will be surrounded by everything good.

I lower Sutton onto the plush throne reserved for her at the head table. She pushes out my matching chair and pats the seat. After placing a kiss on her forehead, I settle in beside my bride. The slow trickle of our family and friends soon filters in.

Sunset creates a natural wonder for our backdrop. A splash of blue and orange illuminate us as dinner is served. We feed each other fried chicken and lasagna, courtesy of Alice's recipes. I swipe marinara sauce off Sutton's bottom lip. She brushes crumbs off my tie. Glasses clink and we never disappoint, exchanging kisses that become more daring with each turn.

When the plates are cleared, Jace and Harlyn stand up beside us. He passes her the microphone. Ladies first. Sutton's maid of honor smiles at us before turning to the small crowd.

"Hey, everyone. I'm Harlyn—Sutton's bestie and college roomie. I met Sutton our first day of freshman year. We were wide-eyed and looking toward the future. Everything was an adventure and we took advantage. Well, mostly." She winks at my bride. Sutton's gaze visibly widens.

Her friend rolls on without hesitation. "She never told me, but there was something always holding her back. That turned out to be a certain someone. When Sutton introduced me to Grady this summer, I finally figured out why she never bothered dating. No one else would matter. You've all seen it, right? Impossible not to with these two. It took them a bit to reach this point, but they're crazy meant to be. I'm honored and grateful to be witness to such a love. So, let's raise our glasses for a toast. To the newlyweds."

We all lift our champagne flutes. Sutton sniffs and wipes at her eyes, wrapping Harlyn in a tight hug. They exchange several unintelligible words. I smirk at their display, a familiar pang bumping off my ribs from missing out on those years. But there's no room for regret, especially not in this space. Jace takes the microphone and clears his throat.

"It's no secret I've always been protective of Sutton." He earns a chorus of chuckles from all of us for that. "No one would ever be good enough for my little sister, right? It's the big brother role. I could pretend to be shocked when Grady told me how he really felt for her. The biggest shock was how long it took for him to admit it. These two are setting the new standard for marital bliss. Sorry, mom and dad. You've been replaced," he laughs. His parents each shake a finger at him.

"So, yeah. There was no use trying to keep them apart. Sutton and Grady are a magnetic force of their own. If I tried to step between them, I'd be shoved out of their axis. That didn't stop me from attempting to be a roadblock. Temporary, of course. Not sure why. My best friend is the greatest man I've ever met. Here we are at their wedding and I couldn't be happier. It's a great joy to see two people find this kind of overwhelming bliss. And on that note, let's drink!" Jace lifts a glass and we all cheers.

I clap him on the back and lean in. "Thanks, man. For everything."

"Meant every word, Grady. Congrats. You two are perfect for each other. Always have been."

"Stop being sappy." I cover the lump in my throat with a laugh. "Girls love a tough guy."

"Well," he rocks on his heels, "lucky for me, there aren't many available options swarming tonight. I can let my inner Prince Charming loose."

And it's true. Besides Harlyn, Molly and Lacie are the only women under forty. The first is still licking her wounds after the shit-storm with Lance. But I'm not sure what the latter's excuse would be. Not sure Jace is all that interested either way.

The moment for our first dance as husband and wife comes next. I hold a hand out for my bride and escort her to the square of wood laid out in the center. *Stand By You* by the Pretenders croons through the speakers set up in the corners.

Sutton rests her head on my shoulder as we sway. "Such a classic staple."

I tuck her tighter against my chest. "Our love will never fade so it's fitting."

"Are you happy, husband?"

"Are you seriously questioning that, wife?"

She tips her chin up and graces me with a wide smile. "Nope, not in the slightest. I just enjoy riling you up. It's sexy when you get all growly."

I bend lower and rumble in her ear. She trembles in my hold. "You in this dress, Sutt? Good Lord. I can hardly contain myself. When you came down the aisle, I had to check my pulse and make sure this was real."

Sutton pinches my arm. "Not dreaming."

"You're the most beautiful bride, baby. I can't believe life gave me you. What did I do to deserve perfection?" I stroke a thumb down her cheek.

She nuzzles into my touch. "You're biased."

"I'm lucky in love, beautiful." I give her a final twirl as the song comes to an end. With another low dip, my lips seal over hers.

"Maybe we can sneak off now," she suggests. Her breathless tone gets me half-hard in a split second.

"Don't you think people will—"

"Mind if I cut in for my turn?" Alice sways onto the makeshift dance floor wearing a wobbling smile and flowing blue gown. She's been crying off and on since Sutton met me at the altar. There's still a ball of tissue crushed in her small fist.

"I suppose, mom." Sutton releases me with a sigh. She

tugs on my lapels and I tip down, pressing our mouths together for a searing moment. "Don't be gone long, Gray."

I grin into our kiss. "Couldn't if I tried."

Alice steps into me, one hand slipping into mine and the other perched on my shoulder. "It's almost criminal to separate you, even for three minutes."

"I can still feel her." I tap the spot over my heart.

Her bottom lip begins quivering again. "Oh, Grady. I'm so blessed to have you in our lives."

"The feeling is very mutual, Alice."

"Is it too soon for me to call you son?"

A broken piece buried deep inside of me wiggles loose. Her words smooth the jaded edges. I slide my eyes closed with a sigh. "Absolutely not."

I receive another watery grin for that. "Okay, good. I don't want to push my luck, but is it too early for me to bring up grandchildren?"

"Ah, maybe?" I allow my eyes to naturally find Sutton waiting in the wings. She winks and blows me a kiss. "Or not."

She follows my line of sight, smiling at her daughter. "That girl has been in love with you since she was little."

A hum vibrates my chest. "I'm finally coming around to believing that. It took a long time, but I realize she's always felt the same as me."

"And you should. You two deserve one another." She gives me a hug as the final notes fade. "Thanks for humoring me with a dance."

"The pleasure was all mine." I glance away before adding, "Mom."

Alice squeaks and waves a hand in front of her watering eyes. "Oh, that's the sweetest gift. Thank you. Okay, wow. I'm a mess. Go get your girl while I clean myself up."

I latch my gaze onto Sutton. "Gladly."

My wife is back in my arms a beat later, where she belongs. We fold into a close embrace while another tune plays. "What did my mother have to say?"

"She wants to call me son."

Sutton blinks up at me. "That's so precious. What did you say?"

I kiss her temple. "Of course. She's always been a mother to me."

"You totally made her year with that one. What else happened?"

"She's ready for a grandkid."

Sutton coughs. "Oh my gosh. Babies? Already?"

I chuckle against her smooth skin. "That's for us to decide. Let's take our time and do whatever we want. Traveling might be fun."

"Oh, that could be exciting. Where would we go?"

I lift her in my arms and spin us in a circle. "Maybe Minnesota. I hear they have a lot of pretty lakes."

She tosses her head back and giggles. "Okay, but not in the winter. It's too cold."

"Don't worry, Sutt. I'll always be here to keep you warm."

BONUS EPILOGUE

Sutton

Happy something #74: Sunshine and rainbows and candy.

GRADY PUTS THE RENTAL CAR IN PARK ALONG THE CURB ON Maple Street. A row of vibrant buildings and lush trees border this side of the road. A front desk employee at our hotel highly recommended we spend an afternoon along this charming strip. We can get the best hot fudge sundae, taffy, nachos, unique gifts, and all that Minnesota has to offer. There's nothing wrong with splurging on this small-town goodness for several hours. That's the tagline for any decent vacation, after all.

He taps the steering wheel with his thumb. "Do you think this is the place?"

I glance out the windshield, an enormous lollipop glowing back at me. The neon sign is a memorable marker to finding the store. "Seems to fit the description spot on."

"Thicket is an interesting name. I wonder what's behind that."

"Guess we'll find out."

I open my door and step onto the sidewalk. Grady gets out to meet me, linking our fingers together. Our stride is lazy while we stroll through the entrance. I almost trip out of my flip-flops when catching sight of the room. Every inch of space is splashed with different shades from a rainbow. The bursts of color pull my gaze from one corner to another, bouncing off the creative pieces adorning the walls.

I'm not sure where to look first.

The candy section takes up the entire front portion. This appears to be a major focal point. I find my gaze swinging to this part more than the rest. There are bins and racks and trays stacked up. An array of sweet treats spills out in all directions. But it's not cluttered. Just the opposite. It appears the shelves and display cases are professionally organized. All of the items have a designated area.

"What is this place?"

I didn't realize my question tumbled out until a woman turns to face us. "Well, hey there. Welcome to Thicket." Her smile is toasty warm as she motions us deeper into the store. "This is our little slice of paradise. Feel free to get lost in whatever capacity that means for you."

I blink at her. She resembles a blonde beauty queen, but all natural. Not a stitch of makeup covers her face. I get this odd urge to hug her, which is weird considering she's a complete stranger. She seems to pull me under this peaceful lull. Before I can contemplate my bizarre reaction further, a ball of zig-zagging motion screeches to a halt in front of me.

When the dust settles, a boy is standing in front of me. His wide grin is missing several teeth. The sneakers on his feet are almost a blur as he bops up and down. I'd peg him to be about seven or eight, still young enough to love the dog cartoon emblazoned on his shirt. He has the kindest blue eyes I've ever seen.

He sticks up a little palm and I offer him a high-five. "Hi! I'm Oliver, but you can call me Ollie. This is the greatest place ever. You'll love it. Right, mom?"

The blonde sways out from behind the counter and joins us. She ruffles the kid's mop of brown hair. "He's my best salesman. Business is booming thanks to you, Ollie."

Ollie beams up at her. "Thanks."

She settles her bright green eyes on me. "Hopefully you weren't expecting a traditional shopping experience. You get a bit of chaos with each visit."

I offer a grin. "This is wonderful. I had no clue what to expect when we pulled up."

"Ah, it's best to just fly in blind."

Grady loops an arm around my waist, remaining silent. I lean into him while keeping my gaze on the woman. "That always works well for us."

"Then you've come to the right place. I'm Braelyn." She places a palm on her chest before pointing down. "And this social butterfly is my son."

I give them a little wave. "I'm Sutton. This is my husband, Grady."

He nods at them, allowing his lips to tip up at Ollie.

Braelyn sighs in that way women do when something romantic happens. "You two are a stunning pair. I can tell you're a very happy couple."

Grady squeezes my hip. "We are."

Seemingly out of nowhere, an extremely good looking man—not Grady hot, of course—appears at the end of an aisle. There's a very familiar protective vibe wafting off him. Piercing blue eyes glare at us before sliding to Braelyn. The frost clears in a snap. Love is thick in the air and I sag against Grady. A high-pitch giggle draws my attention up. Perched on the guy's shoulders is a cute little girl with hearts in her eyes.

"Hey, babe? Where'd you put the juice boxes?"

Braelyn turns to him and I witness that bond only destiny brings. Their eyes connect with sparks crackling into the air. Static creates a low buzz, the lights flicker, and the background tunnels away. I swear a tether snaps taut and latches them together.

"Whoa, is that what happens when I look at Grady?"

"Yes," he murmurs into the crook of my neck.

Dang, my filter is loose today. I really need to watch the whole thinking out loud thing. "That's intense."

He nips at my skin. "Why do you think it's hard for me to look away?"

Cue the swoon. Grady has been on his game lately. Well, since we started dating really. It's been a year of floating high in the clouds.

Braelyn coughs and drags her gaze to us. The shift seems to take a lot of effort, but her smile is easy and light. "This is my husband, Brance,"—he lifts his chin our way—"and the tiny tot is Oaklee."

"Did we stumble into a dream?" I'm mostly joking.

Her laugh is a twinkling song. "Most days it feels that way."

"Uh-huh, yeah. It's so fun in here. This is my most favorite place in the whole world. Hopefully you'll stop by all the time because we're super glad to make new friends. And you're really pretty." Ollie is granting me another gap-tooth grin. This kid is going to be a lady-killer one day.

Once I wrap my mind around his mishmash, I return his joy. "This shop is clearly magical. We're happy to be here. But we live in Wyoming. I'm not sure when we'll be back."

Ollie stares at me. "Uh, that's super far away."

I giggle. "It really is. We drove all the way here."

His eyes stretch wide open. "Wow, that is so cool." He spins toward his parents. "Can we visit Wyoming? Let's take a road trip! Please, please?"

Brance chuckles. "We'll see, kiddo. That would be a long trip."

Ollie folds his hands and lifts them up. "So? I'll take care of Lee. She can sit in the backseat with me."

He earns a sigh from his father for that. "Your sister isn't the issue, little man. Let's talk about it later."

His bottom lip sticks out. "That's your nice way of saying no."

"Okay, moving on." Braelyn claps and focuses on us. "Is there anything particular you're in the market for?"

I take a moment to glance at all the store has to offer. "I'm not sure where to start."

"Oh, oh!" Ollie is leaping on his toes. "Taffy! There are so many choices. They're all my favorite. You should try one of each." His eyes glitter under the fluorescent lights.

Braelyn laughs. "See? He pushes my product without breaking a sweat."

Ollie dashes over to a collection of bins. "Do you like chocolate? Cherry? Blueberry? Butterscotch? Vanilla? Apple? Banana? Root beer? Birthday cake? Caramel?"

Braelyn walks over to him. "Sweetie, you're going to overwhelm them. Let's choose one."

His expression morphs into sheer disbelief. "What? No. That's impossible. How can I decide?"

Braelyn plucks a wrapped candy out of a container and passes it to me. "This is one of my most popular flavors."

I pop the pink piece of candy into my mouth. A burst of watermelon hits my tongue. Almost immediately, my stomach revolts and flips upside down. A gagging heave follows close behind. I spit out the half-chewed piece into my palm.

Braelyn's expression pinches. "Not good?"

"It was really delicious for a split second. Then the taste made me queasy."

Her smile returns. "Ah, that makes sense. How far along are you?"

Now my belly is churning for another reason. "Um, what?"

"I'm so sorry. Are you not pregnant?" She points to my torso—flat and trim, thanks very much. Hasn't this woman heard of girl-code? That's one subject we never broach, unless the evidence is undeniable.

My pulse does a tap dance. I force a laugh while sucking in another deep breath. The nausea fades for the most part. "Nope, not preggers."

She slaps a flat palm to her flushing cheek. "Oh my gosh, I feel terrible. It's just that I was very sensitive to fruit flavors while pregnant with Oaklee. A lot of women who come in have a similar reaction."

Grady's hand settles low on my stomach. "Is there something you need to tell me, Sutt?"

"I don't think so?" But then I do a quick calculation. I've never been one to pay close attention. Over two weeks late. Can that be right? I rub at my forehead. "Is that possible? We just started trying."

"It only takes once, baby."

Baby. A baby? Could it really be? I shake my head, getting way too far ahead.

"So, no pressure or anything, but I happen to have a few early result kits available." She points down a row to the left.

I let my jaw drop. "You sell pregnancy tests?"

"You'd be surprised how often they come in handy. I can barely keep them in stock." Her grin tells me everything I would consider asking.

I turn in Grady's arms, peeking up at him from under my lashes. "Should we?"

He nods and the corners of his mouth quirk. "I wanna know, Sutt."

"There's a bathroom just back there," Braelyn chimes in.

That gets another laugh out of me. "You're very prepared for this sort of situation."

She tosses her blonde hair over a slender shoulder. "Didn't I tell you? Not the typical shopping experience."

"I'm definitely gaining the grasp of that." This place and these people are earning a solid spot into our book of goodness.

Grady grabs a box off the shelf and guides me in the direction Braelyn points. I do my business, limbs shaking to the point my knees begin knocking. The longest three minutes of my life come next.

But the timer eventually dings. When that screen shows two pink lines, our greatest happy something to date settles into our hearts. Our future has never been brighter.

THE END!

Are you curious about Braelyn and Brance?

They're from my standalone romance, *Ask Me Why*. Enjoy this excerpt from the first chapter!

After disabling the alarm, I flip the lights on and watch my pride come to life. I pour everything into this space. If it wasn't for Thicket, I'd be a lost cause. Owning this store gives me a reason to wake up and keep moving.

Other than Sadie, I don't have much pushing me along. My family is all out of state, too far away to be bothered. Not that I blame them. My parents have their own problems to deal with. They don't need to take on more. And it's better for me if they stay away. My siblings are busy finding adventure at every turn. I'm doing my best to accomplish a small semblance of that.

With a slow spin, I take a long look around. Collections of odds and ends cover any available surface. This piece of property is all mine. Well, my name is clearly printed on the lease. But that's a minor detail. In my mind, this space is bought and paid for. Maybe it will be one day. A girl can dream.

That stops me short. Devon was the one who encouraged me to fulfill my fantasies. With him gone, most of those hopes were dashed. Except this one. Thicket is what's left for me.

The morning bleeds into afternoon as it always does. A steady stream of customers keeps me busy without pause so the haunting memories fade into the background. I'm about to start unpacking a new shipment of mugs when a twinge in my chest stops me.

When I blink, a blur of movement outside the window

catches my eye. All I see is a patch of red dashing by in a hurry. I furrow my brow and concentrate on the task at hand. After a quick beat, the welcome chime sounds and a little boy darts inside. I'm guessing he's around four or five, hints of baby fat showing off his youth. His light eyes are blown wide open as he scans the shop from wall to wall. Something grabs his attention and he skips forward. I follow his stare, trying to figure out what he's focusing on.

He dashes down the far aisle in a flurry I can barely track. His tiny feet pound on the floor as he searches the shelves. He zips this way and that, a super-charged pinball darting around the confining alley. His delight is infectious and impossible to ignore. I feel my spirits lifting, just like that.

As I continue watching him hunt, his excitement bounces in every direction. I gladly absorb it all, the layer of ice under my skin thawing ever so slightly. He's bubbling with pure happiness and carefree bliss. I lift my lips in the most genuine smile I can muster. He makes it easier. This kid radiates everything that's good in the world.

Eventually he circles back and screeches to a halt in front of me, slightly out of breath. "Where is it?"

I move from behind the counter. "What're you looking for?"

"Candy! I saw a lollypop on your sign." His chubby cheeks are dented with glee and I feel my smile stretching in return. A mop of brown hair flops over his forehead and he sweeps it away with stubby fingers.

Gosh, he's adorable.

This cutie pie is stealing all my attention so I don't notice the woman standing by the entrance. Until she clears her throat, very loudly.

Our gazes whip in her direction.

"Oliver John, what did we just discuss?" Her mouth is set in a firm line, showing off deep wrinkles.

Oliver's dimples melt away, and he stares at the ground. "I'm not supposed to run off."

"And what did you do?"

"But—"

She holds up a palm. "No buts."

I watch their exchange, the need to intervene compelling me to speak up. "At least he ended up somewhere safe. It's quite all right if he does laps for hours. I don't mind."

The older woman studies me with a wary squint. "You might not, but his father will."

"And that makes you his…" I let my words trail off, hoping she'll fill in the blank.

"Nanny, yes. Although I prefer honorary grandmother. Lord knows the poor child doesn't have any biological ones to rely on. But that's a tale for a different day. I'm Mary, and that little rascal"—she points to the boy beside me—"is Oliver."

"But you can call me Ollie." He grins up at me, the joy reappearing in his expression.

"Nice to meet you both. My name is Braelyn, and you're in Thicket." I motion around the space with a limp flourish.

Mary takes a cursory glance around. "It's charming. There's much to see."

I dip my chin under her watchful eye. "Thank you. I appreciate that."

"Have you been here long?"

"About two years."

Mary nods. "We've never ventured along this street before. But I'm sure Ollie will never forget now that we've found this place."

I feel a tug on my shirt and look down. Ollie's smile hasn't dimmed since being rejuvenated. I find myself grinning back.

"Will you show me where the candy is now?" he asks.

I point behind me, to the row of tubs under the window. "Do you like taffy?"

Ollie's expression morphs into sheer wonder. "The super-chewy stuff?"

"Yes, I have a bunch of different flavors."

He dashes toward the bins. "What's your favorite?"

"The rainbow swirl," I whisper.

Ollie lowers his face closer to the sugary treats. "What do they taste like?"

I swallow the lump in my throat. "Happiness."

His button nose wrinkles. "That's a weird flavor."

I pluck one from the bunch and pass it over. "Try it and see."

He unwraps the colorful roll and pops it into his mouth. Ollie chews loudly, his eyes sparkling bright. "Urm me gesh, whish ish so gerd."

I laugh at his jargon. "You like it?"

"So good," he mumbles.

I tug a paper sack out of the slot and scoop in a hefty amount. This should keep him occupied for at least ten minutes. I grin at that, picturing him gladly munching away. I want to bottle a sip of his energy and drink it later when the blues return.

I glance at him, finding him watching my every move. "This loot is for you. On the house."

Ollie's lips twist in a ridiculous way. "What's that mean?"

"I'm giving it to you," I explain. "For free."

Mary strides over. "You don't have to do that. We can pay."

I wave her off. "It's my pleasure. This little tyke has brightened my day."

"I have?" Ollie squeaks.

"Absolutely," I confirm.

He makes grabby-hands at the bag. I hold it up and out of reach. "I don't want to spoil your dinner."

Ollie pouts, his lower lip trembling slightly. Wow, he's good. My resistance is no match for this kid.

I pass the candy to Mary, giving her control. She mouths a silent thank you and beckons to Ollie. "We should get going. Your dad will be home soon."

At the mention of his father, he begins hopping in place. "Oh, I hope he brings me a surprise."

Mary raises a brow at him. "Isn't this enough?" She shakes the taffy all about.

Ollie seems to ponder that. "I guess." His gaze swings to me. "Can I come back, Miss Braelyn?"

The urgency in his tone takes me by surprise. "Of course, Ollie. You're always welcome here."

"Maybe tomorrow?"

There's no denying him. "I'd really like that."

His grin is huge and honest. "Me too. I can't wait."

As I watch them walk out the door, the storm clouds threaten to roll in. An unexpected wave crashes over me, but I'm not drowning in it today. No, I'm soaring above the violent sea.

Without realizing it, this taffy-loving kiddo gave me a reason to smile.

Ask Me Why **is available now on Amazon!**

MORE TITLES BY HARLOE RAE

GENT: An enemies to lovers standalone

Raven Elliot blasts into town like a wrecking ball—striking and devastating.
With a few simple words, my reliable routine crumbles to dust.

"Is this seat taken?"

I could close my eyes and let her voice wrap around me like a lover's caress.
But this isn't that type of story.
And I'm sure as hell not that kind of man.

She hovers in my space, batting her lashes and smiling shyly.
The glimmer in her sapphire eyes is a promise of peace.
But I'm not falling for it.
And Raven doesn't take the hint.

What starts as a battle of wills, explodes into a turf war.
She stands directly in my path everywhere I turn.
No matter how hard I shove, she won't budge.
Raven seems dead set on driving me insane.
But I was here first.
And I'm not going down easy.

After all, no one ever taught me how to treat a lady.
Read FREE with Kindle Unlimited!

LASS: A friends to lovers standalone

She's the one I've been saving myself for.

Addison Walker is every fantasy I never dared to believe in.
Moving to this town was already monumental.
Finding her removes any lingering doubt.
She's bold and vibrant.
Beautiful and confident.
Far too good for the likes of me.
Luckily, I'm not good at avoiding temptation.
But is she?

My desire is growing beyond control.
I'm done watching on the sidelines.
When opportunity strikes, I eagerly take advantage.
Signing on the dotted line before thinking twice.
The repercussions cross my mind far too late.
When she swiftly sticks me in the friend-zone, there's not a
damn thing I can do about it.

**Addison is just down the hall—might as well be miles
away.**
Every lingering glance drives me to the edge of sanity.
She speaks to my deepest cravings like a siren.
Our chemistry blurs every line.
This battle seems impossible to win.
Yet my determination doesn't wane.
It only takes one night to change everything.

After all, I didn't wait all this time to settle for less.

Read for FREE with Kindle Unlimited!

MISS: A second chance standalone romance

The boy she loved is gone. The man I've become doesn't deserve her.

Delilah Sage was the first girl I loved, my first for many things, but that's only the beginning. She was a warm embrace after especially hard nights, offering comfort where there was only pain. Delilah kept me from sinking and I promised her forever. I should have known better.

I ruined the only good in my life. Now all I have is regret, constant and relentless. My need for Delilah hasn't faded after all these years. She's the only woman who understood me. There's no moving on from that. I've accepted my fate of being alone. This is what I deserve.

Until I'm handed a second chance—whether I want it or not. A job brings me back to the small town I swore would stay in my past. The memories and mistakes are waiting to greet me. I try to keep my distance, but Delilah has always been my weakness. One look won't hurt. How quickly I forget she's impossible to resist.

After all, letting her go was never my intention.

Read FREE with Kindle Unlimited!

Redefining Us
A standalone friends to lovers, military romance.

In order to truly save him, I need to redefine us.

Xander Dixon was my best friend.
Loyal and dependable.
A brave warrior.
A permanent presence in my life until that fateful day he
boarded a plane headed overseas.

Xander's unwelcome silence haunted me for three years…
Until he suddenly resurfaces.
Blinded by misplaced fury.
Trapped in a pool of darkness.
Unable to escape the perpetual pain.

Though it would be easy to walk away, I refuse to give up on
him.
I want to know his misery and torment, so I can rescue him.
Then Xander will finally be mine.

Free with Kindle Unlimited!

Forget You Not
A standalone sweet second chance, military romance.

I didn't believe in love at first sight until Lark stood before me.

Pretty sure I would have married her on the spot.
Too bad fate had other plans.
Duty called and I had to answer—no matter the
consequences.
There wasn't a chance for goodbye, but I'd never forget her.

Time has a way of creating change—but only on the surface.
Even after all these years, I know Lark is mine.
I belong to her just the same.
The moment I see her again, it's a done deal.
All I've got to do is convince her this is forever.
She can push but I'll only pull harder.

I'm not letting our second chance slip away.

Free with Kindle Unlimited!

Watch Me Follow
A stalker, double virgin romance.

Creep. Freak. Crazy Eyes.
I've heard it all.
Over the years, they've slammed me with every demeaning
name in the book.
Their taunts warped me like a steady stream of poison.
Anger replaced anxiety as I started believing the cruelty spat
my way.
Until she showed up and changed everything.

Lennon Bennett is pure innocence—warm sunshine
breaking apart my stormy existence.
She's everything good and maybe I can be too.
For her. With her. Because of her.
Lennon doesn't know I'm beckoned closer with each breath.
She isn't aware that I'm completely consumed with her.
It's become my sole purpose to protect her, by any means
necessary.
But if she discovers the depth of my obsession, it will be the
end of me.
So, I remain in the shadows.
Waiting. Watching. Wanting.
She'll be my first. My last. My only.

Free with Kindle Unlimited!

ACKNOWLEDGEMENTS

Book #8—WOW! It's surreal for me to type that out. I still can't believe I've been fortunate enough to write one book, let alone eight of them. Sutton and Grady have been waiting patiently in the back of my mind since this author journey started. Their story is one I knew would leave a lasting impact on my heart. The road isn't easy, reality isn't fair, and happiness isn't guaranteed. But with the right person by your side, everything is possible. I'm obsessed with how their love conquers so much.

This journey wouldn't have been possible without my amazing team of support. First as always, I must thank my husband. When I get sucked into deadline mode or get lost in my brain, you're always there to work harder than you already do. This dream of mine wouldn't be possible without your unyielding patience and understanding. You and our baby boy light up my life each day. I love you forever and a day.

To the readers, I want to extend a huge and heartfelt bout of gratitude. I wish I could thank everyone individually. Just know how deep my gratitude goes. I'm well aware how many books are available to read. It means everything to me that you chose mine from the masses. Whether this is the first time you've read me or the eighth, thank you so very much.

Kate, Heather, and K.K., you three are my soul sisters. I'm beyond blessed to have found you in the craze of social media madness. The friendship and support you provide me day in and out can never be replicated. I'm so damn thankful to have you in my life. Thank you for always having my back and being there for me. I love you, ladies!

Jacquelyn and Renee, I'm not sure which of us fell for Grady first. All I know is we all called dibs. You two keep me going, giving me that push I'm too afraid to ask for. I'm forever grateful to have found you. This business can be harsh and fierce, but you two are my light. Thank you for always having a shoulder for me to lean on. Love you!

Oh, Talia. Where do I even start? We've been working together for over two years and you never cease to amaze me. Just when I think we've created the best cover yet, you step it up another notch. I really don't know how we will top BREAKER, but I also don't doubt you for a moment. Thank you for being a great friend and sharing your talent with us. I couldn't do this without you. As always, you can never leave me. Hugs and love to you!

Melissa, Katherine, and Keri, thank you for being amazing friends and always encouraging me. Whether it's a simple greeting in the morning or helping me with some major task, you step up and lend a hand. I couldn't manage without you. Hopefully you're well aware how stuck you are with me! I can't wait to hug you all again soon.

Leigh, Parker, and Ava, I'm so grateful to you for all the continuous love and support. Thank you for being so uplifting and being a positive force in this industry. It's rare to find true and genuine friends, but you three are it. Let's plan a retreat, okay?

Nicole, you've been my rock since I started this journey. Thank you for always being there with a kind word or hilarious story. I'll never be able to tell you how much I appreciate you. Thanks for everything, friend.

Lauren, you're seriously amazing. Whenever I message, you're always there for me. Thanks for being my friend. I know we aren't keeping score, but I owe you a lot. Love you!

Peggy, I'm so eternally grateful that you were willing to step in during a crazy time of need. Not only are you one of my close friends outside of this book realm, but you jumped in with both feet to lend a very helpful hand. Thank you, thank you! Sending you so much love always.

Tia, Annie, Ella, Suzie, Sunniva, Michelle, Jane, Meghan, and many more, thank you for being an amazing bunch. Not only are you supportive authors, but I'm also fortunate enough to call you friends. Thank you for all the things. I've lost count of all the ways you guys lift me up and push me forward. I couldn't survive the grind without your doses of sweetness. Thank you, thank you!

Cindy, Shauna, and Megan, I'm always sending so much love to you. I always look forward to hanging out again. Thank you for being part of my support team and being there for me!

Candi and Candi Kane PR, thank you so very much for handling my releases and pre-game craziness. You've been handling my marketing for over a year and I'm not sure how I survived before that. You're such a boss and I love you. Thank you so very much for all you do!

Thank you to all the ladies of Give Me Books. I've been working with you guys for over two years and you always provide amazing release services. Thank you, thank you, thank you!

Having genuine friends in this business is difficult to accomplish and I'm blessed to be part of several groups that keep my author heart happy. THANK YOU Book Babes Forever, Boston Babes, 60K in 30 days, Do Not Disturb Book Club, and KU Explosion.

THANK YOU to Book Cover Kingdom for the GORGEOUS cover. As always, you amaze me.
Thanks to Rafa G Catala, the very talented photographer who shot the perfect image of Adrian. Thank you for giving me a beautiful cover photo for this story.

For my Hotties, the bestest reader group an author can ask for. I can always count on our group to make me smile and boost my spirits. I'm so thankful to each one of you for taking this journey with me. I appreciate you more than words can describe. Thank you for being dedicated to me and our bookish community. I love our special place on social media!

Harloe's Review Crew, thank you so very much for wanting to read and review my words. Somedays, I still pinch myself. I appreciate you going above and beyond to support and promote me during releases. I'm eternally thankful to all of you!

A huge thank you to Stacey from Champagne Book Designs for making the interior of Breaker look its absolute greatest.

And last but certainly not least, a huge shout out to YOU for reading Breaker. I have the BEST readers out there. It's the greatest feeling in the world knowing you chose my book out of so many to read. I mean, wow. I appreciate you so much. Please know that! Just continue loving books and reading for me, okay? You've made me a very, very happy author!

One last thing? If you enjoyed *Breaker* and want to do me a huge favor, please consider leaving a review. It really helps other readers find my books!

ABOUT THE AUTHOR

Harloe Rae is a *USA Today* & Amazon Top 10 bestselling author. Her passion for writing and reading has taken on a whole new meaning. Each day is an unforgettable adventure.

Harloe is a Minnesota gal with a serious addiction to romance. She's always chasing an epic happily ever after. When she's not buried in the writing cave, Harloe can be found hanging with her hubby and son. If the weather permits, she loves being lakeside or out in the country with her horses.

Harloe is the author of the Reclusive series, Watch Me Follow, #BitterSweetHeat Series, Ask Me Why, and BREAKER. These titles are available on Amazon.

Find all the latest on her site www.harloe-rae.blog

Subscribe to her newsletter at bit.ly/HarloesList

Join her reader group, Harloe's Hotties, at
www.facebook.com/harloehotties

Follow her on:

BookBub: bit.ly/HarloeBB

Amazon: bit.ly/HarloeOnAmazon

Goodreads: bit.ly/HarloeOnGR

Facebook Page: Facebook.com/authorharloerae

Instagram: www.instagram.com/harloerae

Book & Main: bookandmainbites.com/harloerae

www.ingramcontent.com/pod-product-compliance
Lightning Source LLC
Chambersburg PA
CBHW050925220726
48290CB00018B/1539